CHEATGRASS

Also by Bart Paul

NONFICTION
*Double-Edged Sword: The Many Lives of Hemingway's
Friend, the American Matador Sidney Franklin*

FICTION
Under Tower Peak

CHEATGRASS

A Novel

Bart Paul

ARCADE PUBLISHING • NEW YORK

First Edition

This is a work of fiction. Names, places, characters, and incidents are either the products of the author's imagination or are used fictitiously.

Arcade Publishing books may be purchased in bulk at special discounts for sales promotion, corporate gifts, fund-raising, or educational purposes. Special editions can also be created to specifications. For details, contact the Special Sales Department, Arcade Publishing, 307 West 36th Street, 11th Floor, New York, NY 10018 or arcade@skyhorsepublishing.com.

Arcade Publishing® is a registered trademark of Skyhorse Publishing, Inc.®, a Delaware corporation.

Visit our website at www.arcadepub.com.

10 9 8 7 6 5 4 3 2 1

Library of Congress Cataloging-in-Publication Data

Names: Paul, Bart, author.
Title: Cheatgrass : a novel / Bart Paul.
Description: First edition. | New York : Arcade Publishing, [2016]
Identifiers: LCCN 2015040028 | ISBN 9781628726015 (hardback) ;
ISBN 9781628726152 (ebook)
Subjects: LCSH: Missing persons—Fiction. | BISAC: FICTION / Thrillers. |
  GSAFD: Mystery fiction. | Adventure fiction.
Classification: LCC PS3616.A92765 C47 2016 | DDC 813/.6—dc23 LC record available at http://lccn.loc.gov/2015040028

Cover painting by Denise Klitse

Printed in the United States of America

For Bonnie and Robert

"... the greeting of heroes was over.
He came back much too late."
—Ernest Hemingway, "Soldier's Home"

"It is thought abroad, that 'twixt my sheets
He has done my office"
—Iago

CHEATGRASS

She drove into the ranchyard at dawn and parked her county SUV under the cottonwoods along the house. Ahead of her across the valley, the sun was about to rise from behind the ridge. She got out, stretched, and trotted up the steps. The pup ran around her when she opened the front door.

"Hey, Dad," she said. "Something sure smells awesome."

She crossed the front room and passed the big table where a coffee mug sat steaming. She took off her jacket and walked to the stove, the pup just behind her.

"Biscuits and gravy," she said. She smiled as she called out. "You must be psychic."

She looked from the kitchen down the narrow hall. "Dad? Don't let breakfast get cold."

She opened a cupboard and took a mug from the shelf. She paused, listening as she poured coffee. She took a sip and set the mug on the counter and walked down the hallway, looking into the bedrooms. She came back up the hall and paused at the half-open door to the bathroom, knocking twice before she pushed the door open. She looked in the medicine cabinet and turned each prescription bottle so she could read the label. She finally picked up the tiny Nitro-Quick bottle of nitroglycerin tabs. The seal was unbroken.

She set it back and hurried through the front room and out the door and down the steps. She broke into a trot with the pup behind her as she explored the barn, the tack room, and grain room, then down the row of empty draft-horse stalls. She was running when she crossed the yard to the shop and looked inside that, and into the open shed next to it. She walked back outside and saw that her father's new pickup was gone. She hadn't noticed that before. She stood there a moment, catching her breath, her hand resting on the butt of her service pistol as she looked out at the pastures beyond the corrals. Then she knelt down and rubbed the pup. It was a crossbred Aussie about five months old.

She stood up. "Dad!" She shouted several more times and noticed she had tears in her eyes. She wiped them with the heel of her hand and ran back up into the house. The coffee mug on the table had stopped steaming in just the few minutes she had been gone and was cool to the touch. The sun was up over the ridge now, filling the room with glare. The bright light caught a single red spot of blood on the yellow linoleum.

"Oh, god," she said. "Dad!" It was more of a sob than a scream.

Chapter One

Captain Cruz sat on the desk drinking wine and watching me pack. She rested her bare feet on the desk chair and dangled her glass in her fingers like the whole thing amused the hell out of her. It was a big rolltop that belonged to a deployed major who sublet me the apartment, and she looked good sitting on it. Nothing in the place actually belonged to me except my clothes, including Captain Cruz. Her clothes were all still scattered in the bedroom. I zipped a 9mm into its case and took it over to the desk to lock it in the drawer. The captain leaned over me so her hair tickled my face and I couldn't miss the way it smelled.

"You're not taking that?" she said.

"I'm just going to visit an old friend."

"An old girlfriend," she said. "That's when you need a gun the most, soldier."

"She's happily married. I told you so."

"And that's why she's texting you. 'Oh, Tommy, come

home. Mama needs you.' I always carry something in my check-in. You never know."

"I get off the plane in Reno, I guess I can find a firearm or two if I need one. I'd sure as hell need one if I ever called that girl Mama. She'd kick my ass."

"You can say her name," she said. "I've heard you say it before."

"Okay. Sarah'd kick my ass. And she's real busted up about her dad. I told you, he just flat disappeared Monday morning. Vanished without a trace."

"Yes," she said. "You told me many times."

"You're a heartless old thing."

She gave a hot little quiver there on the desk. "You know better than that, lover," she said.

We both were still for a minute. You could hear gunfire from down the street in the direction of one of those bars where the soldiers and the locals went to mix it up. This was maybe the third time in a month. She ran a finger down my arm but she was watching the window, alert like she was back in the game. I took a sip of Wild Turkey and watched her close. It was a sticky night in Georgia, and it was only May. She wore red polish on all her fingers and toes when she was off duty. I wasn't used to girls who took the time to do that, but then the captain was no girl.

"So what does she expect you to do that the police won't do?" she said.

"Beats the hell out of me."

"So why do you go?"

"I don't know. We sort of grew up together. Her dad and my dad were best friends. It's like a family thing."

"My husband ever texted another woman like she did you, I'd cut his heart out," she said. "My great-grandpa rode with Pancho Villa, so you don't screw with us. *That* is a family thing."

"You guys were fighting the army back then, and now you are the damn US Army."

"You laughing at me, lover?"

"Hell no. Company commander is a big deal. You oughtta be proud."

"Okay, then," she said, "since you're the only man at Fort Benning better than me." She did some moves with her hair to make sure I was paying attention. "I think maybe that's why I risk another court martial to be with you, *Staff* Sergeant."

"You got more on the line here than me, I know that."

"Don't be too sure, lover. You break my heart . . . all bets are off."

She got quiet again when the sirens blasted by under the window. I let it go and went back to my packing. Like with most real pretty women, folks talked about the captain behind her back. She'd had trouble before, and probably for more than just diddling with somebody below her pay grade, but I never asked her about it. There were lots of stories, but I figured they were hers to tell.

"So how come you don't drive that fine Mustang GT out west?" she said. "If it was me, I'd take a road trip."

"Nope. Gotta get there quick."

"You're in a hurry to get to her," she said.

I tossed her the keys just to watch her stretch for them. "You take a road trip while I'm gone."

"You trust me with that hot car for two weeks?" she said.

"Sure. It ain't like it's a good horse."

"Damn, cowboy," she said, but she sort of smiled. "That's got to be a lot of money to spend on a car."

"It's my only extravagance."

"I thought I was your only extravagance."

I folded the last of my cowboy shirts and laid them all in the check-in bag except a white one I'd wear on the plane. Then I took off my BDU pants and pulled on some Wranglers.

"I always travel in uniform," she said, watching me. "I like it. Nobody ever looks past it to see your face, so it's like camouflage. In airports you blend in to your surroundings."

"You're not the blend-in type."

She liked hearing that. Then she just shook her head when I took my black buckaroo hat and a skinning knife down from the closet shelf. I tossed the knife in the bag and zipped it. The hat still had some sagebrush country dust on it. I hadn't touched it in a long time.

"How soon before we have to leave for the airport?" she said.

"Couple of hours, maybe. It's not even a hundred miles to Hartsfield. Just before sunup should do it."

She pointed to the hat. "You're not going to wear that thing, are you?"

"Not for the next couple hours."

She upended the wine glass and drained it. Then she slid off the desk and held out her hand. I took it. With her standing up I could see the nasty scar under her left breast where they stitched her up after an ambush on the road to Bagram.

"You can call me Mama all you want," she said, "and I promise not to kick your ass."

Mom's Beamer just ate up that grade on the new stretch of freeway that bypassed Steamboat and Pleasant Valley heading south out of Reno. She'd always driven like a madwoman, but since Dad died it was like she'd studied on it, picking up a used 325i on Autotrader and tricking it out just like any other forty-nine-year-old widow would do. It was silver-gray and looked like she'd just washed it that morning before heading for the airport to pick me up. I was half dozing as she took those big sweeping curves on the new bridge at about eighty-five.

"Late night last night?" she said.

"You might say."

"Who was she?"

"Nobody you'd know."

She gave me one of those like-hell-you-haven't-got-beer-on-your-breath looks, like when I was in high school. She'd flown out to DC to meet me when they first sent me home, and she'd chatted up every nurse and doctor and friend of mine at Walter Reed. I guess I really didn't mind it as much as I let on.

"Well," she said, "even with the short notice, it's just great to see you. A sweet surprise on a sad occasion." She started to tear up and reached over to squeeze my hand.

I squeezed back, then let it go so she wouldn't rear-end a motor home. "Good to see you too, Mom."

I looked down on Washoe Valley, and over to that timbered mountain to the west that hid Tahoe, counting the seconds until she did that mom thing again.

"How did you finagle getting leave so quick?" she said. "You won't get in trouble, will you?"

"Company commander likes me. I said it was a family emergency."

"Did he believe you?" she said.

"Oh, yeah."

"You could have said it was for medical reasons," she said. "You still limp."

"Not so's you'd notice."

"Like heck," she said. She was quiet for a bit. "You look awful, Tommy."

"Sometimes I don't sleep so good."

"Like never," she said.

"You think there's a chance Dave's still alive?"

"I just don't see how he could be."

"Sarah thinks he is."

"But she has to, honey," she said. "She's got to have hope or just go crazy."

"She said the sheriff's office thinks it's foul play, but she told me Dave's doctors said maybe he had some sort of stroke. Wandered off. Maybe some new deal with his heart."

"Right now it's Sarah's heart I'm worried about," she said. "You stay out of her life, young man. She's over the moon about this guy Kip that she married, and he's real good to her and a great provider. You had your chance with that girl and you blew it when you reenlisted."

"Nice, Ma."

"Well?"

She just drove for a while. She thought the world of Sarah Cathcart and had her own hopes for the two of us, I guess. When we were halfway down Carson Valley, I got out my phone to text Sarah I'd landed and would see her that afternoon. I saw I had a text from Captain Cruz but I didn't check it out just then. Mom stopped at the JT Bar in Gardnerville, and we went in for an early lunch. I dug into my steak sandwich and beer and fries, and she started telling me stuff I already knew—stuff about her new boyfriend, Burt Kelly, who was a Marine mule packer and instructor at the base out by Sonora Pass, and how two months before she'd moved off the ranch in Jack's Valley where she was bookkeeper to move in with Burt at the Marine housing in Shoshone Valley just down the road from Dave Cathcart's, and how she hoped I was okay with it all, as it had been almost eight years since Dad had died and she had to get on with her life.

"That's what Sarah's got to do," she said, "get on with her life and, well . . ."

"She can't till she knows what happened to her dad."

"What has she asked you to do?"

"Nothin' yet. They figure why anybody'd want to harm him?"

"Sheriff Mitch thinks it might have been some sort of random home invasion thing," she said. "Gone bad."

"Sheriff Mitch."

"Now, Tommy," she said.

"Dave wouldn't have just walked out without a fight."

"There's a bad element creeping into our part of the

country that just wasn't around when you were growing up. At least we didn't notice it out on the ranch." She looked kind of mopey and sad again, like she was lost in the past. "It's those drugs. Those and the lack of decent jobs. That does something to people."

"I guess."

"I don't know how we deal with that," she said.

"Keep an eye out for strangers, I suppose."

"You're the stranger now," she said. Her look was as sad as I could remember.

I paid the check, and we hauled ass south, up into the Pine Nuts on the Reno Highway, then past the State Line Lodge and down into California. The big irrigation reservoir was blue and shimmery like always with some white-caps in the breeze, but lower than I remembered. I watched a yellow cloud of dust at the far end of the reservoir. It was the Hoffstatler place, or what was left of it.

"The hell?"

"It's so sad," Mom said. "It happened when you were in Jalalabad. The LA cousins wanted to cash out, so when they couldn't find a buyer in this economy, they outvoted old Thor and sold the water rights to the restoration project. It just broke his heart. I think that's what killed him."

"What restoration project?"

"The Frémont Lake restoration project. They buy up water rights on the East and West Frémont watersheds so they can raise the lake level out by the Indian reservation— reduce salinity for cutthroat trout and all that. Hoyt Ber- glund's the rights acquisitions honcho for Fish and Wild- life. You remember Hoyt. He worked for the irrigation district back when your dad first started at Allison's." Just mentioning Dad seemed to make her sorrowful. "That seems like such a long time ago."

A big gust swirled that yellow cloud into a pillar of dirt hundreds of feet high, like all that was left of that ranch was getting sucked up into the sky. Mom slowed down as the dust devil swallowed us up, shaking the car on its shocks till we couldn't hardly see. She was just creeping along, and the road there was narrow and curvy and high, so it was a long drop down to the water's edge. When we got further along we could see the ranchland at the north end of Shoshone Valley. The pasture grasses had dried up and what little was growing out of the hard dirt was just cheatgrass and rabbitbrush. The West Frémont River curved through the center of the dry ground then ran straight into the reservoir, running past the old headgates, ditches, and diversion canals that had kept the place rich with grass for a hundred and fifty years. The only green now was along the river's edge.

"Damn, I hate to see that. Hoffstatler's was one of the first ranches that split off when old Tom Rickey went under a hundred years ago. Dad said Will James rode colts there."

"It's all so sad," she said.

The wind hit us again and a torn bit of yellow police tape snagged a wiper blade and trailed alongside the car, snapping in the air. By now we were south of the reservoir driving along the edge of the dead ranch with the foot of the Sierra rising high on our right. We passed a stone building that had been part of the old Rickey cattle empire and could see the fallowed ground up close. Mom pulled over under some dying cottonwoods, got out, and untangled the police tape from her wiper. She had thirty feet of it in her hand and looked pissed as hell. After she stuffed it in the trunk, she got back in out of the yellow wind.

"I don't know why I baby this darned car in this hard country," she said.

Then we were out of the fallowed land and just as suddenly the valley off to our left was green with spring grass. A narrow, fenced gravel road lined with trees sloped away from us down toward an iron bridge over the river then across the center of the valley, and I could see red cattle grazing and see the Cathcart headquarters under the big cottonwoods with their gray trunks, and leaves thick and light green shading the barn and sheds and corrals, and the sandy pink and white peaks of the Monte Cristos rising beyond the pastures and the sage hills off to the east.

I guess Mom caught me looking and began to chatter, as if that would keep me from thinking of Sarah and Dave and my dad, and all the rest that was gone.

"It's only a matter of time until this looks as horrible as Hoffstatler's," she said.

"What do you mean?"

"I mean Dave was planning on selling his water rights, too," she said.

I couldn't think of a thing to say to that.

"Burt's kept your old Dodge Ram in good order," Mom said. She sounded happy to be talking about him. "He starts it up every week or so, and he changed the oil when he heard you were coming home."

"It's not exactly home."

"Well, it's the best I can do right now," she said, sort of snappish.

"Okay. I'm sorry. Thank Burt for me."

"You can thank him yourself," she said. "Be nice, Tommy. He's a good guy, and he wants to be your friend."

"I know. We knew each other when he was packing out of the Summers Lake outfit when I was in high school and I packed for Harvey. Before Burt went back into the service. He's okay."

By now Cathcart's was behind us. She was quiet for about as long as she could stand.

"I try not to compare Burt to your dad," she said. "He's a fine man, but he's not Leland Smith."

"Who the hell is?"

We drove farther south toward Rickey Junction until I saw a cluster of apartments and cars on a bench above the highway on the right. Mom slowed down and pulled up the access road to the Marine housing complex. It just depressed the crap out of me.

"It's funny," she said, "but the last two months is the first time in my life I haven't lived on a ranch."

We got out of the car and went inside their place to meet Burt. He was a big, curly-headed Irishman in black-rimmed glasses who, from his years in the saddle and all the times he got tossed out of one, carried himself more like a packer than a Marine. We said hi and drank iced tea and BS'ed about folks we knew and about my latest little hoo-rah with a Taliban IED, and what my plans were now that I could get out of the service again if I wanted. Burt had been in Desert Storm and got himself a Purple Heart while he was there, so I wasn't telling him much he didn't already know. He was trying too hard, but he was doing it for Mom so I couldn't complain. I figured he might be a few years younger than her. He called her Deb and she called him Hon and she looked girlish around him and happier than she had in years, so I guess her smile was because of more than just the damn car. I sure as hell hadn't made her happy since I got back from my second tour—before I re-upped for the third.

After a while I told them I best be getting on down the road to see Sarah. Burt told me my truck was topped off with diesel and ready to go. I thanked him and we shook, and I gave Mom a squeeze and said I'd call when I knew my supper plans. My old Dodge Ram hadn't really got any better looking with age and appeared pretty shabby parked next to Burt's immaculate F-250. I'd had that Dodge about ten years, give or take, since I was seventeen, and it was plenty used when I got it. It needed a paint job and probably new tires from all the sitting around, but it was so familiar I could hardly stand it.

I sort of poked around in it before I fired it up. The dash was dusty and cracked, and there was a dirty pair of Ray-Bans hanging from the mirror that had belonged to my partner Lester Wendover who'd got killed almost two summers before, and a topo map of the Toiyabe National Forest under the visor. Behind the seat I found a Filson's catalogue, a copy of *Range* magazine with a Kurt Markus photo of a Nevada cavvy on the cover, some wire pliers, jumper cables, and a mostly empty box of Remington .270

soft points for my dad's old deer rifle, plus a red silk wild rag of Lester's that made me think of Captain Cruz's toenail polish. The wild rag had been folded so it wasn't as dusty as you'd think. I shook it out, three foot square, then folded it crossways, wrapped it once and a half around my neck and tied it on. I caught a look at myself in the driver's side window glass and almost choked, it reminded me of Lester so. But if you couldn't see me hobble about and didn't know any better, you'd almost think I'd never left that country. I fired up the pickup, put on my own Ray-Bans, and drove off to see Sarah Cathcart.

Chapter Two

Whatever it was that Sarah thought I could do to find her father, I didn't think I was the one to do it. We had gotten so close and then so crossways after Lester was killed and I told her I was reenlisting that I didn't see a way to mend what was pretty much all my doing. Me feeling sorry as hell didn't make the world over.

I turned off the northbound Reno Highway onto the gravel lane about ten minutes later. I was just creeping along, figuring what I would say and wondering why I hadn't stayed at Fort Benning. I pulled up under the cottonwoods before driving on to the house and just took it all in. It was a really fine spring day, and I'd forgotten what a nice clean place this ranch was, small and well-kept, and how much I'd missed this country—the look of the horses in the corrals, the sound of a calf bawling and a dog barking, the breeze off the mountains, all that crap. I remembered the text on my phone that said it was from Cruz, Ofelia. All she'd written was, *Where are you, Lover?* I texted back, *Home.* I tried not to look at old messages, especially the one from Sarah that brought me here.

At the far end of the ranchyard just past the barn I could see a new doublewide mobile home that wasn't there two years before. Probably newlywed central. Sarah's Silverado pickup was parked alongside, and I gave that end of the yard a wary eye. Behind an open-walled shed at the near end of the yard I saw a ratty travel trailer that I didn't remember either, and a beat-up Chevy Blazer parked next to it. It wasn't like Dave to have such junky-looking equipment on his place. Two men stepped out of the trailer and looked me over as they walked out to the open shed. I started to laugh. The two were pumping iron. They had a whole weight set in the shed—bench press, heavy bag, tower, and the works, and these boys were huffing and grunting through their reps in the early afternoon like they had nothing better to do. I laughed because on most ranches a guy would be working that time of day— digging a posthole, bucking some bales, running some cattle through the chutes, cleaning out an irrigation ditch, welding a backhoe bucket, or maybe shoeing a horse. Some damn thing. Anything. There's too many ways to break a sweat on a ranch that a guy doesn't have to look very far, so these two just struck me funny.

One was short and shaved-headed with a goatee hanging off his chin as long and skinny as a hot dog. The other was taller and scowly like he thought he was something out of an action comic. Neither one was Sarah's new husband as I remembered him, but then I'd only seen that guy once or twice. These two looked up sort of unpleasant-like as I drove by and parked over at the house that Dave had vanished from. I could see torn pieces of yellow police tape blowing along the porch that no one had bothered to take down.

I got out and stood in the cottonwood shade in a warm breeze. Then the shade seemed to flutter and shift, and I heard a slapping, flapping sound. I looked up and saw half a dozen buzzards at the very top of the tree. One was spreading its wings, and the rest sat silent, looking down. The wingspan looked to be at least five feet, and it gave me the fantods. Buzzards are common in that country, with their red bald heads and featherless necks, and they'll take over a cottonwood and after a time they'll kill it with their droppings. But these weren't like anything I'd ever seen. Their heads were as black as their bodies so you couldn't see their eyes, and they looked like shadows against the sky.

There was a chain-link kennel alongside the porch with a half-grown blue merle Aussie wagging his stump at me. I let him out and he ran past me and jumped the steps to examine a bowl by the front door. He licked the empty bowl, then he watched me as I climbed the steps. I sat down on the top one, facing the yard, and let the pup crawl over my lap while I waited for Sarah to get home from work.

She pulled up in her sheriff's SUV about twenty minutes later. She didn't get out of the car right away. I couldn't tell if she was on her radio or phone or only postponing the inevitable. She finally got out and just stood there in her deputy uniform and sunglasses. Her hair was pinned up and she looked grim-faced, but she still fairly took my breath away. When I came down the steps, she walked up and hugged me and started to cry. Then she pulled back and slugged me in the chest as hard as she could. The punch like to knock me down.

I had to catch my wind before I could say a word. "I'm here, just like you asked."

"I know," she said. She wiped her eyes with the back of her hand. "I know there are some things I can always count on you for. A couple, anyway."

We stood there and looked each other over, just as awkward as could be. I don't really know what I expected.

"It's good to see you," she said. "You don't look any the worse. In those clothes it looks like you never left."

"Yeah, well. I'm so sorry, Sarah. Tell me what you want me to do."

She didn't say anything, just walked past me up the steps and into the house, and I followed. I never was very good at sitting in somebody's living room making bullshit small talk and this was the second time I was trying it in an hour, camped on the edge of Dave's recliner with my hat on my knee, drinking coffee that Sarah'd made and feeling awkward as hell. I listened as she told me firsthand about the morning Dave disappeared.

"I'd just come off a graveyard shift," she said. "It was my turn in the rotation. Dad had said he'd have breakfast waiting when I got home. Since his heart attack, I check on him every day as soon as I get off work, no matter what time. But after I got married, I . . ." She looked around the room. "I didn't live here anymore. Kip and I got that new mobile home. For a fresh start. Anyway, when I came in,

I saw Dad had breakfast ready. Biscuits in the oven, gravy in the pan, coffee poured and hot. But Dad was gone. Just . . . *gone*. His heart meds weren't touched. I looked and looked, and then I finally saw a single drop of blood in the kitchen." She took a breath. "It tested out as the dog's, but I didn't know that. I thought it *must* be Dad's." She looked over at me just as clear-eyed as can be. "I drink too much coffee. You want a beer, instead?"

"Sure."

She got up and took my cup into the kitchen. I remembered this room from when I was in high school and I'd offer to help at Dave's brandings because I knew that Sarah would be home from college. She and her dad and some neighbors and Lester and me, all smelling like burned hair and hide, blood, sweat, and manure, all eating the lunch that Sarah had cooked the night before, sitting here, talking over the bawling of the cattle with our plates on our knees, like Sarah and I had just been doing.

She handed me a beer and plopped back down on the couch across from me. The beer was Sierra Nevada. That would be an upgrade for Dave.

"I called our office in Piute Meadows right away, then I waited outside," she said. "I couldn't stand to be in the house alone. It seemed to take Mitch and Jack Harney forever to get here from Piute Meadows. They worked up a missing person's file and Jack contacted the FBI field office in Sacto." She was picking up speed. "They offered any assistance we asked for, like cell-phone tracking, forensic accounting, and kidnapping protocols if it turns out to be that. And they had a Nevada guy from the South

Lake Tahoe office here by the afternoon since those guys were closer. Mitch isn't exactly the poster boy for interagency cooperation, but the Feds were kinda reassuring to me, so I was glad to have them on board. Since I'm law enforcement, they were super helpful. The guy from Tahoe even knows who you are, and that you and I . . . you know. Anyway, by then I'd got hold of Kip, so he was back from Reno."

I must've given her a funny look.

"He'd spent the night up there at some nutritional supplement convention," she said. "He's into bodybuilding big-time. That's why he moved those two guys in a couple of days ago to be like security guards here at the ranch in case we're dealing with foul play or . . . god knows what."

"Okay."

"Quit the Mister Inscrutable crap," she said. "Kip figured as long as I was working graveyard, I wouldn't miss him."

"Did you?"

"Don't make me sorry I asked you to come."

"So why did you?"

"I haven't felt safe from that moment I knew Dad was gone till I saw you sitting on the porch just now," she said. "It's not rational, but there you have it."

"Fair enough."

"You have a certain reputation," she said. "You scare people." She looked at me over the top of her beer and took a sip. "That can be a good thing. Even the FBI agent said so."

"You got the whole county sheriff's department behind

you. Plus all these ironpumpers and the FBI. You don't need me."

She got up from the couch.

"Fine," she said. "I don't need you, and you don't want to be needed. You think you can trouble yourself to help me tag some calves, then?"

"Okay."

"Since Monday, I'm already behind on cow work," she said.

"This time of year I don't doubt it."

"Even after his heart attack, Dad still put in a day's work. Just let me change my clothes."

She took the empties to the kitchen, circling me, keeping her distance, then headed out to the doublewide. I waited in the yard. When she came back, we walked out to the corrals with the ironpumpers watching us. It was midafternoon by now, breezy and nice. We walked amongst the milling horses, and she pointed out her Dad's old roan rope-horse for me to ride as she caught hers, a classy bay mare I didn't remember from before. I stopped to look at a big ratty-maned sorrel colt that was watching me walk through the bunch. Sarah stopped what she was doing to glare at me.

The sorrel was a five-year-old gelding out of Idaho I'd started for Sarah's dad before I left. It had been his surprise for Sarah. The horse looked like his winter coat hadn't quite shed out or felt the touch of a brush in a while, and he was unshod and rough-footed. Sarah watched me looking him over as he and I got reacquainted.

"I quit riding him, okay?" she said. "A while ago, actually."

"Mind if I use him instead of Dave's roan?"

"Do what you want," she said. "I haven't touched him in over a year. How long has it been since you've been horseback?"

"Over a year."

"You'll be quite the pair," she said. "He might just be a tad fresh. You might get yourself piled."

"If you want, I'll trim these feet before we go."

"Suit yourself," she said.

This whole homecoming deal was going along great. I haltered the sorrel and followed Sarah out of the corral. I gypped him around a bit waiting for her to find me nippers and a rasp before I tied him in the barn. It just took ten or so minutes to even up his hooves and take off the flares as Sarah saddled up, not saying a word. That horse had always been good about his feet. I looked up and saw those weight-lifters still watching us from the shed. When I had the sorrel squared away I poked around in the saddle room for the rig I'd left there but couldn't find it. I hoped the husband or these two honyockers hadn't borrowed it or hocked it or something worse. I did see a brand-new basket-stamped Wade from Tip's in Winnemucca on a saddle rack. The letters KIP were tooled into the cantle leather, and it didn't look the slightest bit used.

"You can use Kip's rig if you like it so much," Sarah said.

"I'd rather use my dad's if it's still here."

"It's in the house—in my old bedroom," she said. "It'll take me a minute to load the tagging bag if you think you need to go get it."

I hustled over to the house. I knew right where her

room was but I'd never set foot in it, though I'd imagined doing just that a thousand times. It was spare and no nonsense, but next to a desk was my dad's old saddle with the Visalia tree sitting on a wooden rack, as clean and well-oiled as the day it arrived from the maker in Oregon and my dad picked it up at the Greyhound desk in Piute Meadows back when I was probably still trying to pedal my Hot Wheels across a rocky barnyard. And my chinks were hanging off the saddlehorn like I'd just left them there myself. I stood there taking it all in, looking at her stuff, and afraid to wonder why she kept my rig in here with it. She had ordinary things, like a poster from the Elko Cowboy Poetry Gathering a few years back and a few framed pictures and ribbons on the wall. College rodeo stuff. She kicked ass in the barrels and had the pictures to prove it. A couple of years back, I'd given her a pair of teamroping buckles for safekeeping that Dad and I'd won at a Fourth of July jackpot when I was thirteen. I looked around for those, but I didn't see a trace.

There were two photographs on the desk. One was of her mom Lorena, who died over twenty years before when Sarah was little. You could see where Sarah got her looks, and why Dave had never remarried. The other picture was of Sarah, Lester Wendover, and me with some friends at the Deer Hunters' Dance in Piute Meadows the fall Lester and I graduated high school. I don't remember even being in any picture, but there we were. Lester is standing between Sarah and me wearing his big hat and a plaid shirt and the red wild rag I was wearing now. Sarah's boyfriend that month

---

is standing next to her. He was a ski instructor and French, and we all hated him on sight. Everyone is laughing at the camera except Sarah and me. We're both looking past Lester and the boyfriend at each other, like there was nobody else in the picture, like nobody else existed.

After I brushed the sorrel, I eased Dad's rig up on him. Sarah walked out of the saddle room looking calm and pretty and handed me a hackamore. She was wearing a new pair of *armitas* over her jeans with long fringe almost to her boots. She wore what looked like my dad's teamroping trophy buckle under them.

"Pretty *armitas*."

"Wedding present," she said. "Elkhide. From my . . . from Kip."

"Make 'em himself?"

She gave a little snort. She saw me looking at the buckle.

"You mind?" she said.

I just shook my head.

"It reminds me of him," she said. "You're not the only one who misses Leland."

She tightened her cinches and tied on the cantlebag with the tagging gear. I gypped the gelding around a bit more before I got on. I never would have done that when I was eighteen.

"Not the Tommy Smith I remember," she said.

"Yeah, well."

"Does the new wound still bother you?"

"Hardly notice it."

"I bet," she said.

We rode out east past the corrals, through the horse pasture, and up a long slope into a field where willow grew tall along a big ditch and where a new mama cow could get off by herself to calve.

"Dad had most of them tagged already," she said. "They've been calved out for a week or so, but the last ones slipped by me."

"Those gym rats in the shed didn't help you?"

"What do you think?" she said. "They're friends of Kip's from Silver Springs or some place. Not exactly ranch-raised, but at least they don't appear to be tweakers. Kip said they could help with maintenance around the place once they settle in."

"So, where is old Kip today?"

"In Carson," she said. "He has a meeting up at a legislator's office, probably followed by drinks, dinner, that whole thing. He's trying to get support for an Eastern Sierra veterans' jobs program."

"Can't argue with that. He's real go-getter, I hear."

We circled through the stock. Sarah was quiet, watching the cattle like she was afraid to talk. These were first-calf heifers, and they kept them close in to keep an eye on them. Dave's older range cows were mostly out on his winter permit in the Nevada desert thirty miles north, experienced old girls who could get by in hard country. We were just riding along keeping to our own thoughts, and I shook out my loop and swung it to remind the sorrel what-was-what. I was figuring it would've been about time for Dave to gather the pairs off that permit, but to me, that was all untraveled country.

"You're right," Sarah said. She'd been quiet for a long time. "Kip says he likes to lead by example."

I didn't even remember what we'd been talking about.

"So what about you?" she said. "Did you get the college money you reenlisted for?"

"Not exactly."

She looked like that was what she expected me to say.

"I still have some medical stuff to clear up."

"The limp," she said.

"That's part of it."

"So," she said. "Nothing, then."

I told her I'd been looking into officer candidate school with the help of a female captain who'd gone that route. She kind of smirked at that.

"I hope that all works out for you," she said. "Since you gave up so much for it."

We picked up half a dozen pair and eased them toward a wire trap where one rider could hold them while the other roped. Some steers grazing just over the fence raised their heads to watch us. Sarah told me to build a loop and get to it. It felt so good I was excited and rushed it. My toss was pathetic, and my arm felt like a dishrag. Even the sorrel was disgusted and skittered off to the left when the loop landed in the grass.

"Definitely not the Tommy Smith I remember," she said.

Now I took my time thinking about what I was doing and eased up to a little bull calf, then stopped thinking entirely and threw all relaxed, like I'd been at it all afternoon. I got both hind feet at the hocks and dallied and was feeling pretty brash until Sarah stepped off her horse and hustled down my rope. Then I felt like a prize chump. I watched her grabbing the calf's foreleg and flank, jerking it off its feet then laying it down easy with a knee on its neck as I kept the rope tight. I got off, backed the sorrel a step and rooted around in her cantlebag for the applicator and tags. I wrote the cow's ear-tag number on a blank yellow tag and clipped that in the calf's ear. The tagger itself was new and worked so slick and easy I thought I must be doing it wrong. I was keeping Sarah waiting longer than I should have, and I thought she'd be peeved when the sorrel stepped forward and put some slack in the rope. But all she did was have some sport with how rusty I was. When I was done, Sarah let the calf up and it ran back to its mother.

"Next time, you rope and I'll flank. Don't know what I was thinking."

"I'm fine," she said. "I'm perfectly capable of tagging by myself if I have to."

"But you're not by yourself."

She got back on her horse.

"What are the green tags for? You and Kip get your own brand?"

"Boy, nothing gets by you," she said.

I started to ease another pair away from the fence, watching to see if she was going to take her rope down.

"I'm not handling this very well," she said.

"It's okay. You been through hell the last few days."

"I mean the 'seeing you again' part," she said.

Then she gave me a what-the-hell look and we got back

to it, both of us kidding each other now and then, more skittish than the way we used to, but not so bad either. We'd finished with the calf of a green-tagged heifer when Sarah looked up west. The two ironpumpers were bouncing out our way, all ballcaps and muscle shirts, sitting two gentle horses at a lope like a couple of sacks of walnuts. Sarah sort of tensed up and started shaking out a loop to catch the last untagged calf in the trap. The two gunsels kept coming, and some of the heifers scattered along the fence. I edged the sorrel crossways to slow them and Sarah made her throw. She got one hind foot, and I got off. The two were right with us now. I handed my *mecate* to the tall guy sitting a dun mare and smiled nice as you please so he'd hold the sorrel and stay out of our way, then I trotted down Sarah's rope and flanked the calf. Sarah was all business as she got down and clipped that tag on. When we were done, we stepped aboard and I thanked the guy for holding my horse.

"Anything else Delroy and me can do for you, sir?" he said.

Sarah got a cranky look but didn't say anything.

"Sarah and I are going to ride down this ditch a ways to make sure no calf got left behind in the willows. You boys might want to check the cattle in this next field. They should be starting to calve out right about now."

"We'd be glad to . . . Sergeant," the little one called Delroy said.

I kind of frowned at that. We watched those honyockers ride up to the gate, get off and walk through, then get back on and bounce away.

"When do you think they'll figure out that there are no calves to be had out of those *corrientes*?" Sarah said. Her father had summer-pastured Mexican steers for a Reno stock contractor as long as I could remember.

"Not till we're back on your porch getting outside of a couple more beers."

"I blocked out what a smart-ass you are," she said.

We hit a high trot across the pasture back toward the corrals, and I asked her how they knew who I was.

"Kip probably told them you'd be here," she said.

"How did Kip know?"

"I told him you were visiting," she said. "Why wouldn't I?"

I'd had the feeling maybe she hadn't told the new husband I was coming back to that country, or at least that she hadn't asked me to come. Maybe that was just my wishful thinking.

"Those two always seem like they're checking up on me," she said. The afternoon wind picked up and spun the dust over the Hoffstatler ranch. "Sometimes I feel like a stranger on my own place."

We braced ourselves as a wave of dust hit us, turning our faces from the wind.

"I suppose you heard Dad was thinking of selling our water rights," she said.

"You going to?"

"That's his decision, not mine," she said. "But everyone's got an opinion. Some folks said with this drought Dad better sell them quick while they're still worth a bundle." She squinted like the dust hurt her eyes. "You know I have to believe he's coming back. If I don't have that to hang on to, I'll just go crazy."

"I know, babe."

"Don't call me that," she said.

"So, is that why you wanted me here—beside the fact I scare people?"

"In a way, yeah," she said. "Moral support. Even if they don't say it to my face, everyone thinks he's dead. You're the only person I know contrary enough to think maybe he's not. I hope so, anyway."

A bigger gust hit us, and we hunkered down inside our hats and collars.

"The water rights thing was Kip's idea at first," she said when the wind died. "He said Dad could finance a whole new future for me—after Dad was gone. Kip was talking an equine event center, covered arenas, clinics, and all that PR stuff that he's so good at. Dad's not as hidebound as he lets on, so he was intrigued. This is a small place. Even with the permits it's never been easy to make it go. Just as hard in my granddad's day. You know that. Dad thought Kip's idea might give us a better life than just a cow-calf outfit scraping by. I'd be free to quit the sheriff's office—maybe have kids."

She was looking straight ahead so it was hard to read what she was thinking.

"Dad was real high on me marrying Kip," she said. "You need to know that."

"Look, Sarah, all this is none of my business. But you know my dad had more respect for Dave than just about any cowman he knew, and that was saying a lot, so don't get pissed off. I guess I wonder if the best legacy for you and any kids you might have wouldn't be to hang on to those rights. Keep this a working ranch."

"Well," she said, "if I had a different husband, that would surely be the case." She goosed her horse and left me in the dust.

Chapter Three

We rode into the yard holding on to our hats in the stiff gusts. Sarah pulled the mare up as we rounded the horse corral. A second county SUV was parked in the shade facing hers. Mitch Mendenhall, the Frémont County sheriff, was sitting with a deputy inside the SUV out of the wind, talking on his radio. He'd been sheriff since I was in high school.

"I've seen about enough of him the past couple of days," Sarah said. "Since Monday he treats me like a civilian."

Mitch was parked at the base of the buzzards' cottonwood. Sarah rode over to the barn and stepped down from her horse, and I followed. I watched Mitch and the deputy get out while I pulled off my saddle and blankets. The wind seemed to piss Mitch off. Watching the deputy walk up to me and give me a two-handed handshake just pissed him off more. The deputy was Jack Harney. He was a Piute team-roping pal of both Dave and my dad and the chief investigator for the sheriff's office.

"Hey there, Trouble," Jack said. "Heard you was back."

"So, Sarah," Mitch said. Then he said it again louder.

That just made Jack laugh.

Sarah came out of the barn after hanging her bridle up. She stopped on the dirt ramp leading into the barn alley and stood there watching Mitch.

"Kip home?" he asked.

Sarah shook her head no. "In Carson," she said.

Mitch ignored Jack and me when he talked to her. "His phone doesn't answer."

She looked west at the sun. "By now he's probably having drinks and dinner at Adele's," she said. "Schmoozing that state senator he knows. He doesn't take calls in restaurants."

"He's a class act." Mitch finally looked over at me. "She said you'd show up."

"And a damn cheery howdy to you, too—Sheriff."

He stood there staring at me for a minute, kind of huffing. He had a bunch of papers in a file folder and looked down at them.

"Hey, Sarah, can you give this stuff back to Kip then?" he said. He held the file out to her. "It's the cell-phone tracking the Feds did for me."

He was still talking when Sarah slapped both hands over the file and yanked it away.

"He's *my* father," she said. "I just might be the one to see if . . ."

You couldn't make out the rest of what she said. She walked across the yard to the doublewide and climbed the steps, her spurs ringing. The cheap doors and door frames of mobile homes are so light that they don't slam hard, but Sarah did her best.

"This has been real hard on her," Mitch said.

"No shit, Mitch."

"Don't you come back here with that chip on your shoulder," he said. "I'm not cleaning up another one of your messes like when Lester got shot."

"Go to hell."

I'd said it as nice as could be. I even smiled. Jack and I walked across the yard to the barn, and I unsaddled Sarah's mare, then he and I led the horses into to the corral and turned them loose. I crossed the corral and opened the far gate to let all the saddle horses out into the pasture for the night. We walked back toward the barn and waited for Mitch to back his SUV away from the trees. He stopped hard next to us. We let the dust spin over us as Mitch rolled down his window. Jack gave me a grin and got in the passenger side.

"Look," Mitch said. "You and me got to be on the same page on this deal. For Sarah's sake."

I didn't say a word, but I must have nodded. There were already big black and white glops of buzzard shit on the hood of his department vehicle. It was hard to believe this guy won countywide elections three terms in a row.

"But just remember," he said, "there's a spotlight on us here. One wrong move, and we all look like chumps." He backed away from me then put it in gear, heading for the lane. He drove fast enough to disappear in his own dust.

I walked up the steps of the doublewide and knocked. Sarah had slammed the door so hard it bounced back open, but I didn't want to just walk in on her in her new place. I really didn't want to go in at all. She didn't answer the second knock, so I went in anyway. She was sitting on a stool at a counter that separated the kitchen from the living room, and she could see out the window to the barn where Jack, Mitch, and I'd been talking. The light from a small lamp was shining on her face.

"Don't mind Mitch," she said. "He knew you were coming. He just got grumpy when I told him I wanted you around."

"I thought old Kip got those ironpumpers for that."

"They're a joke," she said. "But the husband's impulse was duly noted." She got me a beer, then sat back on the stool.

I looked around for some sign of her in the living room.

"I know," she said. "It has all the charm of the lobby of a Days Inn. We're working on it, but we haven't been here long."

"I didn't say a thing."

"You didn't have to," she said.

There were pictures on the wall, but mostly of Kip, and mostly signed by somebody famous. The only picture of Sarah was from her wedding, taken under some trees by herself, and she looked so beautiful and so happy I didn't linger on it. I looked at a picture of Kip in a big Nevada hat, wild rag, Confederate cavalry goatee and mustaches, grinning like crazy standing next to Buck Brannaman at a horse gentling clinic. Another picture was of him with Sam Elliott on a movie set. There was one of him in a

Hawaiian shirt and ballcap, holding a surfboard with some TV star. And a picture of him with Delroy, the gunsel with the hotdog goatee, both leaning on the open passenger door of a small plane. And finally, a photograph of him in a suit with the new Nevada governor. A wooden plaque with a gold-colored horse trailer on it said good things about the Tule Lake Trailer Company from the Fresno Chamber of Commerce.

"It's like you're married to half a dozen different guys."

Sarah gave me a look. She switched off the lamp and swiveled on the stool to face me.

"They told me there are a few basic ways they'll be looking at Dad's case," she said, "so I want to bring you up to speed."

"Who's 'they'?"

"FBI. Mitch too," she said. "First is kidnapping for ransom, but it's been days now, and there's no demand yet." You could see she was trying to keep the deputy part of her in control.

"If we get a demand," she said, "we'll focus on that tack, demand proof of life, negotiate payment or whatever."

"Okay."

"The second possibility is he was taken by someone. With intent to do harm—" She made a little choking sound. "And he's already dead." She squared herself, a deputy again. "That, of course, is a totally different scenario."

"Yeah."

"Third is that he somehow wandered off. They say most adult missing persons are due to dementia—the wandering off thing—or substance abuse or schizophrenia.

So we can rule those out. But maybe he had a stroke or another heart attack, loss of blood to the brain. Who knows? He's stronger than he looked and might have been able to really cover some ground."

"That makes sense."

"If he fell or passed out," she said, "animals might . . ."

I thought about the buzzards in the cottonwood, but I didn't say anything. Besides, Sarah knew how easy it was to spot carrion in this country.

"Anyway," she said, "we'd know. We-would-know."

"Since there's no word yet from kidnappers or critters, what do you think of your 'doing harm' idea?"

"I try not to think of it at all," she said. "It's too grim."

"Anything in that financial stuff that applies?"

"No. Dad was frugal. I always knew that. That's about it."

"What about the water rights?"

"I don't know what you mean," she said.

"Could the money from that deal factor in to his disappearance?"

"I don't see how," she said. "He didn't have it yet."

We heard a noise outside and she leaned toward the window to look, as twitchy and watchful as Ofelia Cruz. It was getting dusky and she flipped on the yard light.

"Any word from the husband?"

"No," she said.

"Worried?"

"Not really, but since Monday . . ."

"Kip armed?"

"No," she said, like that was some crazy notion. "He's in awesome shape. I don't think he's ever even touched a gun since his discharge." She looked like she was trying hard not to cry.

"Tommy, I feel so helpless."

She kept staring out the window. It was just the two gym rats riding back from their circle through the steers.

"You want me to make sure that pair of top hands get their horses squared away?"

"That would be great," she said. "I'm full of sand and need a shower. We can talk more at dinner, okay?"

"Sure."

I watched her unpin her hair and shake it out as she moseyed down the hall. I'd be lying if I said I didn't wish I was following her. She began unbuttoning her cowboy shirt before she disappeared into the bedroom. I went outside with my beer and sat on the steps watching the weightlifters unsaddle and lead their horses to the corral gate.

"Some guys think they're pretty damn funny," one said.

"Some asshole," said the other one.

They'd passed me at a distance so I didn't know who said what, not that I cared. They looked like they had things handled, but I waited a long while out on the steps just enjoying the evening and how it smelled, and the sounds of those two horses running across the empty corral on their way out to the pasture to join their pals. I was a long way from Georgia and glad of it—for now. I texted Mom that I was having dinner at Sarah's, though she'd probably figured that out hours ago.

A new black GMC pickup with a destroyed tailgate pulled into the yard and two big cowboys got out, joking with the two ironpumpers. The cowboys looked either Indian or Hawaiian. It was hard to tell from a distance. They were semi-drunk, and the gunsels would have a ways to go to catch up. The buzzards in the treetop were just dark shadows against the last of the light, but the slamming of a truck door made the shadows shift and sway in the branches. The tailgate of the cowboys' truck was bent in half at the middle like somebody had tried to unhook a gooseneck trailer and floored the GMC forward without lowering the tailgate first. Could happen to anybody, I suppose. Finally I went back inside.

"I thought you'd got cold feet again and headed for the airport," Sarah said. She was standing at the stove in shorts and a tee shirt and wet hair, whipping up some fajitas and not looking at me. The shower seemed to have perked her up.

"I'm not going anywhere, Sarah."

She finally turned and looked me over.

"God, Tommy," she said. "How long's it been since you slept?"

"I slept on the plane this morning."

"In the fluorescent light you look all gray," she said.

"I figured getting here quick was more important than a week's sleep."

She gave me kind of a sweet look then and dug at the skillet with a spatula, moving the food around in the oil and looking out the window into the yard from time to time. She set plates on the table with tortillas and salsa and hot sauce, limes and guacamole, then brought out two more beers and we sat down.

"Surprised?" she said.

"At what?"

"Dinner," she said. "I know what you and Lester used to say. That I'd better marry some camp-cookin' cowboy like one of you two young rascals or I'd starve to death, I was such a lazy hand in the kitchen."

"I never said any such thing."

She looked happy for about half a second.

"Well I'm glad to hear you never said that to my wife, Tom." It was Kip Isringhausen, standing just inside the front door watching us eat.

Chapter Four

He was shorter than I remembered. There was no telling how long he'd been standing there. Sarah got up and gave him a kiss. He still had that brushed back goatee and mustache like some serious young buckaroo, but he wore a business suit with gator-hide Luccheses and looked prosperous as hell. They talked for a minute between themselves while I fiddled with a tortilla. When I looked back, she had her hand on his chest the way wives and husbands do. Then Kip came over and shook my hand like we were old saddle pals.

"It's sure good to see you back safe, Tom," he said. "I know Sarah was one worried girl when she heard you were wounded again, right, doll?"

Sarah brought out a third plate then sat down without looking at us. "Yup," she said.

"Sarah said you were in town," he said. "So what brings you home?"

"I was visiting my mom. She just moved into a new place at the Marine housing unit a couple of miles from here."

I wasn't sure exactly why I was lying. But then I still wasn't sure exactly what Sarah had said to him about the old boyfriend thing either.

"Well, I know you and your folks were like family to Sarah and Dave," he said. "I bet you've got your own opinion on this whole sad mess."

"Sarah was just filling me in."

He went over to the kitchen and built himself a Maker's Mark on the rocks. He held up the bottle and I nodded yeah.

"I thought you were having dinner up at Adele's, hon," Sarah said.

"Senator Edmunds got stuck in conference," he said. He studied me for a minute. "I'm working with a guy I know in the Nevada legislature trying to fund a bi-state jobs program for returning vets here in the Reno-Bishop corridor. I got a lot of serious inquiries on my website." He handed me the whiskey and sat down with us at the table. Then he held his glass up in my direction. "It's the least I can do."

"Kip got a medical discharge from the Marines nine years ago," Sarah said, "He was trapped in a fire during a training exercise at Parris Island."

"Must have been bad."

Kip waved it off. "None of that seems very important on account of the past few days."

Still, he yanked off his tie and opened his shirt so we could see some nasty burn scars across his six-pack. I just sipped my whiskey. I wasn't about to drop my Wranglers and show him mine.

"Well, you made it to Afghanistan for the both of us," he said.

I drank some more bourbon and just nodded while he tucked in his shirt. I hated crap like that.

Sarah said she wanted to talk about something nice during dinner, which pretty much left out war or pain or death. We settled in to her fajita burritos. She was always a good cook, no matter what she said. We talked about basic training and water rights and different whiskies and where I bought the white cowboy shirt I was wearing until the food was about gone. Unlike most folks in that country, Kip didn't talk at all about horses. When Sarah brought up the young sorrel I'd ridden that afternoon, he acted bored. He was clueless that the horse had been something between the two of us, and she was only mentioning it to let me know she was still pissed I'd left. He asked if I wanted my drink freshened and I said sure.

"So when are you guys going to gather your cows off your desert permit?"

"That's Sarah's deal," Kip said. "I think it's coming up fast though, right, doll?"

"We have to have them off the permit by the end of the month," she said.

"Like I said," Kip said, "coming up fast."

"If I'm still around then, I'll give you a hand. I always wanted to ride that country."

Kip looked at me like he never figured he'd ever have to see me again, much less have me hanging around for a week or two. He took a plastic bowl from me and spooned out more guacamole, though I saw he hadn't eaten much of anything. He started talking again about Dave and what the options were, whether Sarah wanted him to or not. He was definitely a guy who liked to talk.

"Since there's no sign of struggle and nothing Sarah can find that was taken," he said, "the FBI guy said we can probably rule out what he called a crime of opportunity." He sipped his bourbon but kept semi-ignoring his fajitas. "You know, home invasion, a burglary gone wrong, that kind of thing."

"But somebody took Dad's new truck," Sarah said.

"Well," Kip said. "Maybe. They said it might turn up if he got forgetful and wondered off."

"Truck could've been taken even if his disappearance had been a planned thing."

"You could be right, I guess," he said.

"So if it was for anger or hate, did he have any enemies? And if it was for money, who stands to gain?"

"Dave Cathcart had nothing but friends," Kip said.

"Tommy was wondering if Dad wanting to sell his water rights had anything to do with all this," Sarah said.

"Nobody kills someone over water," Kip said.

"In ranch country it used to be considered a leading cause of death. Right up there with fighting over women."

Kip was stone quiet for a second, wondering if he'd been insulted. Then he laughed and looked at the two of us like he'd caught us flirting. "I'd rather fight over a woman any day. How 'bout you, Tom?"

"That would be way past my pay grade."

Sarah got up looking tense and started clearing the plates.

"Well, I still think Dave just wandered off," Kip said.

"If he had," Sarah said, "the vultures would let us know."

"So, what's the deal with those ugly suckers?"

"They're migratory," she said, "so they're on their way north. But they're way, way further north than they should be. I looked them up. They're black vultures—*Coragyps atratus*."

"Never heard of them."

"None of us had," Kip said.

"They range as far south as Chile or Tierra del Fuego," Sarah said, "but traditionally no further north than, say, Nogales."

"What the hell are they doing up here?"

"It's crazy," she said. "It has something to do with droughts, flooding in Arizona, winter habitat and all that." She looked out the kitchen window. "We'd seen them once before. More than twenty years ago when I was just a kid. Then two days before Dad . . . before he disappeared, they show up again." Her voice got faint. "They landed in the same tree they took over all those years ago. Like they'd only been gone an hour." Then she couldn't talk any more.

Kip didn't seem to notice. "They give me the creeps," he said. "I wanted to take a shotgun and clean them out, but Sarah wouldn't let me. She says there's some law says you can't kill 'em. Isn't that so goddamn typical?"

"Federal law. 1918."

"Go, Tom," Kip said. Then he got an edge in his voice like maybe I was messing with him. "How the hell would you know that?"

"You pack in deer hunters, you got to remind them that some scavengers are off limits."

Sarah stood up. She looked like she was going to cry.

"I shouldn't have brought it up," she said. "I'll be right back." She disappeared down the hall.

Kip tossed down the rest of his drink. We could hear Sarah crying then a door shutting.

"I'm glad you're here," he said.

That sort of surprised me.

"I worry about her," he said. "I mean, how do you handle it if there was someone out there who hated your father enough to do him harm? I can't imagine losing a father."

"Yeah. Gotta be hard."

"But she's tough," he said. "I can't tell you how tough that girl is."

He freshened his drink and held up the bottle, and I shook my head no. Sarah came back in, her face bright like she'd doused it with ice water.

"Tom and me were talking about his deployment as a sniper," Kip said.

"Which one?" Sarah said. "He's had so many."

"Dave said you were big stuff as a sniper," he said. "Some kind of hero. He sounded real proud of you."

"Just a job."

"I'm trying to picture you in your ghillie suit," Kip said, "lying still for hours till you made your shot."

"Ghillie suit?" Sarah said.

"Yeah," Kip said. "It's a super camouflage outfit. Sticks

and rags and native foliage so Tom here would look like that scarecrow from the Oz movie—except with an M-one-ten. That about right?"

"Actually I always thought guys wearing them looked like an old hay bale popped open and left out in the weather." I was surprised he was so up on all the sniper stuff. "And I like the old bolt-action M-twenty-four myself."

"Why the hell?"

"More like my deer rifle."

"You're a crazy bastard," he said. "Did you make your own camouflage suit?" he said. "I read some guys make their own."

"Maybe should've, but I never used one. Some places you'd have to make one out of sand."

"You two are pathetic," Sarah said. "Like a couple of little boys." She went back to rinsing plates in the kitchen.

"Any chance of a redeploy when you get back to Benning?" he said.

"Not unless I begged for it."

Sarah clanked a dish so hard on the sink I thought she'd busted it. Kip looked clueless. He pointed to my empty glass.

"So how do you like that?" he said. "The Maker's Mark?"

"It's good. Tastes sort of like Wild Turkey."

"I told Sarah the exact same thing," he said, "but even smoother. And I like it totally better than that gnarly old Jack Daniel's."

"Oh, Uncle Jack and I go way back. That and Crown Royal. Sour mash, Canadian, it's all good."

"But this is ninety proof," he said. "More bang for the buck."

"One way to look at it."

"So what did you drink in Kabul?" he said.

"Blood of my enemies, mostly."

He was pretty sure I was trifling with him then.

"Okay, smart guy," he said. "You were deployed in both places. What's the biggest difference between the terrain in Iraq and Afghanistan?"

"Afghanistan's taller. Mountains look just like Lone Pine."

He sat quiet for a minute clenching his jaw and looking at his phone. Then he gulped down the last of his whiskey and hopped out of his chair. "Wow, buckaroos and buckarettes. How'd it get so damn late? I gotta get a jump on tomorrow." He went to the sink and grabbed Sarah's hand. "So, Tom, can you let yourself out?"

Sarah looked poleaxed. He just pulled her out of that kitchen right past me, heading for the hallway.

"Make sure you come see us before you head back east." He looked all happy again. Then he led Sarah off down the hall and that was that.

I stood there a second feeling like a prize tool. Then I got the hell out of that place.

I walked toward Dave's dark ranch house in the yard light's cottonwood shadows. On a bare limb at the top of the one cottonwood I could see a single vulture silhouetted against the sky. I went up the steps to Dave's porch and pulled off the scraps of yellow police tape draped over the rail, just mad as hell. I was wishing I'd helped Sarah clear the damn table and not knowing why I didn't, and wishing I'd stayed in Georgia and was damned sure why I hadn't. And that "buckarette" bullshit was something Lester used to say that Kip must've heard from Sarah, so that just galled the crap out of me, too.

Parked next to my old Dodge there was a new Diesel Ram 3500 Dually. They were pretty much the exact same truck, with barely twenty-five years and fifty-five thousand dollars separating them. Kip might have parked so far from his doublewide so we wouldn't hear him drive up and he could slip in quiet the way he did—like he wanted to see if Sarah was up to something with me. Or he might have wanted to show me that his was bigger and more pricey than mine. Or, maybe he was as good a guy as everybody said he was. Maybe he was just stopping by to make sure his weightlifting pals were squared away, all tucked in for the night. Maybe it was me that was acting like an asshole.

Either way, he'd had the last word, and I still didn't have a clue what I could do to help Sarah find her dad. I shoved the bunches of police tape in my truckbed under the spare. As I drove off I noticed that the pickup of the two Indian cowboys was gone.

Chapter Five

Fifteen minutes later I pulled into the Marine housing unit, creeping up a little drive and finding a place to park close to Burt's apartment. It wasn't yet ten and the place was quieting down fast, with lights going out all around me. Mom had given me her keys so I could let myself in. Their place was on the ground floor, facing back toward the main road. I turned a couple of keys before I found the right one. I don't think she'd ever lived in a place before where she locked her doors.

I stretched out on the bed she'd made up for me on the couch in the spare bedroom they used as an office and stared at the ceiling. I must have slept a bit because when I woke up it was after two. I got up and explored the little room but didn't see many traces of what used to be my life. In the closet I found my dad's old Remington .270 that he'd given me before he died. I turned off the light and set the rifle on the rug next to the couch so I could reach down and touch it if I felt like it. I looked at my phone to see if I'd missed a text from Captain Cruz. There was a message, but it was from Sarah from about eleven thirty that night. She said, *Breakfast MT about 7?* That would be the Mark Twain Café in Piute Meadows about forty miles south. I spelled out *Affirmative* and tried to get back to sleep without looking at the message from her that brought me there, and without thinking of Sarah and Kip behind that closed door. I had about as much success as you'd figure.

I was up early for coffee with Mom and Burt. A young Marine packer with a shaved head and tattooed sleeves named Eddie showed up to carpool Burt to the base, and I could see folks in uniform outside starting their cars in the predawn. Even after we talked mules over more coffee for a bit, I was still on the road by six. Forty-five minutes later I'd passed through Rickey Junction on my way out of Shoshone Valley, wound through West Frémont Canyon, passed the Sonora turnoff leading to the Marine base, cruised down the slope from Hell Gate Pass through the Basque sheep outfit, and then rolled out into Piute Meadows. I could see the headquarters of Dominion Land & Cattle straight ahead, and the old 1860s house under the poplars where the highway took a hard turn to the left. I got closer and could see the new tin roof on the fresh-painted house. Before Dominion bought the place from John Wesley Allison's widow, the house was where Allison's ranch foreman lived. From four years before I was born until I was almost nineteen and he died, the foreman had been my dad, and that house was the only home I ever knew. It was behind me in a flash as I made the turn and headed straight across the pastures into Piute Meadows two miles ahead.

By quarter to seven I was camped at a window table at the Mark Twain Café, drinking more coffee and watching the street. I was fiddling with my phone when an older couple I knew who had a livestock vaccine business stopped by the table to say hi. We talked for a minute before they took a booth. I went back to my phone, to the text from Sarah I got a few days before.

Dad's been taken. I need you. Come home as soon as you can.

Love, S

That was all. I'd already read it a thousand times.

A couple of minutes later Sarah walked through the door dressed for work. It was funny. Neither of us could ever stand being late. I set the phone on the table before she could catch what I was looking at.

"Sitting with your back to the wall like Wild Bill Hickok, I see." She leaned down and gave me a half-assed kiss on the cheek. I caught the vaccine lady sneaking a glance.

"Thanks for coming," Sarah said. She looked like she'd slept even worse than I did. "Just to set the record straight, nothing happened last night after you left—between Kip and me. He did that just for show."

"He's your husband, for chrissakes. You don't owe me an explanation."

"You're getting one anyway," she said. "Even if you don't deserve it."

"What do you mean?"

"You were rotten to him last night," she said. "If someone was that snarky to you, you'd take 'em out."

"Sorry. I'm not handling this 'seeing you again' business too great either."

"Good," she said.

"Can you just tell me what's going on?"

She waited until the waitress set coffee in front of her and freshened my cup. Sarah didn't look happy.

"I left Kip about three weeks ago. I moved back in with Dad."

"Jesus, Sarah."

"That's why the morning he disappeared, Dad was cooking me breakfast at the house. I was living there."

"And that's why Kip was in Reno?"

"Yeah," she said.

"What the hell happened?"

"It wasn't anything I could put my finger on. I guess I'd been second-guessing myself. Wondering if I'd made a mistake committing to this great guy when maybe I wasn't over a certain irresponsible . . . somebody. I don't know. It'd been gnawing at me for a while. Then I was lying in bed one morning watching him get out of the shower, preening in front of the mirror and talking nonstop about his plans and himself and all the cool things he'd done. He'd left me in bed on my day off when we might have had some time together. Instead of spending the morning with his wife, he'd gone out to go lifting with his dork pals in that dirty old equipment shed."

"I thought the gunsels had just moved in."

"They've been practically living with us for months," she said. "That's why they had all those weights already here." She looked out the window at a stock truck rattling by. "Anyway, Kip had come back inside about nine thirty to shower. He was wired like crazy, and all of a sudden I was spooked. I looked at him like some suspect, not like my husband. It was creepy. I'd heard everything he'd said dozens of times, but I realized that every time things were a little different. Details were changed like he was just making stuff up as he went along, or maybe testing me to see if I'd notice the changes in the story. It came to me that I didn't know this guy at all. I lived with him and slept with him and made plans for the future with him, but all of a sudden he was like a stranger. I thought back and remembered that if I ever asked him a question, he took it as a threat and got mean. Sometimes worse than mean—totally untracked."

She stopped when the waitress came back and took our order.

"Later that day, we were at the barn and I asked him something about that trailer company he used to own. The ranch needs a better stock trailer than my barrel-racing rig, and I wanted his opinion. I thought he'd be flattered, but that set him off and he came after me. He was in a rage, saying I was spying on him. I ran into the kitchen and locked the door but he jammed his hand through the glass and unlocked it and kept on coming. I thought he was going to hit me, but then he got sweet and apologetic and wanted—" She stopped talking. She looked whipped. "You know what he wanted."

"Did he hit you?"

"No," she said. "No man has ever hit me, and no man ever will."

"Good."

She looked like she'd talked too much.

"Anyway," she said, "I needed some breathing room. Thinking room. So I moved out."

"Selling that trailer company—it set him up pretty good?"

"Well enough, I guess," she said. "He always seems to have money—for the mobile home, for his veteran's deal and trucks and gifts. Nice clothes, nice dinners. First class airfare to Vegas for the NFR."

"Big rodeo fan, huh?"

She looked sort of embarrassed. "You know, the things guys do to impress."

"I guess I don't."

"Bull," she said. "You used to try to impress me."

"I was just a kid."

She started to say something, then didn't.

"So," she said, "did you believe his story about Parris Island?"

"Not really."

"Why?"

"I figured he was bullshitting. Doubtful he would have trained there if he was from that little Swedish town outside Fresno."

"Kingsburg," she said.

"He'd more likely have started his Basic at the Recruit Depot in San Diego, not South Carolina."

"I'm not surprised," she said. "He likes to make himself the star of every story. But he did get those scars on his belly somehow."

"Yeah. So maybe it's nothing, Sarah. We all have stuff in our stories that don't track."

"I just felt in my gut that I didn't really know him," she said. "Maybe I just fell for the image—the charming, successful guy." She looked just about drained. "And the life he could offer. Anyway, I told him I needed some space and moved back in with Dad."

"What did Dave think of all this?"

"Dad thought Kip walked on water. It was almost like he pushed me into . . ." She quit looking at me. "Into his arms. I think Dad was wanting grandkids."

I didn't say anything.

"Dad got to know Kip first," she said. "He helped Dad with all sorts of stuff. Putting on training clinics, jackpot ropings—all the stuff Dad loves."

"He knew a lot about those, did he?"

"Not really," she said, "but Kip's a diabolical organizer and an awesome talker. And Dad genuinely liked him. He thought they were going to be a team. Kip took an interest in everything Dad did. He acted like spending his life keeping Dad's dream alive was all he wanted. It flattered Dad."

The waitress brought Sarah's omelet and my chicken-fried steak, and we got to it for a bit.

"When he was courting me after you left," she said, "he seemed too good to be true."

I wasn't touching that. "Was he mad you moved out?"

"He was cold," she said. "As cold as I've ever seen anyone."

"You hurt his feelings."

"*That* is really touching, Tommy," she said. "Coming from you."

"You ever consider that you figuring you might not love this guy, then leaving him, might have triggered something—something that ended with Dave getting taken?"

"No," she said. I was annoying her again. "That would be too much of a leap."

"What about selling his water rights? Would that put Dave crosswise with anybody?"

"No," she said. "Why would it?"

"I got no idea. I'm just throwing stuff out there. I thought that's maybe why you asked me here."

She looked at me like I was about the dumbest son-ofabitch she'd ever seen.

"I told you yesterday why I asked you. To have you here right by my side to scare the crap out of anybody messing with my father—or me." She gave me a snarky look. "Hey, sweetheart, nobody does it better."

I wiped my sourdough toast in the gravy and looked out the window.

"I'm sorry," she said. "That was mean."

"When did you move back in?"

"When I got your message a couple of days ago saying you were coming," she said. "I only wanted to deal with one crisis at a time."

"How'd he react?"

"Weird," she said. "Both possessive and standoffish.

Like he's punishing me by refusing to touch me. And he's gotten even weirder since you showed up. He knows our history, so I guess I can't blame him for that."

"And how'd you react?"

"*Relieved.* Jesus, Tommy, what kind of question is that?"

She picked up my phone and started fiddling with it, not really paying attention. When she saw me tense up as she scrolled around my messages it seemed to make her happy.

"Who's Captain Cruz?" she said.

"One of the company commanders at Fort Benning."

"Nice underwear," she said, "and great boobs. She a sniper too?"

"She wishes she was. Helluva shot, though."

"She misses you, 'lover', but she doesn't know how to spell Ophelia."

"It's Mexican. Ofelia."

"Whatever," she said.

I took the phone back.

"Oh shit."

"What?" I whipped around to see what Sarah was looking at.

"My husband just drove by." She didn't say anything else, just sat there afraid to move.

"It's okay. We're not doing anything wrong here, Sarah."

The café was at the east end of town, the last building on the south side of Main Street before the river bridge. The parking lot was around back. Across the side street was the tall old Masonic Lodge, so once you drove by the café on Main Street it would be hard to glance back for a good look at what cars were parked there. I flagged down the owner for a coffee to go.

"Get to the office. Start your day. When you see Kip next, tell him we had breakfast, or don't tell him. Whichever. I'll cruise down and see where he is, and maybe him and me will shoot the breeze. I'll be polite as hell after grinding his nuts last night."

"Okay," she said. "Okay."

We walked to the door, and she took the coffee from the owner and headed out to the parking lot. It bothered me how spooked she looked.

I joked with the owner like nothing had happened and sat back down by the window to finish my breakfast. I watched Sarah's truck pull out of the lot and turn left opposite the Ponderosa Motel just across Main Street. The waitress brought the check, and I handed her my card. Then I got out my phone and texted a guy I'd known at Walter Reed who was serving in the Provost Marshall's office at Pendleton and asked him to find out what he could about a Marine named Kip Isringhausen.

Chapter Six

I turned on to Main Street myself a few minutes later. I could see Kip's white Ram a block away parked in front of the Sporting Goods. I pulled over a few cars behind it and walked up the sidewalk like I hadn't a care, then I stepped inside. Kip was standing at the counter buying something from Nick, the owner, who was just opening up. Kip was dressed like a city boy on vacation with hiking shorts and boots and a fisherman's shirt. He looked up when he heard the little bell over the door and smiled almost like he was expecting me. I waved and browsed among the flyrods and shotguns, just passing the time. Nick shouted hi, and I shouted back while I took a nice Lamson reel out of its box. The Sporting Goods was small and cluttered and old as hell. It had been a lunch counter, a saloon, a billiard parlor and another saloon, and had a justice court on the second floor until about 1900. An acquitted murderer coming down the stairs from that court had been attacked by a mob and beheaded out in the street. But that was a long time ago. Nick and his parents had owned the store as long as I could remember, and the pine floorboards were worn deep between the nailheads.

I eased up to the counter and saw Kip buying 9mm ammo.

"Hey, Tom," he said. "Long time no see. Hope you didn't think I was rude last night. The last few days have about wrung me out."

"I bet."

"Yeah," he said. "I was whipped and ready to hit the rack."

Then I saw him smirk like some high school jerk who'd been telling his boys about nailing the cutest cheerleader. I almost took him out right there.

"Stocking up?"

"Yeah," he said. "I just bought a new SIG. Since the thing with Dave, you can't be too careful."

"What kind of SIG?"

"A totally sick P-two-two-six Blackwater," he said. "A righteously fine piece." Talking about the pistol seemed to make him happy.

Nick brought him a handful of cash in change, then reached over the counter and shook my hand and told me how good it was to see me safe. He was about twenty years older than me and looked like an eighth grade history teacher, but a lot of what I learned as a kid about fishing and shooting in that country I learned from Nick.

"Got one myself."

"A SIG?" Kip said.

"A nine millimeter. A Beretta."

"Which one?" he said, "The M-nine?"

"M-nine-A-one. Pretty basic, though."

"Do you have it with you?" he said. "I'd love to burn some powder with you before you leave town. You could check me out on it. You could teach me a lot, I bet."

Nick sort of smiled at that.

"Until the FBI gets a handle on the Dave thing," he said, "we don't know what the hell we're up against, so I wanna be ready."

A Mexican-looking girl stepped out from the rear of the store to wait on a fisherman back by the old glass-front drink coolers.

"Left the Beretta back in Georgia, sorry. You might want to try those Remington rounds with the nickel-plated casings in that new SIG. Lower friction coefficient. They'll feed and extract real smooth, and you'll never jam."

Kip grinned at Nick. "I said this guy could teach me a lot." He held up his fist at me. "Combat experience. No wonder the bad guys you tangled with up at that pack station never had a chance."

I fist-bumped him in spite of myself. He picked up the box of cartridges.

"Can I trade up, Nick?" he said.

Nick said sure and brought out the nickel-plated rounds. He re-rang the sale and recounted Kip's change. The girl smiled at us as she went behind the register to ring up the fisherman's Bud Light.

"Maybe we can figure a way to shoot a bit before you go, anyhow," Kip said. "I'm new to all this, but there's obviously some bad actors on the loose."

"So you don't buy the Dave-wandering-off scenario now?"

"Hey," Kip said. "I think we've got to consider every angle."

"Well, if I have some time to go shoot, I'll give you a yell. Maybe tomorrow."

"Great," he said. He was looking the girl over as she walked around us, then he gave me a look.

"Sweet," he said when she disappeared into the back room. "*Ay Chihuahua.*" Then he headed for the door. I just shrugged, but Nick looked peeved. He leaned both hands on the counter, watching Kip cross the sidewalk.

"Good to see you, stranger," he said. "We hope you're about done with your foreign adventures."

"You and me both."

Nick looked out the window as Kip fired up his Ram. "That guy's a character," he said. "A steady customer, always friendly, and always pays cash. But he knows Conchetta's my niece and he's still being a crass jerk. On the other hand, a few more like him and I'd retire."

"You'll never retire."

"So, can I get you anything, my friend?"

"I guess I'm handled. I don't know. Probably could use a sixpack."

"What's your poison?"

"Sierra Nevada?"

"Kip's favorite," Nick said.

"Then Coors'll do."

"It's funny what he said about just buying that SIG," Nick said. "He's had that pistol as long as I've known him."

He rang me up while I snagged a sixpack from the cooler and fetched it back to the counter.

"Take 'er easy, Nick."

"You too, Tommy. Welcome back."

I started to walk out when I saw the two Indian cowboys who'd been visiting the ironpumpers the night before. They'd walked up from the General Store and were climbing in the cab of the GMC with the ruined tailgate. I turned around and saw Nick heading toward the back of the store where they stocked clothes and waders and such. "Hey, Nick, who are these guys?"

He came back and stood next to me.

"The two Indian guys in that black pickup."

We looked out the window at the GMC pulling out into Main Street.

"The Miller brothers," he said. "A couple of real mean drunks. They got arrested on some assault thing with Jedediah Boone last year."

"Jed's been bad news since the third grade. He'd wipe his boogers on the little kids."

That made Nick laugh. We watched the GMC make an illegal U-turn.

"Say, Nick, do you have a box of those Remington two-seventy soft points?"

I drove west to the end of town. Instead of going straight out on the Reno Highway the way I'd come, I turned right and cruised the back streets to see if Kip or the Miller brothers were still around. Piute Meadows is barely four blocks wide, so it didn't take me but a minute, but I still felt

I was going nowhere fast as my dad used to say. I eased by the sheriff's office and saw Sarah's Silverado parked in the lot, then I drove out into the big meadows to hunt up some friends.

The Summers Lake Road turned one way then another every mile or so southwest across the valley. Four miles from town I passed the lane of the Bonner & Tyree ranch. Three more miles and I turned right off the pavement past some fishing cabins then climbed up a washboard logging road that angled across the face of the ridge. I could see the whole valley down to my right. After a mile or so the road turned left into Aspen Canyon. I crossed and recrossed the creek on Forest Service bridges before I got to the first drift fence. Beyond the locked aluminum gate was the Bonner & Tyree grazing permit, and down to the right was Harvey Linderman's pack outfit, Aspen Station.

At the fence a dirt road made a hard right down the hill to the creek. I hadn't got far before I hit another locked gate and a sign that said DOMINION LAND & CATTLE— PRIVATE PROPERTY. I rooted around under a couple of rocks until I found the key. I got back into the truck and could see that the meadow straddling the creek was full of cattle, not Harvey's horses and mules. At the bottom of the slope I crossed the bridge and turned left through the aspen along the fence to the pack station, but it was gone. Harvey's trailer at the end of the road was gone. The tin snow-survey hut in the aspen next to the trailer was gone. And the wood pack platforms had been burned where they sat. Only the corrals and loading chute and the refrigerator box off the back of a milk truck we used for a saddle shed were still standing. The corrals had been rebuilt by somebody with money. They'd replaced the long wood hitching rack and grain trough with welded pipe. The refrigerator box was half-hid back amongst the aspen, the painted sides mostly bare sheet metal with rusty streaks and the doors padlocked together with a big chain. I got out of the truck and sat on a log with a Coors and just about cried. I worked here all through high school and one summer two years ago when I was back from my second tour. This place had meant the world to me. But nothing lasts forever.

I looked out over the meadow at Dominion's cattle. This piece of ground had belonged to Allison's when my dad ran that ranch, and they'd leased it to Harvey since before the crust had cooled. Dominion bought Allison's three years before, so they must have finally canceled Harvey's lease and kicked him off. I drained my beer and looked out across the meadow to the creek where we'd walk out with the dogs before sunup and run in the stock, and I remembered how the horses and mules would charge out of the tamarack through the creek crossing to the corrals with the dogs on their heels.

I took a last look and got in the truck. When I came to the bridge, I got out again and walked out on the planks. It was nothing but the undercarriage of an old railroad freight car that Harvey had hauled up there somehow. I'd stood on that bridge one night with a rifle in my hand thinking I was going to make my stand right then and there and save the world. My world, anyway. It didn't quite work out the way I planned—for me or for the guys trying to cross that bridge.

I got out one last time to drive through the gate and lock it behind me. When the road topped out at the trailhead, there was a pickup parked against the hill under the trees that wasn't there when I drove in. It was the Miller brothers' GMC. They must have followed me from town. And I must have been losing my touch. I pulled up next to the drift fence gate and shut off my engine and rolled down the windows. No one was in the GMC cab and there was no sound except the wind in the Jeffrey pine. I got out and walked over to the truck. The cab was full of fast food and beer trash. I didn't see any weapons, but there was an empty 12 gauge shell box smashed on the floormats with the Subway wrappers and MGD bottles. There was a beat-up drink cooler in the truckbed along with some tools. Finally, I could hear a hammer pounding from the direction I'd just come. The Miller brothers arrived directly.

They walked up toward me along the fenceline on the other side of the wire. One carried a hammer and a number ten can that probably had fence staples in it. The handles of wire pliers stuck out of his back pocket. The other guy carried a shovel and wore a Ruger revolver on his belt.

"We're fixing fence for Becky Tyree," one said.

"I don't recall asking you what the hell you're doing. But the fence don't need fixing."

"Well, we're tellin' you," the other said. They started climbing over the H brace next to the aluminum gate and had a slow time of it. They obviously didn't have a key to the gate.

"Becky Tyree wouldn't hire the likes of you to drag off a dead cow."

"You go to hell," the first one said. He was panting from his climb.

"Say hi to Jedediah for me. And make sure he don't wipe any boogers on you."

The second one put his hand on the butt of his Ruger.

I turned my back on them and walked over to my Dodge and got in. They took a couple of steps toward me but didn't seem to have the stomach for much more. I could see them rooting in their cooler in my rearview as I drove away.

I bounced back down the logging road, dust trailing above me. On the downslope toward the valley I passed an old Toyota pickup heading upslope with a Mexican guy in a straw hat behind the wheel. He waved and I recognized him from a few years back as Dominion's irrigator, a guy named Francisco. I crossed the creek and turned in among the fishing cabins alongside Summer's Lake Road, backing my truck around so I was hidden from anything coming up behind me by a big clump of granite. Pretty soon the GMC rattled by me, and I waited until they hit the pavement. They stopped there for a housekeeping minute to throw their trash out the cab windows into the sagebrush.

I stayed on their bumper for about a mile, cruising at seventy through the sage. The pavement straightened out and you could see the Bonner & Tyree headquarters about a mile beyond. I eased off then and let the two drunks pull ahead fast on their way toward town.

In a couple minutes more I turned into Becky Tyree's

ranch. In the distance down her lane was a big old house in some poplars with a screened side porch. I saw three riders coming up from below the barn behind two cow-calf pairs. When they got closer, I got out of the truck.

"Jay-sus Chroist," one of them said. "Look what the dog drug home." It was Harvey Linderman, closing the corral gate from the back of a big old gelding. The other two were Becky and her half-Piute son, Dan, who was ten or fifteen years older than me. I walked down to the barn with them as they unsaddled and we talked. It was the first time I felt comfortable since I stepped off the plane the morning before.

Becky gave me a long hug and told me they'd all been worried about me there in Afghanistan. Then she asked me as easy as she could what brought me back into their country.

"Got a message from Sarah. She asked me to get on out here as soon as her dad disappeared."

"That's what I hoped happened," Becky said. "I'm glad you two are talking. She needs you now."

"I don't know what I can do."

"Just being here for her is important," she said. We all walked out of the barn toward the house. "Hearing you were back is the only bright spot in this whole mess."

"I don't know if her husband or Mitch'd agree with you."

We went inside and washed up, and Dan and Becky heated up a mess of leftover chili and corn bread and invited me to lunch. We all danced around the Dave thing at first. It was just too grim to talk about all the time. Becky asked about my mom, and I asked about the pack station. That was like I figured. Dominion had stopped renting Harvey the site in the canyon so Dan had hired him to irrigate that summer and let him lease pasture for his stock while he figured out his next move. I asked him if he was getting out of the outfitting business for good.

"Chroist," Harvey said, "since the economy went into the shitter, it's anybody's guess. I got a bunch of hunters booked this fall, so me and Dan will pack them out of Hell Gate into that Little Frémont country in late September. Always plenty of deer up there. I don't know if it's going to be worth it to even get the permits, though."

We jawed about this and that until we got to what brought me back. I told them what I'd learned from Sarah and Mitch about the FBI and their theories and protocols. It was Harvey who first brought up Kip Isringhausen, and everyone around that table took a deep breath and stopped looking me in the eye.

"You've met him," Becky said. "Haven't you Tommy?"

"Had dinner with him just last night. Cheerful bugger—considering the situation."

"And easy on the eyes," she said.

"He's a world-beater," Dan said. "He'll tell you so himself."

"Yeah. I guess he and Dave were pretty tight."

I saw Becky and Harvey trade a look.

"Ran into him in town again this morning. At Nick's. Wants to go shooting with me."

"Hell," Harvey said. "We should warn that city boy to watch his back."

"Hey, Tommy," Dan said, "you're not going to go shoot Sarah's new husband are you?"

"You two," Becky said. She glared at them both and went to rap Harvey's knuckles with a spoon, but he yanked his hand back. His beer gut kind of shimmied when he tried not to laugh at her.

"Kip seems like he means well," she said. "He called me last month to see if Dan and I could help Dave when they gather his desert permit. Dave was talking about getting his cows out before the BLM deadline because they were running out of feed. Kip seemed real concerned about Dave not overdoing things with his bad heart and everything."

"When Kip says he'll do something, he does it," Dan said. "I'll give him that."

We were all quiet for a minute.

"Anybody here know a couple of big old guys with the name of Miller?"

"The Miller brothers?" Dan said. "Oh yeah, Tommy, I know 'em. A pair of no-accounts from Indian Camp in Shoshone Valley. Pretty good cowboys when they were young. Later they worked for a hay outfit when they were sober till they beat a guy half to death when they weren't. You know those lowlifes, Tommy?"

"Nope. They're friends of some guys Kip knows."

"Friends of Randy Ragazino and Jedediah Boone, too," Dan said. "So don't you turn your back on 'em."

"They just followed me up Aspen Canyon and back."

"Did they give you trouble?" Dan said.

"Uh-uh."

"Their last name is Sam or Tom or Jim," Harvey said, "one of them traditional Piute families. But they been called the Miller boys since they were young ones 'cause they were weaned on Genuine Draft. Started as a joke, but they been called that so long most folks don't rightly remember their real name."

We finished and Dan got us some more coffee. The late spring afternoon wind had kicked up with some bite in it, and they were all glad to linger inside a bit. I asked Dan if he had a pistol I could borrow in case Kip and I did go terrorize some targets before I left. He said a Smith & Wesson .22 Mag was all he had ammo for at the house, but I was welcome to it.

From tiptoeing around the subject of Sarah's husband, now it seemed like that was all these folks could talk about. Harvey was joking about a Ford flatbed Kip had bought from some guy in Fallon for a work truck for Dave, but it had one thing wrong with it after another.

"Talk about him doing whatever he'd brag he'd do," Harvey said to Dan. "When he had to replace the clutch and rebuild the transfer case the same summer, he said the next damn thing to go wrong with that bastard, he'd rip the steering wheel right off the column, and I should remember I'd heard him say it."

"He's stout," Dan said, "but nobody's that stout."

Becky stood up and put the plates in the sink. Then she leaned back on the kitchen counter and watched us like she had heard all this before.

"Well, a couple weeks after that, the alternator went," Harvey said, "and I saw that sonofabitch jump in the cab and grab that wheel and go for it. His veins were popping and his face was purple, but damned if he didn't rip that goddamn wheel right off the column." He laughed. "That wheel was bent half-over. I never seen anything like it. That is one stout boy."

"Sounds like roid rage," Dan said. "You about ready, Harv?"

"Let's get to it," Harvey said.

The two of them said their good-byes to me, grabbed their hats and headed out the back door to doctor a cancer-eyed cow they'd just brought in. Becky was leaning her hands on the counter, staring out the window toward the barn watching them go. She turned and saw me get up to leave. At around sixty, Becky was still a real pretty woman, tall and shapely and full of life, with a long braid down her back like a girl, though the braid was mostly gray.

"Wait right here," she said. She headed for the dining room door.

I sat back down to finish my coffee and listened to her footsteps on the stairs. I'd sat at this table with my dad and the Tyrees when I was little and their world was all I thought I ever wanted to know. In a couple of minutes Becky came back into the kitchen with a cloth sack and set it down on the table in front of me. It thunked when it landed.

"This was my late husband's," she said. "It's kinda low-tech, but it's got more oomph than a twenty-two."

I pulled a Colt single-action Army .45 out of the sack. It was in a plain leather gun rig with three cartridges still in the loops. I looked up at Becky to see if she was serious. Old as it was, this was a pretty serious piece of hardware.

"Dave's been kidnapped or worse," she said. "Sarah's in some kind of trouble, and now you're back, looking as grim as the wrath of god. Don't think I'm a crazy old woman, but all this gives me a bad feeling."

"Me too, I guess."

"Anyway," she said, "since you and Dan were talking guns."

"Yes, ma'am. I know."

I pulled the pistol out of the holster and half cocked it so I could spin the cylinder across my palm and listen to that old gunfighter sound that no other revolver quite makes. I lowered the hammer and set the gun on the table and slid a round out of the loops. The brass was sticky green with verdigris from the tannins in the leather.

"Those are wrecked," she said, "but I know Nick stocks these Long Colts in town."

"Little WD-40 and a rag and these are good-to-go. But I might be wanting more than three."

"That sounds ominous."

"Yeah, well. We don't know what we're dealing with here."

"Right enough," she said.

It did start to worry me that old Becky was thinking the way I was thinking—that Dave had been taken and was probably dead, and that this wasn't the end of it. More likely just the beginning of something we didn't understand. Becky had seen a lot in her day, and not all of it good. Her late husband was a legendary horse trainer in our part of the country and well-loved, but he had his dark side, and had done time.

"You got any thoughts on Dave selling his water rights?"

"I think it's nuts," she said. "I blame the husband for dangling dollar signs over a sick old man's head."

"No argument here. Does Hoyt Berglund still have that environmental consulting office in town?"

"Just across from Nick's," she said. "You passed it getting here. You going to talk to him about Dave?"

"Thought I might."

"Good," she said. "That restoration plan is going to ruin this country."

I put the Colt back in its holster and the whole rig in the sack and got up, nodded thanks, and headed for the door. I had almost made a clean getaway before she said a word.

"Tommy," she said, "I'm just sorry as can be about all this business with Sarah. You two were meant for each other, and everybody in this valley knows it."

"I know it too, ma'am. I just don't know how to make it right."

"You'll figure it out," she said. She nodded at the sack in my hand like my whole life was inside it. "Or it'll get figured for you."

Chapter Seven

The one-story building sat on a corner across a side street from the firehouse. There was no sign that you could see driving by, but I remembered the building had been a thrift store for years and a liquor store owned by Lester Wendover's grandfather before that. Lester's dad used to tell us that, when he was in high school, he'd pick an argument with his old man to distract him while his pals shoplifted Jim Beam half-pints. Then he and his friends would stuff the half-pints in their boot-tops before local dances. When they were good and drunk, they'd start hellacious fights with boys from Rickey Junction.

I was almost to the door before I saw a brass plaque that said BERGLUND CONSULTANTS. Seemed like overkill on such a crappy unpainted little building, especially as there were no other consultants besides Hoyt. A girl who looked about fifteen was sitting at a computer. She told me that Hoyt was "out in the field" today. When I asked where, she said she didn't rightly know. She did say that he'd be by the Hoffstatler ranch tomorrow and offered me directions. I asked if I could look at the maps on the wall for a minute. Hoyt had maps of both the East and West Frémont drainages. They were covered with clear plastic sheets so he could color and outline the parcels, and just looking you could see how the acquisition was going. On the Shoshone Valley maps I could see Hoffstatler's outlined and shaded in red—a done deal. I could see several more red parcels downstream for thirty-five miles until the two rivers joined. It was forty miles more to the desert lake.

To the left of Hoffstatler's parcel, the Cathcart ranch was shaded in gray. I asked the girl what that meant. She said it meant the parcel was still in play. She said Dave Cathcart was real positive about moving forward. She didn't have a clue, but that didn't make her much different from anybody I'd talked to since I touched down.

I went out to the sidewalk into the early afternoon wind. I took my jacket out of my truck and crossed Main Street. I passed the General Store and was about to head up the side street to the sheriff's when I turned for a last look at Hoyt's shack, wondering how a genial doofus like him ever got the water acquisition job in the first place. A block down from his building I saw a sheriff's SUV parked next to the Mansion House Hotel. It was Sarah, watching Main Street for speeders and cell phone desperadoes. I waved until she saw me, then kept on to the sheriff's. Parked outside the main entrance was a new Impala. Taped in the corner of the windshield was a card with a logo and the words *Federal Bureau of Investigation—Government Owned Vehicle*, just as plain as you please.

When I got inside the building, I could see Mitch sitting in his office talking to a guy in a sport coat and jeans. I stopped about six feet from his door.

"So Mitch, how's the Dave Cathcart thing going?"

"It's going real good, Tommy," Mitch said. "Now, why don't you run along and leave us to it?"

"I will when you get Sarah in here. It's her father, for chrissakes."

"Don't start," Mitch said. "I keep Sarah in the loop, so—"

The guy got up. "You must be Smith," he said.

I told him I was.

"Pleased to meet you, Sergeant."

We shook, and he said he was agent Aaron Fuchs from the FBI's South Lake Tahoe office there to advise. He said he'd heard of me but didn't say how.

"You're the Marine sniper, right?" he said.

"Army."

"Anyway," he said, "your reputation precedes you. Want to sit in?"

Mitch didn't look happy anymore. The agent started to fill me in on what new information they had about the disappearance, which was precious little. There had been a lot of calls claiming Dave Cathcart sightings that turned up dry. His red Chevy pickup had been seen from Fallon to Placerville. Folks had come to the Tahoe office with theories and guesses that had just wasted their time, but he said they had to follow up every one. He did say that they'd located a joint bank account that Dave had opened with Kip. Each guy had put in a grand, but there weren't any withdrawals, and he asked me as a family friend if I knew why Kip and not Sarah was on the account. All of this really frosted Mitch.

"Before I forget," Fuchs said, "did you ever find his cell phone?"

Mitch shook his head. "My guys combed that place," he said, "but even just the barnyard is huge. I'm sure Sarah had Kip and Tommy workin' together, looking under every rock."

"From what we could tell, his phone battery is dead," Fuchs said. He was fiddling with an iPad. "So we may never find it." He looked at Mitch across the desk. "And you got the message off his landline, right?"

Mitch looked flummoxed. "No."

Fuchs tapped the screen and set the iPad on the desk. It was Dave's voice, but it sounded frail and drifty:

". . . Sarah? Pick up if you can. I went and told him. Said I just couldn't do it—couldn't sell the water. It'd kill the place. It might die anyhow with the goddamn never-ending drought and nothing but cheatgrass and ground hornets like a goddamn plague— Hold on. Maybe this is him on the other line . . ."

"That was the night before he disappeared," Fuchs said.

There was a long busy signal, then silence. The three of us just looked at each other.

"He'd changed since you saw him last, Tommy," Sarah said. She was standing just outside the door. "He must have made that call to the house right after I left for work that night. Nice of you to wait for me, boss."

"Swear to god, Sarah," Mitch said. "I just heard that for the first time myself."

"I won't even ask why that is," she said.

"Hell, I don't even think about landlines anymore," Mitch said. "Who uses 'em?"

"So who's the 'him' Dave's talking about?"

"What do you mean, Tommy?" Sarah said.

"Who was it he told?"

"Hoyt?" she said.

"Or Kip? Or some third person we don't know about?"

"Now don't go making this more complicated than it is, Tommy," Mitch said.

"It's a real good question, Sheriff," Fuchs said. "We're just seeing the tip of the iceberg here, which is common with these kinds of cases."

He reached out and played Dave's message again. Sarah looked sad and started walking down the hall towards the restrooms. Fuchs took the iPad and got up to leave. He told Mitch he'd be in email contact the next morning after he got more information from their Sacramento office. Then he and I shook again.

"I'm sure the Isringhausens are glad to have you around," he said.

Mitch snorted at that. We both watched agent Fuchs go, then Mitch looked up like he was surprised I was still there.

"Okay," Mitch said. "You wanna know what I think?"

"Can't wait."

"I don't think Dave just got demented all of a sudden and wandered off," Mitch said. "And since we got no ransom demand I think we can rule out kidnapping. You heard the guy—tip of the iceberg. I think the old boy just took a timeout. Just bailed on the whole deal. You heard his voice. He sounds tired. Wore out. Too many decisions. Too many people pulling him in too many directions and too darned old to deal with it." He waved his arm around the room, then leaned toward me. "And I think old Dave needed a breather from his daughter's sticky domestic situation. A situation all bollixed up 'cause of the torch that girl still carries for you."

"Bullshit. Sarah's as honorable as they come."

"Yeah, but you're here, aren't you?" he said. "Big as life, sticking your nose in Cathcart business even as we speak. I just got a call from Hoyt Berglund's office girl. The kid says you were just there poking that nose of yours in the darned water deal, and was she even supposed to talk to you about it? And did she tell you too much already? So that's it. I think Dave just walked away from it all. From the whole mess, you included, hotshot. I bet the Feds find a secret bank account in Vegas or some dang thing. He's probably down there now with a drink in his hand and a keno girl on his lap."

"You think he'd walk away from his place? From his daughter?"

"Yeah," Mitch said. "That's exactly what I think. If her love life's about to turn into a clown show now that you're back, why not?"

"I don't mean to sound critical here—Sheriff—but

Dave's life, or any of the family ranchers around here—it ain't like running a Starbucks. Dave's dad came into Shoshone Valley in the Depression. Sam Cathcart was a kid mustanger and bronc rider from down around Bishop whose old man had been a muleskinner on the aqueduct. There was damn few decent cowboying jobs then, so mustanging was one way not to starve, but it wasn't pretty. They'd steal empty five gallon lard cans from behind cafés and cut an X in the tin, then bury the cans real shallow in a brush trap they'd built leading to a waterhole. They'd run some scrawny band into that trap, and if a horse stuck a foot in that can, they couldn't pull it out so they were easy to rope. It didn't matter how cut up they got—they were going straight to the killers anyhow for dog food. Sam was so poor he ran mustangs on a borrowed horse and saddle. When he finally saw one worth keeping, he roped it out in the open, snubbed it up tight and ran it across that rocky desert behind his horse till it about dropped. After he gentled it, he rode that broomtail bareback all the way up into this country 'cause Shoshone Valley was where he wanted to settle. Sam lived in that stone barn out at Hoffstatler's—lived on soda crackers and beans when he could get 'em and starved when he couldn't and saved every goddamn penny. When he saved enough, Sam bought the place Dave has now. If you think Dave could turn his back on all that his old man did to build that ranch, you're nuts."

"Whoa, big fellah." It was Kip. He must have walked in during my little rampage. "You been holding *that* in for a while. Shit, dude, say what you *really* think."

I had to laugh at that.

"Where's my bride?" he said.

"In the ladies," Mitch said.

"So, we still on for tomorrow?" Kip said. "Shoot some targets or tartlets—whatever you got?"

"Midmorning? Sarah asked me to take a ride through those heifers of Dave's right after breakfast. Might have to tag a couple."

"Let me know," Kip said. "No sweat. I got an appointment here tomorrow to talk to a lady at the courthouse about canceling a colt gentling clinic Dave and I were putting on at the county arena. And thanks for helping Sarah with the cattle. Definitely not in my wheelhouse."

"Hey, Kip," Mitch said. "You agree Dave mighta just wandered off, right?" He was fiddling with his desk computer.

"Yeah, like a stroke or something," Kip said. "I don't think we can discount it."

"Looky here on the computer, Kip," Mitch said. He looked up when he heard Sarah walking toward us in the hallway.

Kip walked around the desk to look at the screen. "I heard of him. Does Sarah know?"

"Know what?" Sarah said.

Kip was still staring at the screen. He didn't see her squeeze my hand when she walked by, or see how surprised I was when she did.

"Say's here they found Randy Ragazino dead out by Frémont Lake, on the Rez," Mitch said.

"Isn't that a little out of your jurisdiction? Wrong state and all?"

"Copper County's just giving us a heads-up, Tommy," Mitch said. "Ragazino's been in all kinds of drug dealing and low-end crap for years with your pal Jedediah Boone."

"They're not pals," Sarah said, "and you know it."

"Says here Randy died from a massive blow to the face," Mitch said. "Smashed cartilage, brain trauma and stuff. Copper County says Boone is definitely a party of interest." He looked at me just insincere as hell and smiled. "If anybody could take you out with one punch to the face it'd be your pal Jedediah."

"My god, you know not to discuss crime-scene details, Mitch," Sarah said.

Kip started staring down at his phone like he hadn't heard much of what Mitch said anyway.

"Do you still want to go get a late lunch?" Sarah said.

"Can't, doll," Kip said. He looked up from his phone. "Gotta zip back up to Carson. I just got rescheduled." He kissed her on the cheek. "Sorry—don't wait up."

Sometimes Sarah looked like every man on the planet just pissed the hell out of her.

Chapter Eight

The wind was still the next morning and it was overcast like a spring storm coming. I had breakfast early with Mom and Burt, then told them I'd be out for most of the day. Eddie, the young Marine, stopped by like clockwork to fetch Burt. The kid and I talked a bit while Burt got his stuff squared away. Young as he was, Eddie was in charge of the operation where Burt taught packing. He said he was from Spink County, South Dakota, and had never been deployed to anyplace where folks were trying to kill him and never done any packing before he joined the Corps, but he'd taken to the life and to the country. I asked him if I could come up to the base and check out their setup some day before I headed east.

"Folks around here always joke about government mules, so I'd actually like to see some that weren't just in a Fourth of July parade."

"No problem, sir," he said. "Just let Burt or me know, and we'll give you the tour."

Damn Marines were always polite as hell. I recalled I hadn't got a reply from my Pendleton guy on Kip yet. I was probably being too suspicious because it was him not me behind that bedroom door with Sarah. Burt kissed Mom good-bye and he and Eddie hit the road. I stood with my arm around Mom's shoulders at the front window of the apartment as she watched them cross the asphalt to where Eddie had left his Tundra parked out by the Dumpsters and big propane tank. She seemed pretty damned content for the first time in a long while.

I drove into Cathcart's yard with my spurs on by seven. Kip's big Ram and Sarah's Silverado were both gone. She'd told me she had the early shift, and I figured that Kip hadn't come home yet from his business in Carson City though it was barely an hour's drive north. Sarah had corralled and thrown hay to the saddle horses for me before she left, and told me where to find her cantlebag with the tagging stuff in the saddle room.

I caught her dad's roan ropehorse, saddled him and grained him in the barn. Then I snooped around a bit. There was no movement at the ironpumpers' little trailer, but their old Blazer was parked behind it. I walked close and stopped to listen, then banged on the door. The sun broke through as I was thinking of some bullshit excuse to be bothering them, but I didn't really care what they thought. It was past seven and high time these two honyockers got started on whatever foolishness it was they did all day. When no one answered I went inside and looked around, but just for a second since it stunk so bad. Except for open pill bottles that looked to be steroids, Bowie knives, a machete, some bodybuilding magazines that looked kinda suspect, lots of weed, an old AK-47, and some straight porn, there wasn't much out of the ordinary. I left the door open when I went back outside so they'd know they'd had company.

I rode the roan out through the heifers. Sarah had given me the ear tag number of one with a prolapsed uterus she'd brought in to doctor a few days before and wanted me to check on. I found one bagged-up about to calve that I'd look at again later in the day. Off by herself at the edge of the willows I saw a brockle-faced heifer that had calved a few hours earlier. She hadn't quite cleaned out yet but you could see she'd been sucked. The calf looked healthy and was lying in the sun and stood up when I rode closer. I roped the calf and stepped down. The roan kept the rope taut as I shooed the cow off, flanked the calf and tagged him. I let him up and watched him run off to his mama, thinking of all the times I'd done this with Dad, and thinking of all the times since he died that I'd gone halfway around the world to not think about any of this at all. I coiled my loop, put the tagger back in the bag, reset my saddle and stepped aboard. I circled through another half dozen until I found the prolapsed heifer, and to me she looked good as new. Sarah had, as usual, done a fine job minding her calvers. I always thought she would make a rancher and was wasting her talent as a deputy, but then she and I never listened to the best things that each of us told the other.

I headed north toward the fence that separated this field from Hoffstatler's. In the distance I could see a truck that belonged to Fish and Wildlife. I got closer and could see Dad's old water buddy, Hoyt Berglund. He was standing with his fists on his hipbones staring down at a dry ditch. He looked up at me like we'd been in the middle of a conversation—like he'd just asked me a question and was waiting for the answer.

"Hey, Hoyt. Been a while."

"Tommy Smith," he said. "Tell me, how does a guy lose an entire crick? I seem to have misplaced the sonofabitch."

He reached up and we shook. I got down from the horse and he showed me the bone-dry, ten-foot-wide watercourse. We walked up it together, poking the gravel with our boot toes. Then I hobbled the roan and we walked over to the truck and sat on the tailgate. He had a four-wheeler strapped down in the truckbed. He asked how my mom was and if I was done with the Army and home for good. Then he asked what was going on with the Dave Cathcart investigation, and I said damn little. He handed me a water out of his cooler and offered to share some beef jerky and trailmix. It was only nine in the morning so I passed, but he dug right in.

"Your dad ever tell you about the time we caught Hornberg diverting Power Line Crick back in the seventies in that bad drought?"

I said I'd heard the story a lot, but Hoyt told it to me again anyway.

"Folks just go crazy over water," he said at the end of his story. "Makes 'em nuts. Sleepless nights. They think they never have enough, even with the best prior rights. And in a bad year everybody is watching their neighbor, suspicious as hell." He took another bite of jerky and talked while he chewed. "Can't blame 'em. If somebody diverts your water even for an hour, it's gone for good. Gone-for-good. You can stop 'em, but you'll never get that water back."

"Like that saying that you never step in the same river twice."

"I have no idea what you're talking about," he said.

He started back in on his dry creekbed. It was from a drainage just east of us up in the Monte Cristos called False Spring Canyon, and now no water was flowing down.

"When I negotiated the rights with the Hoffstatler family," he said, "it had a small flow. It fluctuated, but it was steady enough to monitor."

"Is it the drought?"

He shook his head. "That would reduce the flow, but it's spring fed even in dry years. It's unpredictable, but despite the name, it don't just disappear."

"What are you going to do?"

"I don't know, Tommy," he said. He turned and looked back at the canyon mouth. "I got to find the problem or the whole project looks sorta foolish."

He'd taken to wearing floppy fisherman's hats and mom-jeans since I'd last seen him, and his face was pink and scabby and his teeth long and yellow just like I remembered, so I let that comment go.

"What about Dave's rights? Where does that stand?"

"He told me he'd finally decided against selling," Hoyt said. "Told me he wanted to keep the place a working ranch, which I sure understand."

"He tell you by phone or in person?"

"He told me in person."

"You remember when?"

"It was maybe the day before he came up missing, or the day before that," he said. "Funny thing about that, though. A couple hours after we talked he sent me some texts saying he'd changed his mind. Had a 'change of heart,' he said. Those were his words. I thought he was gettin' loopy. Wanted to know how quick he could get the money, so I said soon as I get the paperwork we can start the ball." Hoyt studied on this a minute. "He wouldn't be sending me them texts if he was dead, would he? Unless it's me getting loopy. If I get that way, you just shoot me, okay."

"Do you know if he talked to anybody else?"

"Couldn't tell you," he said.

"You still have those texts on your phone?"

"Sure, I guess."

"Can I see 'em?"

"Don't see why not," he said. "What for?"

"To see if somebody was scamming you."

This notion seemed to trouble him. He fiddled with his phone and finally handed it to me.

"Take care of these messages, Hoyt. The FBI will want to see 'em."

"Well, shit," he said. "If you say so."

"Did Dave ever get any money?"

"Not yet," he said. "If he ain't dead, once he sends in the paperwork, it's a process. You're thinking like maybe Dave went 'poof' before that text got sent?"

Out of nowhere Hoyt started telling me about a deer hunting trip he, Dave, and my dad took in the Ruby Mountains before I was born. I'd heard that story before, too. We were still sitting on the tailgate, and he was right at the part of the story where the mountain lion sauntered out of the range teepee. Then Hoyt's mind meandered back to wondering what happened to his missing creek.

I looked over my shoulder at the four-wheeler. "Looks like you're planning on tracking it to the source."

"I don't guess I got any choice," he said. "You wanna give me a hand unloading that sumbitch? It weighs a young ton."

He had a pair of two-by-twelves he used as a ramp. We anchored them and winched the four-wheeler down with a come-along he kept in the cab. He said the truck belonged to the government, but the four-wheeler and the come-along were all his.

We got it out on the dead grass and he fired it up. He checked his spare gas can while I stowed his two-by-twelves. He throttled down and pointed to a ridge off to the southeast.

"See that green V of the canyon mouth with the yellowish burned-off mountain behind it?" he said. "That's False Spring Canyon." He secured a coat and more water bottles and jerky on the four-wheeler. "I might get back late, but I'll call you in the morning. You don't hear from me, send in the cavalry."

"You worried?"

"Don't laugh. Hell, folks say I'm the kiss of death for ranching properties, and don't I know it. Lucky somebody hasn't plugged me by now." He sounded jokey, but he looked dead serious. "Still, it's a job-a'-work and if I don't get to it, somebody else will."

"I don't hear from you, the cavalry it is."

"Good to see you, kid. Say hi to your mom."

He revved that sucker and bounced out across the dead field going about eight miles an hour. I sat the roan and watched him clear the pasture and start climbing through the sagebrush. At the rate he was going, I wondered if he would even make it to the mouth of the canyon before dark. While I watched, I texted Kip Isringhausen. I told him that I could meet him at the Sporting Goods in Piute Meadows in an hour and a half. Then Dave's horse and I rattled our hocks back to the ranch.

I was trotting easy toward the barn and saw a car parked in front of the ironpumpers' trailer. It was an old American sedan with more primer than paint—from a distance maybe a sixties muscle car. Maybe a GTO. A guy came out of the trailer, a big muscled-up guy bending low. He was shaved-headed with a stubble goatee and a bright white tee shirt and prison tattoos on his arms and neck. When I rode closer, I saw that the car was a GTO. The guy saw me and grinned. His teeth were white as his tee shirt.

"Goddamn Tommy Smith," he said. He spoke soft, but I heard him across the yard.

"How's it hanging, Jedediah, you old peckerwood?"

"Can't complain," he said. "I heard you were back. Young Tommy Smith, back from the wars."

"What brings you here?"

"Looking for the two assbites who live here," he said.

"They owe you money?"

"Something like that." He laughed. Then he nodded north. "See you huddling with old Hoyt out there in the tall grass."

"You know how it is. When you been away, you got to say hi to everybody once you come back or they get their feelings hurt. Like you when you got back from Soledad."

"Tell me about it," he said. "Everybody wants a piece of you."

"They want to share those *good* times."

We both laughed at that. It was pretty common knowledge he'd had a bad time in Soledad.

"You should watch it, brother," Jedediah said. "Old Hoyt's not very popular. You may not want to be seen with bad companions."

"Little late for that. What's wrong with Hoyt?"

"Why, he's the devil," Jedediah said. "Tempting honest ranch folk with easy money, then sucking the life out of their land like some water vampire."

"Your concern for the traditional life is touching as hell."

"The old ways are the best," he said. "That's why I stick to selling weed. I'm just an old-fashioned guy."

"Right. Weed. And guns and meth and stolen cars."

He laughed in spite of himself. "Been a couple of years since I saw you. Sorry to hear about Lester. He was hella fun to fight with."

"He could take either one of us."

"And did," Jedediah said. "Repeatedly." He got a cagey look. "So what brings you here? Still sniffing after that hot Sarah C?"

"Old habits."

"You staying here at her place?" he said. "Just you and her—and that new husband?"

"Nope. Only checking cows for her. I'm staying at my mom's just up the road."

"The Marine housing unit," he said.

"Yeah."

"That Sarah," he said. "A righteously fine piece." He gave me a real cocky look. "Or so I hear."

"Watch it."

He walked over to the GTO and opened the door. "Take it easy, brother. You don't have Lester to back you the way you did in high school." He gave me a little salute and started to get in the car.

"Yo, Jed."

He stopped halfway in.

"Give my best to Randy Ragazino."

Jedediah turned slow with his mouth open, almost like he was panting. Then he tried to turn it into a smile. "So, soldier boy. You think *you* can take me?"

"I guess we'll see."

He semi-laughed. Then he got behind the wheel of the GTO, fired that monster up, and stuck his head out the window. "I guess we will, Tommy. I guess we surely will."

I unsaddled the roan and turned him into the corral, then got in my truck and drove down to Piute Meadows.

Chapter Nine

I was looking at a long text from Captain Cruz. I barely got it read before I lost service in the canyon. She said that a boy from Three Rivers, Michigan, just back to Benning from Kandahar had a meltdown and shot his wife and her tennis friend on the base before taking himself out. She ended with, *Girl played with fire and got burned.* Stories like that always depressed the hell out of me, and I wondered why someone who had seen what Ofelia had seen would even talk about such stuff. All I texted back was, *How's my car?*

I beat Kip to the Sporting Goods by half an hour and bought a box of .45 Remington Long Colts, a cheap cooler, and some ice and beer from Nick's cute niece. Even with the text from Captain Cruz, I hadn't given a single thought to smooth olive skin since I saw Sarah cooking fajitas in her shorts two days before.

I was learning that Kip was one of the always-late people. Finally, the bell over the door jingled and in he came like now the party could start. Today he was decked out as Mister Buckaroo, with good quality boots, wild rag, vest, and palm leaf hat. He carried a zippered bag that I figured held all the stuff for his SIG.

"Where to?" he said.

"The point of the hill out towards Summers Creek."

"I'll drive," he said.

"I got to stop in at Becky Tyree's after, so why don't you just follow me." That was sort of the truth, but I could tell it didn't make him happy.

"Good enough," he said. "I gotta make it short, too, 'cause I'm meeting that babe at the courthouse to cancel the colt gentling clinic. I think the first time I met you was at one of those clinics right before you went back into the army."

"Might have been somebody else."

"I don't think so," he said. "You're a memorable character."

I climbed into my truck and headed out the Summers Lake road with Kip on my tail. I didn't much like being a memorable character, leastwise not to him. He seemed to know too much about me already. A mile west of the Bonner & Tyree lane, I turned off the pavement onto a wagon road at the base of a sagebrush hill. I got the gate and pulled up and waited for him to close it. We drove out for half a mile till we got to an old dump against the slope. Kip looked at the scrap lumber, bits of broken equipment and rusty cans.

"What's this?" he said.

"You said targets, but bottles and beer cans are more fun. You hit something, it jumps."

"Suits me," he said. "From what I heard a couple of years ago, Tommy Smith hits something, it dies."

"Don't believe everything you hear. I don't."

He set his bag on a board and took out his gear. He had a slick little nylon holster for the 9mm, camo earmuffs from Cabelas, and a pricey pair of shooting glasses. I watched him Velcro the holster to his belt. He pulled a full magazine out of the bag, dropped it in his vest pocket, then took an empty magazine and loaded it with the nickel-plated rounds he'd bought from Nick. I got us a couple of Coors from my truck and handed him one. He opened it and scrunched his face.

"How can you drink this fish piss?" he said.

"Suits me."

I guzzled some as I took the cloth bag off the truck seat and pulled out the gun rig. I had to laugh at the look on his face when I broke out the box of .45s, flicked open the loading gate, and slipped five of those fat suckers into the cylinder, leaving the hammer on the empty chamber. I'd cleaned and oiled the Colt at Mom's the night before, so I was good to go.

"Where the hell did you find that relic?" he said.

"Around."

"I can't believe I brought my state-of-the-art Navy SEAL piece out to a real live dump," he said.

"Once upon a time this bad-boy was state of the art for the Army." I took my skinning knife off my belt and slipped the sheath on the holster belt so everything would ride easier. Kip studied every move.

"Yeah," he said. "Custer's army."

I buckled the gun rig on.

"Can I see the knife?" he said.

I held it out to him. He turned it over in his hand, reading the etched writing on the blade.

"Puma Trail Guide. Bone handle—very cool," he said. "Where'd you get it?"

"Indian guy I packed with. Been to Vietnam. When I signed up he gave it to me for luck. And the handle? Stag, not bone."

"Whatever. The Indian ever kill a gook with it?"

"I expect."

"You stick any towelheads?"

"Nope."

"Come on," he said. "Bet you did."

I could see him getting excited. I took the knife back. He shoved the fresh magazine into the SIG with the heel of his hand and patted his vest where he'd slipped the other, then set his beer on the hood of his truck and started rooting around in his bag again. I finished my beer and climbed up through the junk and lumber, setting bottles and cans and bits of tin up as targets once I was about twenty yards upslope. When I looked back, Kip was putting his earmuffs on, still watching everything I did. When I got a bit further on he shouted up at me.

"What exactly did Sarah say to get you back here?"

"She just asked, is all."

"I think you heard she'd moved out," he said, "and

you thought you were gonna come out here and snatch her right up."

"She's back with you now."

"Hold that thought, dude," he said.

I was watching my footing on the old lumber then I heard boards rattle. I looked back. He'd pried out a section of rusted iron wagon-wheel rim. It was curved and about four feet long. Kip gripped the ends and pushed his hands together, bending the iron. He didn't look to be straining much. He saw me looking and grinned, tossing the bent rim out in the sand. I turned back, making my way up through the piles of old boards. I heard him rack the slide on his SIG but I didn't look up. I didn't want to let him think he could get to me. He shouted again.

"You could drill somebody out here and the corpse might not get found for years."

"Nice thought."

I just kept climbing. I was glad we had both our trucks with us. He might manage to shoot me, but he couldn't drive both trucks out of there. I got to the front end of a red-rusted postwar Chevy when I heard the pop and ping of him glancing a round off the car fender. It was about six feet to my left, and the deflected bullet could've cut me down kneehigh. That's when I did look up.

"The hell?"

Kip just looked curious. "What?" he said.

"You *know* what, city boy. Shooting at somebody's not very smart."

He pulled down his earmuffs. "What? I don't know what you're talking about."

"You just skimmed a round off that fender."

"No I didn't," he said.

He grinned this terrific grin through that little beard, and I wanted to shoot him right then and get it over with. I settled for stepping over the broken boards to the fender. I ran my finger along the shiny crease in the old steel that 9mm round had made and held it up, covered with rust.

"Right here, smartass."

"Oh," Kip said. "*That* fender." He pulled a bottle of Maker's Mark from his bag and guzzled some. When he was done, he grinned up at me.

"Had'ya going," he said.

This was either the most confident son of a bitch I'd ever met outside of combat or just flat batshit crazy. I wiped the rust on my jeans and started back across the boards. Then Kip put another round right through that fender about a foot from the first hit. The bullet made that steel ring. I finally turned and looked down at him.

He was all fake surprise like he didn't mean to do it, but he'd pulled the earmuffs back up over his ears and was grinning like he couldn't wait to try it a third time. I jumped off the lumber into the sand and pulled the Colt, thumbing back the hammer as I raised that beast.

"Safety one-oh-one, dipshit."

I squeezed one off at eye level, just showing off. The .45 made a louder, hollower bang than his 9mm, and it skittered that Coors can on his truck hood over the fence into the pasture, but not before Kip got a nice little beer mist. We stared at each other with our pistols in our hands, and I was half expecting him to up the ante. My god, he looked ready, rocking the SIG in his hand like dying would be all part of the game. Everything Sarah said about him at breakfast made sense. He grinned like it was all a huge joke—or like he was reading my mind.

"You shoot that thing pretty good," he said.

"I was way off. I was aiming at your head."

"You're a funny guy, Sergeant," he said.

When it seemed like we were done testing each other and he was back on planet Earth, I walked toward him. He pulled the Maker's Mark from his bag and offered it to me. I took a drink and handed it back, then he took another. I told him that once he emptied each magazine we could compare the casings to see if there was any difference in the scoring between brass and nickel. I was just bullshitting. I had no clue if we could tell a bit of difference, but I wanted to see how far I could string him along.

He reset his ear gear and stepped into a pretty fair combat stance with his hands in just the right position and took three quick shots. He hit one bottle twice, breaking it down to nothing and looking pleased.

I turned sideways and sighted down that seven-and-a-half inch barrel. This time I nicked my own empty Coors can and it flew off into the sagebrush. He took two more shots then waited for me, and we fell into a back-and-forth rhythm, him taking two to my one. Like we had been gun buddies since we were kids. Like each of us didn't at least have the notion of blowing the other guy's brains into the sand.

Shooting pretty quick, he'd hit something seven times

out of eleven, which wasn't bad for somebody whose business wasn't shooting. I'd got four out of five, just goofing, squeezing them off gunfighter style.

"You do pretty good for a guy whose wife said he didn't even own a firearm."

"Our women don't know everything about us," he said, "do they, Tom?"

He popped off his last couple of rounds fast into the woodpile, not really aiming at anything, just watching the splinters fly. He pulled down the earmuffs again, casual as could be.

"You don't ever use these?"

"Nah. Your hearing is another weapon. Best not disable it."

"You learn that in the army?"

"Deer hunting."

"Christ, are you hardcore." He pulled the bourbon from his bag and took another swallow. "I can almost see why Sarah had a thing for you." He didn't offer me any. "Almost." He looked at me just standing there after I opened myself another beer.

"How long will it take you to reload that thing?" he said. "It'll be dark in another eight hours." He popped out his empty magazine and rooted in his vest pocket for the other one.

I was half turned away from him, holding the Colt by the frame with the barrel pointing straight to heaven. It took me maybe three seconds to flick that ejector rod five times through the turning cylinder and shuck my spent brass, and not much longer to drop five more live ones through the loading gate and snap it shut.

Kip was still talking as he racked his slide again. He about jumped when I spanged one off the bent wagon wheel rim while he was still finding his footing.

"Holy shitballs, Batman," he said. "How the hell did you do that so fast?" He looked shook.

"Talk less. Shoot more."

He took his first shot. I must have rattled him, because I saw a puff of sand off in the sage with no sound he'd even grazed anything. We emptied our loads a second time, and he watched me kneel down and pick up one of his spent casings.

"What're you doing?" he said.

"Comparing the nickel and the brass."

He studied me close as I picked up one of the brass shells with just my fingers touching the ends.

"There are itty-bitty marks from the loading and eject-ing, see?" I was just making stuff up. I picked up a couple more, then moved on to the nickel-plated. I couldn't see a shit worth of difference. They looked the same to me as they did in the box. I held one up to the sun. It was all sil-very, and I handled it like cut glass.

"Go ahead. Check it out for yourself."

Kip picked up one of the nickel-plated and looked at it. Then he looked pissed. He wiped the casing with the end of his wild rag and tossed it in the sand.

"I know what you're doing, dude," he said. "You want my fingerprints."

"If I wanted your fingerprints, I'd swipe something from your house. Paranoid, much?"

"Paranoid, hell," he said. "My father-in-law disappears and two days later my wife's old squeeze shows up and starts snooping around."

"Dave and my dad were best friends, that's all."

"Everybody thinks that old bastard was a goddamn saint," he said. "They don't know shit."

"Was?"

He acted like he didn't hear me.

"You ought to keep those shells. You could start reloading and save a bundle. Economize."

"You know what you can do with those shells, Sergeant."

"My mom's boyfriend is a reloader. I'll give 'em to Burt."

"Ah, the new Marine boyfriend," he said. "Semper fi."

He said it real crass. I wondered what else he knew about my family.

"Musta bollixed up your plans when Dave changed his mind about the water sale."

"You hick, you couldn't figure my plans in a lifetime," he said. "All you see is what I want you to see." He started messing with his phone. Then he looked up and laughed.

"You can stay out here all day with the trash if you want," he said. "I gotta boogie. That county girl is waiting." He ejected his magazine and popped in a loaded one from his bag, then holstered the SIG.

"You were right, Kip. That's a *righteously* fine piece."

He moved toward his truck without taking his eyes off me or his hand off the holster. I dropped another five rounds in the Colt just for show.

"How about you stay out of my business and stay away from my wife," he said.

"Any problem you have with her didn't start with me."

"Then how about you just go to hell."

"Hell's empty. All you sonsabitches are up here."

He flipped me off and got in his truck. I listened to that big Cummins rumble as he drove away. It was like we were in the seventh grade, but with better weapons.

I finished that second beer. Three certifiable crazies, and it was barely lunchtime. I watched Kip's dust, knowing he'd have to stop at the paved road to open the gate and knowing how pissed he'd be. I picked up his spent brass and dropped them in a paper bag. Then I crawled through the barbwire into the pasture to pick up his Coors can and bag that, too. Just to be sure.

Chapter Ten

I drove into Becky's yard and saw Dan at his computer on the porch updating spring calving records. I told him I might need to borrow his flatbed and gooseneck the next morning, and he said no problem. And I asked if I could keep the .45 a few days more. He didn't inquire as to why, but he looked serious and asked if I was okay. I said I just had a crazy hunch about something and would need to check it out horseback. He said he'd have the trailer hooked up and the diesel topped off just in case.

I found Sarah in her county vehicle parked in front of the Indian curio shop, watching for speeders for the second time in two days. She looked bored and sad and told me she felt Mitch was punishing her for bringing me into his private sheriff's business. I started to say I was sorry, but she wouldn't have any of it. I told her I'd just been shooting with Kip. She took off her shades and rubbed her eyes then asked how that went.

"He showed me that weird side you told me about. Dropped the mask. Like he didn't give a shit anymore. But he knows what he's doing with a nine-millimeter."

"He was a Marine," she said.

"So he says." I handed her the bag with the spent shell casings and the Coors can.

"What's this?" she said.

"Kip's fingerprints. Agent Fuchs can run 'em for us."

"Why?" she said. "What are you up to?"

I told her about my talk with Hoyt, and with Jedediah. She wasn't quite ready to make a connection between her husband and questions about the water sale, or her husband and bad companions. But she was getting there.

"At the least, that boy has some serious steroid problems. Let's just check his record so we can see what we're dealing with."

"Okay," she said. "I'd hate to think that you're putting him in your sights because—"

"'Cause I'm jealous?"

"Yeah," she said.

"Been my experience, when people drop the mask they get dangerous. They don't give one shit anymore."

"I'd like it better if you were just jealous," she said.

"I've already dropped my mask on that one."

"Okay," she said. "You win. I'll get this to Fuchs. I'll have him run the prints."

"And have him check Hoyt's cell phone as soon as Hoyt gets back tonight."

Me telling her about the texts that were supposed to

be from her dad but couldn't be just brought all the grim-ness back.

"You working tomorrow?"

She said she was.

"You might want to take a sick day."

"What are you up to next?" she said.

"What you asked me to come here for, I hope."

She nodded and reached out the open window to squeeze my arm. Then I stood back as she put on her shades and took out after a camper going forty in a twenty-five zone. I didn't have a chance to tell her I wanted to ride up to False Spring in case Hoyt found anything interesting up there.

I parked by Dave's corrals and caught and saddled the sorrel. It was about four in the afternoon. I rode out at a high trot to the willow field where the heifers were calving. I checked them all, some close, some off against the far fence, their calves just little ears sticking up in the late afternoon sun. The prolapsed heifer looked good. The brockle-face and her new calf were doing well. The heifer that was about to drop that morning had got herself a nice little bull calf. I jotted down her number but wasn't going to tag it myself off such a green horse. Actually, I had other plans. I stretched in my stirrups and looked north to see if I could spot Hoyt's truck. The sun was off to my left when a shadow crossed over and I heard the flap of vultures' wings. Up along the willow ditch I could see a coyote eating something–probably the fresh afterbirth of the new calf. Three vultures cruised by low overhead and the coyote tucked and ran. It disappeared into the willows, then came out the other side of the ditch and disappeared a second time. I looked back and the birds had settled in on the afterbirth. Four more glided by just overhead and began to circle the calf. I gigged the colt and we pushed the calf and cow toward the ditch. I was hollering and wishing I had a shotgun, federal law from 1918 or no federal law. I pushed the pair down the ditch bank until they were hid in the thickets where the vultures couldn't fly. Then I topped out of the ditch so I could check the rest of the cattle. I'd never seen carrion birds so aggressive.

I rode north, keeping the willow ditch on my right, eyeing it for brushed-up heifers. The sun was still high enough that Hoyt would have a lot of daylight left to find his way back. I hadn't left Dave's property yet when I saw Hoyt's truck sitting right where it'd been at nine that morning. I crossed Hoffstatler's pasture at a walk, watching the ground and the trees along the river. I stopped thirty feet away from the Fish and Wildlife truck and got off the horse. I hobbled him and walked the rest of the way to the truck, looking for tracks. Besides Hoyt and my boot tracks and the tire marks of his four-wheeler, I saw three other sets of boot tracks walking around the truck. It looked like whoever it was stayed a while, poking around, maybe looking in the cab. I saw vehicle tracks in the dry ground about twenty feet on the other side of the truck, and a shiny new black cap from a bottle of Miller's Genuine Draft lying all careless-like, face-up in the dead grass.

I unsaddled back at Dave's but kept the sorrel tied in

the barn alley. I looked in the saddle room for horseshoes and tools. I found some scattered shoeing stuff of Dave's, then got started. The only thing that keeps you in shape to shoe horses is shoeing horses, so I took my time, keeping an eye out for Kip, the ironpumpers, or the Miller brothers. Hoyt had all those rascals interested in what he was doing out in that barren field, though I wasn't quite sure why.

Sarah pulled into the yard about thirty minutes later as I was clinching the second front foot with a driving hammer. If Dave had alligators or a clinch block, I hadn't found them.

"Planning on riding some rough country?" she said.

"You never know."

Sarah watched me until I set the foot down. She disappeared down a row of stalls, and I could hear her rooting and clanking in the grain room. She came back lugging my shoeing box with all my tools.

"You left this stuff at the saddle shed at the pack station when you reenlisted," she said, "like you expected that not a single thing would change while you were away. When Dominion kicked Harvey out, I thought this might get lost in the shuffle when they tore the place down. I didn't want you to come back and get all pissed when you found some Dominion cowboy using your nice aluminum shoeing box and dulling up your GE nippers." She set the box down. "Not that I ever thought you *were* coming back."

"Well, thanks for that—I guess."

"I'm going in to shower and change," she said. "If Kip's not back from Carson, you want to get some dinner?"

I said I did and went back to shoeing. I dusted the

sparrow shit and feathers off the box and got the sorrel squared away with my own tools. Then I turned all the horses out. By six we headed off for dinner in Sarah's truck. On the way I had her detour up the lane to Hoffstatler's. We could see out across the pastures from the deserted barnyard. Hoyt's truck hadn't moved. I told her what I thought it all meant, and that if the truck was still there in the morning, I wanted to ride up to False Spring to see what happened to him. Then we headed up the Reno Highway to grab a couple of rib eyes at the State Line Lodge.

"You're really serious that Dad's disappearance is connected to this water business," Sarah said. We were eating our salads and drinking some wine, sitting in a booth by the big windows.

"I don't see how it couldn't be. It'd be the biggest change he had in his life"—I looked through the glass at the reservoir—"since you got married."

She gave me a hard look.

"The water might be only half the reason, though." The lodge and casino were on a bluff above the lake. I'd never seen the water so low.

"If Hoyt's not back," she said, "what do you think you'll find up at False Spring?"

"If I knew, I wouldn't have to go."

"Well, if you go I'm going with you," she said. "I'll take that sick day."

The waiter took our salad plates and set down the steaks.

"If Kip pulls in when we're loading or sees Dad's rig gone, I don't quite know how I'd explain that," she said.

I told her I was borrowing Dan's truck and trailer for just that reason. We kicked around a couple of possibilities of where we could load the horses in the morning without getting seen.

"So," she said. "What would be the other thing you think might be the cause of Dad vanishing?"

"Rather not say till this shakes out. Don't want to piss you off."

"Since when?" she said.

After dinner we made the same detour to Hoffstatler's barnyard and saw the same thing—the truck right where Hoyt left it. I called his cell and it went straight to voicemail. Then I called Dan Tyree and told him I'd see him dark and early. He said he'd leave the rig at the county arena to save me driving out to the ranch.

At her place Sarah and I walked back down the lane into the ranchyard. We stood under a cottonwood by the porch of Dave's house. Across the yard the doublewide was dark and the ironpumpers' trailer was dark and just as I'd left it after talking to Jedediah. Even the vultures' cottonwood was still. The night was warm for early May, and we talked about the past and about horses, and not about the fact that after several days with no word she might be ready to accept that her father was dead. She told me it was comfortable to see me shoeing one of her dad's horses and asked if I remembered the time I drove into this yard with Lester and my own dad when she was in college and shoeing her barrel-racing mare. Lester had made a crack that made her so mad she threatened to part his hair with a rasp.

"Whatever he said really chapped my hide," she said.

"All he hollered was that you were too good-looking to be shoeing. We were only maybe fourteen, and you were so pretty we couldn't stand it. He didn't mean nothing by it."

"So you do remember," she said.

We stood close in the dark. I was gamey with the smell you get from horses' feet and corral dust and your own sweat, but I could smell her skin and her hair fresh from washing. I remembered everything we'd ever done together, but there was no point in telling her now. She let the pup out of the run and fed it while we talked about the next day. Then I squeezed her hand and got in my truck and drove up the lane toward my mom's.

Sarah and I were on the phone by five thirty in the morning. She told me she had walked out north of her house before she went to bed and had seen a bit of light out across Hoffstatler's field by Hoyt's truck. The light had moved and flickered like a flashlight or a phone, and then was gone. She'd looked outside in the gray dawn just before she called me to see if Kip's truck was back from Carson. It wasn't, so she was alone in the doublewide, and I was glad of it. She told me she'd throw some hay in her pickup and scatter it along the fence half a mile from the corrals so we could catch the horses and load them in Dan's trailer without anyone even noticing.

I had breakfast with Mom and Burt while I explained

what I was up to. I gathered my gear, including Dad's .270 with my Leupold scope, saddle pockets with a whiskey flask and box of shells, and a jacket. I was on the road to Piute Meadows by six.

I pulled alongside the county arena by six forty, parked my truck, and locked it like I was back in Georgia. I secured my gear on Dan's flatbed and found the key under the floormat. The arena was at the edge of town a couple of blocks past the jail, with no houses close. I was back at the south end of Shoshone Valley by quarter to eight. I never did get a call from Hoyt that morning.

Sarah was waiting for me about a quarter mile up a curvy back road, parked where she couldn't be seen from the highway. We'd planned our rendezvous like a couple of cheaters. She looked calm and pretty and was wearing her new *armitas*. We loaded our saddles, blankets, bridles, a couple of brushes, and a can of grain into Dan's rig.

"You drive. You know the road."

"Okay," she said.

She drove north up the paved road through the sagebrush east of the valley floor. I poured myself some coffee from her thermos and caught a hint of her scent again mingled with the smell of the coffee. There were a few newer houses along the way, but mostly the road was isolated, far from ranch headquarters and houses and corrals. We pulled even with Dave's place down to our left when the road turned to gravel. Sarah parked, and we walked down a dirt lane to Dave's horse pasture. About twenty head were along the fence eating the hay she'd scattered that morning.

We caught her bay and the sorrel and I looked across the pasture to the ranchyard as we brushed their backs. Everything looked quiet and still. I saw a bird circle the buildings. It could've been a red-tail or it could've been a vulture. It was too far off to tell, just a tiny cut in the sky. We saddled up, loaded the horses, and got rolling.

A mile further on, Sarah turned up a rougher road that forked to the right and climbed bare hills. She pulled the rig around on a rise ten minutes later, giving us a view of the valley. We unloaded the horses without saying much, and I caught her watching me lift Dad's rifle scabbard from the flatbed.

"Expecting trouble?" she said.

"Just cautious. If I was expecting trouble, I'd have brought Becky Tyree's forty-five as well."

I buckled the scabbard on the offside then pulled the box of soft points from the saddle pockets. I took five rounds out of the box and put them in my shirt pocket, then put the box back and buckled on my chinks.

"So what if Kip comes home while we're out here?"

"I texted him I was taking a day off," she said. "Told him I needed to clear my head, so I'd offered to help Harvey check trail up on the Little Frémont for deer season."

"Yeah, with opening day still four months off, I bet Kip totally believed that."

"He doesn't really savvy the rhythm of this country yet," she said. "You can imagine what he'd think if he saw the two of us here, though. He'd think I'm sneaking you off into the tall pines for a little adultery." She turned away from me and buckled on her service belt and pistol. That cop rig looked out of place hanging around her hips over the fringed waist of those pretty *armitas.*

"He already thinks so."

I tied my jacket on the saddle and stepped aboard. This was her home country so she led the way. The road dropped down into a dry wash, and from then on we were out of sight of the valley. It got rough as we climbed, and the wash widened and deepened into a canyon with low hills on our right becoming high ridges topped with piñon against the sky. We took our time, our eyes on the stream-bed that had sent Hoyt Berglund here. We passed a sign that said we were entering National Forest. Even at a walk, we were making good time on the rough road.

We stopped after a bit to let the horses blow. Across the streambed we could see a hole in the bank with a yellow warning sign and a big mound of sandy orange mine tailings.

"Even in dry years," Sarah said, "there's at least some flow coming down the canyon this early in the season. I guess Hoyt was on to something."

"Where does this streambed drain?"

"About half a mile north of where we parked," she said, "it hits the ditches on the Hoffstatler ranch."

"How much further to the actual spring?"

"Another mile or two."

"Why'd they call it False Spring?"

"It's historically intermittent." She looked me over then. "It's just not very dependable," she said, "as springs go."

"So how long have we been in Nevada?"

"Since before we got out of the truck."

We rode on a while longer. I was looking at the road and any signs of traffic.

"Who uses this other than four-wheelers and bottle hunters?"

"Probably miners and woodcutters," she said. "Just like in the old days."

"Not a lot of call for heavy water use, then."

"Nope."

I got off my horse and handed him to her so I could study the ground. There were all sorts of tire tracks both old and fresh. Some looked like Berglund's four-wheeler, and some were new to me. I walked ahead a bit and Sarah followed. A wind picked up out of nowhere and we put on our jackets. I looked around at the ridges. If anyone was up there, we'd be hard to miss. Sarah watched me pull the Remington from the scabbard and pop the magazine and load it with the rounds from my shirt pocket.

"What do you think?" she said.

"Busy place. Been a Dually truck up here. And a couple of four-wheelers."

I slipped the loaded rifle back in the scabbard and got mounted. Up ahead we could see where the hills were burned clean to the sand, leaving black stumps and not a trace of new growth. I looked back and saw the creekbed thick with willow in the damp spots. On the right we saw a larger mine with falling-down, corrugated sheds against the bluff and part of the hoisting works still standing. Rusty bits of machinery lay scattered in the wash. Beyond the mine the road ran through a muddy pond the length of a truck, then curved to the left and dipped down out of sight. Sarah pointed up a steep draw filled with willow and wild rose all the way to the ridgetop.

"There you have it," she said. "False Spring."

Tall grass grew around the puddle and a steady trickle of dirty water oozed into it from above. The fire in the canyon had burned right to the willows' edge. On the downhill side of the draw was a piñon-covered rise cut by a jeep track that climbed into the trees and disappeared. For the first time we saw bits of human trash along the road. A white paper sign on a stake said that the area up the jeep road was a federal mining claim, but the spaces for names, addresses, and boundaries were all blank.

"Springs are usually fresh and clear," Sarah said. "This runoff looks vile."

I could see bits of scattered small animal bones near the water's edge. A dead crow barely broke the black surface of the puddle.

"Smells funny, too. Maybe they're using chemicals for mining."

We rode past the claim notice and up the jeep track. Human sign was everywhere now—empty cans of beans and fruit and salsa, plastic water bottles and cellophane wrappers, beer cans and boxes of rat poison. And we saw what might've been blood. I bent down and looked at a dried smear in the grass about half a foot long. Sarah handed me a ziplock from her cantlebag and I tried to gather what I could on the blade of my skinning knife. It had been sticky and goopy, like calf snot, but dried hard.

"Human?" Sarah said.

"Can't tell." I bagged it as best I could without touching it, then handed it up to her. "Could just be rabbit guts."

She wrote on the ziplock with a Sharpie. The jeep track climbed another hundred yards, then crested a ridge. From there a game trail covered with human tracks dropped into the willows.

"Tommy," Sarah said. She pointed ahead.

I saw a cross made of white pipe about three feet high at the top of the ridge just off the two-track. White-painted two-by-fours made a kind of enclosure on the ground, and inside the enclosure were shotgun shells, Bic lighters, and plastic flowers arranged like some sort of shrine. Or like a grave. Sarah got off and handed me her mare as she knelt down to read a little wood sign about the size of your hand.

"'Wendy Hammond.' That's all it says."

"There are Indian graves scattered all around this country, especially near creeks and springs, but that's no Indian name I ever heard."

"And no Indian grave," Sarah said. "It could just be a local's joke."

"Or a warning."

She got back on her horse. We followed the trail down into the thick willows where there was the rank smell again and the ground was torn and muddy from what looked like four-wheelers. With the heavy growth we couldn't see far in any direction. The wind in the branches made moving shadows on the mud.

"Pretty," Sarah said, "but creepy."

"No argument here."

"I thought for a sec I saw somebody moving back up there," she said. "Probably just my eyes playing tricks." She rested her rope hand on the butt of her pistol.

"Funny how wet it is here and how little flow there is downstream."

"Yeah," Sarah said. "Funny."

We pushed through another fifty feet until the thicket opened up. The willows had been chopped down and hollowed out to make a big clearing that you couldn't see from the road. In the opening we saw a generator, gas cans, Wal-Mart sleeping bags, more trash and toilet paper scattered everywhere, plastic chairs, a half-collapsed wall tent with a hole burned in it, blue tarps, and black plastic water lines with the smell of wet earth mixing with the smell of human shit. We saw rows of holes and then scattered plants along the edge of the clearing that hadn't been ripped out by their roots yet, and smaller clearings cut in the willows beyond where we could see. Above us on a rise was a dam made of boulders smeared with rough concrete. It was a crappy-looking job, but it held back a small pond. Scum floated on the surface and more black plastic hoses gravity-fed the plants that had been growing downhill.

"Terrific," Sarah said. "Goddamn pot farmers." She scrunched her nose and pointed up at the pond. "This dammed-up mess is the actual False Spring, for what it's worth."

"Explains why Hoyt's water disappeared."

"And now Hoyt's disappeared," she said.

"Yeah. Looks like whoever farmed this bailed in a hurry."

"Maybe that's who I saw down there in the trees." She was only half kidding.

"You get those spent cartridges to agent Fuchs last night?"

"Yeah," she said. "I put them and the beer can in an evidence bag and told Mitch I found them around Dad's porch when I was re-checking the crime scene. Told him I'd texted Fuchs to pick them up from him."

"I guess even Mitch can't screw that up."

"Mitch loves the forensic stuff," she said. "He thinks he's Mister CSI."

"I never asked you—I know you told Kip I was coming, but how did the husband actually know you contacted me in Georgia?"

"He snoops on my phone," she said.

The cold breeze ruffled a blue tarp in thick wild rose. That woke the horses right up. I stepped down into the goop, pulled the .270, handed my horse to Sarah and walked closer. I stopped when I saw the bottoms of cheap boots sticking out and could see the soaking wet cuffs of the pants. I pushed the edge of the plastic tarp away from the body with the rifle muzzle.

"Is it Hoyt?" she said.

"No."

It was a Mexican-looking guy, kind of heavy and maybe forty years old lying on his back. His face was crusted with blood and he stunk bad.

"Your radio work this far out?"

"It should," Sarah said. "I'll call Mitch while you think

up a story for Nevada deputies of what the hell I'm doing up here."

"You're helping me look for Hoyt on your day off, remember? Like any other civilians."

I hunkered down, watching her study the whole clearing from the back of the mare as she pulled her radio from her belt. In spite of the mess and the stink and the mud, you could see it had been a really pretty place once, with the willow and rose and a few elderberry and the spring flowing clear under the pale sky. I peeled the tarp the rest of the way off the body.

"Holy crap. Call for a medevac."

"You're kidding," she said.

"This guy's still alive."

Chapter Eleven

I heard Sarah tell the dispatcher in Piute Meadows to get hold of the Douglas County sheriff in Nevada and have them line up both an evac chopper and emergency medical personnel. Her dispatcher must have given her grief, because Sarah said sort of testy-like that we would need a response damn fast as we'd stumbled on a crime scene with a bad casualty, and that Hoyt Berglund was a possible missing person, and Mitch should know about both ASAP. Sarah gave our general location and said that she'd radio back in a few minutes with specifics once we got the guy stabilized.

I squatted down and studied the muck and growth around where the Mexican lay and saw a bright bit of wire about as thick as a guitar string tied to a stout willow a foot off the ground. The wire stretched tight from behind where I was standing to just inches from the guy's boots. Then I heard Sarah's bay mare step just to the side of me in the mud.

I started to yell Sarah's name but only heard the shotgun blast and felt the rush as Sarah's mare scrambled, running and falling sideways, covering a quick thirty feet to the edge of the clearing. The sorrel jumped back, scared from the muzzle blast, and followed the mare. I saw the Mexican's eyes open wide for a second and saw Sarah land on her left side with the mare on top of her, then she disappeared as the horse thrashed to gain its feet. I stumbled to her through the muck and grabbed the mare by her getdown rope, calming her as best I could. Sarah rolled to her hands and knees and took inventory for broken bones and buckshot. Where the mare had finally fallen at the edge of the willows was rough dry ground and Sarah had landed hard. I saw her feel for her pistol.

"Jesus, baby, are you hit?"

She gave me a strange look when I called her that and didn't answer.

"I'm sorry. I was just afraid . . ."

She didn't say anything for a second. "It's okay," she said. "What happened? Who's shooting?"

"Nobody. Just a trip wire. A booby trap. You okay for a second?"

"I'm . . . fine."

I led the mare and caught the colt and tied them both to a couple of piñon outside the spring, keeping my eye on the ground for more traps. The mare had a little blood on the back of her left front pastern. It looked like she'd got a foot over the wire. I took a bottle of water from Sarah's cantlebag and a pair of fence pliers from her saddle sheath, gave Sarah the water, and scouted around.

The trip wire had looped through a ring nailed into a burned piñon stump then doubled back to the willow. The end of the wire was wound tight around the trigger of a Mossberg 12 gauge braced and tied between two wooden stakes, with the cut-down stock butting against the stump, the muzzle pointing toward the Mexican's boots. One of the stakes had been pulled loose by the mare, and the wire was slack now. I put on my gloves and took the pliers, cut the trip wire and unwrapped it from the trigger.

"Careful," Sarah said.

"Your mare got her foot over that wire and yanked the setup just sideways enough so we didn't all get gutted. We were right in the line of fire, otherwise."

"It's my fault," she said. "It's the first thing I should've looked for."

"It's the fault of the pricks who did this, not you."

I used her pliers to free the 12 gauge from the stakes, then looked it over. With its short barrel and stock, it made for a pretty handy street-sweeper sort of weapon. I shucked the shells and put them in my jacket pocket, then leaned the shotgun against the stump.

"How you doing?"

"I could use whatever's in that flask you brought."

I went over to the horses, snugged up their knots, and pulled a silver flask from the saddle pockets. It was engraved with the name of my unit and my initials and had been a gift from Captain Cruz. But whiskey is whiskey.

Sarah sipped some Wild Turkey and caught her breath. We tended to the wounded guy as best we could, cleaning up his mouth and nasal passages, looking for any other wounds, sitting him up enough so he wouldn't drown in his own blood and snot and getting him warm and hydrated without trying to move him. He was shivering now but still pretty much out of it. He couldn't talk, but he could swallow a bit and we'd both seen worse. When we got him squared away, Sarah hobbled after me over to the horses and I pulled off my saddle. She looked me in the eye and put her hand hard on the back of my neck for a quick second, and just nodded, like the two of us were okay again—at least for now.

I checked the cut on her mare, then took the folded Navajo from off my saddle pad to wrap the guy. I was cinching back up when Sarah called me over. She'd limped up the slope into the piñon. I thought she'd found another booby trap.

"Look here," she said. She was standing next to a nylon camp chair with Tecate cans and cigarette butts scattered all around.

"The hell?"

I stood close, looking where she was looking. There was an opening in the trees that gave us a view down the canyon and of the road curving away for more than a mile. Up-canyon a little rise hid the road. Beyond that we could see it twisting out through the burned-over country until it disappeared.

"You found their lookout."

"They sure could've spotted us coming," she said. "Maybe I did see somebody moving down in the trees."

We were studying the country when we heard a motor off in the distance.

"If that's the medevac chopper," she said, "they sure got airborne fast."

"Sounds more like a plane."

We scanned the sky until we saw it—a little single engine reddish-colored thing with an overhead wing dipping down as it cruised east over the mountains up above us.

"Where do you think it's heading?" she said.

"No clue."

"Anyway," she said, "false alarm."

We walked back down past the horses to the guy and wrapped my saddle blanket around him best we could. I hate to say, I kept the tarp between his rank jeans and that nice Navajo. I didn't want to have to burn it when we were done.

"Hoyt must have surprised some bad characters yesterday," Sarah said. "You think he's in trouble, don't you."

"Oh, yeah. Lethal or not, he's definitely in trouble."

She looked at the guy on the ground. "I guess this one was just the cheese in the mousetrap."

We sat on our jackets on either side of him in the willows so he could sense he wasn't alone. Sarah radioed in our exact location. She had to cool her heels while her dispatcher tried to reach the right folks in Nevada.

"There's sandwiches in my cantlebag," she said to me.

I brought the food and some water bottles and waited for her to finish. Then we ate a little. The mess and the smell and the gurgling sounds from the Mexican didn't do much for our appetites. It was almost noon when we found him. It was pushing one when Sarah got radioed from a Nevada deputy that the chopper was airborne and he was close behind.

"I'm going to walk down to the road and find a landing spot," she said. "Then I'll guide them in."

"I'll go. You're all stove-up."

"I want to get out of this place," she said. "It gives me the creeps."

She stood up and stretched, wobbly and sore from her wreck. Then she disappeared into the willows on her way to the jeep track.

She was gone four or five minutes when I heard her scream.

I hustled to the horses and jerked the .270 from the scabbard, then pushed out of the willows and down the hill. I got close to the road and called her name.

"*Tommy*," she said back. Her voice came from up the road. It sounded weak and terrorized.

I slopped across the edge of the muddy pond on the road, then climbed up around the bend. Sarah stood with her back to me on a flat spot on the road, her hands at her chin and her hat on the ground. I could hear her hyperventilating. Twenty feet beyond her was the burned-out shell of a pickup. I put my hands on her shoulders and she turned and hugged me hard. She gasped and sobbed and tried to talk all at once.

"It's Dad's," she said. "Dad's truck. And he's *inside*."

It was Dave's new Ford, or what was left of it. The truck Mitch and Sarah and the FBI had all been looking for. She said my name over and over, then just collapsed on the road. I knelt and held her as best I could until she was breathing steady.

"Let me go look."

She nodded, and I got up and walked to the truck. It was facing up-canyon, away from us, but already I could see where the heat had distorted the steel. Any rubber or plastic was long gone, and with the tires just smoldering black marks on the dirt the whole truck looked smaller. Through the back of the cab I could see the body behind the wheel. It looked smaller, too. I circled to look at the corpse up close. It was burned to the bone, and it leaned to the side like there wasn't much left holding it together—like it had been dead a thousand years. I walked around to the front to look in where the windshield used to be. The skull was all caved in where the nose and mouth had been, and it had a bullet hole smack in the middle of the forehead.

Chapter Twelve

"You bet," the Nevada deputy said. "It was me who was first on the scene with Dave Cathcart's body, okay?"

The guy sitting in the Douglas County sheriff's Chevy Tahoe talking on his radio was somebody Sarah and I semi-knew called Roger Parrott. He was speaking so loud about her dad's corpse that Sarah could hear every word until the sound of the chopper covered him up. He'd pulled up to the burned-out truck just minutes before the evac flight, and agreed to the landing spot we'd picked. Two EMTs got out of the chopper after we guided it down. I told them where the Mexican guy was, and they pulled out a long-board stretcher and started to follow me. They were jokey and matter-of-fact until they saw the burned Ford and the shriveled corpse and Sarah standing to the side looking shocky and devastated. They asked me if the body was her missing father. I went to Sarah and put my arm around her shoulders, and whispered that I wanted to borrow her radio. She gave it to me, then she led the EMTs and the deputy up the jeep track to the clearing. She was warning them about more booby traps, but her voice was faint and they might not have heard. I got hold of Agent Fuchs and gave him a rundown, then caught up with the others. We got to the clearing and the EMTs tended to the guy while Sarah showed Roger the pot farm layout, including the 12 gauge, which he picked up with no concern for fingerprints.

The EMTs worked on the Mexican a good while before they called us over. Roger told us that the Reno DEA office had a team on the way to take evidence of the pot operation and the Douglas County medical examiner was on its way to catalogue the scene and remove the body in the truck.

"I'm going to want to take Sarah out of here before all that gets rolling."

"She could help answer their questions big-time, though," Roger said.

"Assuming that's her dad, she'll need some time to regroup."

"She had to know this was how that kidnapping deal would end," he said.

One of the EMTs was a guy around my age. The other was a woman with a brown ponytail about ten years older than Sarah. They said the guy would probably live, and showed Roger, Sarah, and me just how they wanted to ease him on to the long-board. Then we lifted him slow, and the five of us carried him out of the clearing and down the jeep trail to the road. We tried not to slip on the steep ground and dump the poor bastard. He was hefty and all dead weight, so we had to set him down more than once. The woman and Roger teased each other all the way down about who their exes were sleeping with and about their kids who went to the same high school in Gardnerville and what sports the kids would play in the fall. We got near the pickup and were huffing. Sarah let us go on without her. She turned away and started walking back up to the horses. On the hike down she hadn't said a word.

We transferred the guy to a gurney, and the EMTs stowed him aboard the chopper. They went to work with IVs and monitors and such, getting him stable for the eighty-mile flight up to the hospital in Reno. Roger and I hiked back following Sarah, watching her climb up the jeep track, stiff from her wreck but moving fast. She never once turned around.

"So who besides the DEA and Forest Service does your department notify about a deal like this?" I handed Roger the shotgun shells from my pocket.

He took the shells and looked at me like I'd asked him some big secret. "It's more like who don't we notify, okay," Roger said. He barehanded the shells into an evidence bag. "We got this interagency drug task force going, with us, Copper County, Carson City, Frémont Lake Tribal, plus the DEA. Oh, yeah, the Nevada National Guard, too. Every-freakin'-body. Too many chiefs and not enough freakin' Indians, okay."

"Sheriff Mitch?"

"Shit yes," he said, "or he bitches all to hell. Thinks he's the Super Chief of Frémont County and us other agencies are just sorry-assed braves." He was back to joking again.

Sarah met me horseback coming out of the clearing and handed me the sorrel. I checked my cinch and stepped up. I told Roger that he could find us at Dave's, and we left him there to poke around. I noticed Sarah had reset my Navajo and tied my coat behind the cantle. And I noticed that she didn't give Roger the ziplock with the blood smear. I looked back and Roger was on his radio again.

We heard the chopper revving up a few minutes later. The canyon amplified the sound as it flew over our heads, gaining altitude to clear the ridges.

"Do you think that was Jedediah's pot setup?" Sarah said.

"He was on your place yesterday and seemed pretty interested in what Hoyt was up to, so it's likely."

"That being his business," she said.

"And Randy Ragazino getting killed kinda tells us there was trouble in reefer paradise."

"Hoyt should've taken some law enforcement with him," she said. "I wonder if we'll find him alive either."

"Hard to tell."

"Who was Roger Parrott talking to just now?" she said.

"Probably his boss."

"Thanks for getting me out of there." She looked like death. It doesn't matter how much you steel yourself to accept something like that. It just doesn't.

We saw the first DEA crew a few minutes later, two guys and a woman in their DEA windbreakers and agency truck. They stopped and I rode over. They were from the Reno office, like Roger said. I told them that Dave's missing person's case and the pot farm up the road were connected somehow, and that Jedediah had been on Dave's ranch the day before. They were scribbling fast. I told them about the disappearance of the federal water guy, how that was connected, and said the FBI should be along directly.

"We've got a lot of questions," the lady said. "We really need you to come with us to the scene."

"This is Deputy Cathcart from Frémont County. It's her dad's truck that burned and likely his body inside. I'm riding with her back to their ranch. The deputy on site can tell you how to get there."

They were a little sniffy, but we just rode off down the road. The Douglas County Medical Examiner van was close behind them with two more sheriff's SUVs following after, but none of those stopped.

"It's a good thing you checked for tracks on the way up," Sarah said. "There won't be a trace left now. And did you see how Roger handled the shotgun? What a bozo."

We rode down past the first abandoned mine and then past the National Forest boundary sign. We were quiet a long time.

"I should've listened," she said. "Dad had been sad and depressed when I moved back in with him. He was sorry my marriage had tanked. He never talked about it, but I know the vultures really got to him, too."

"What do you mean?"

She waited a second. "I told you we'd seen them once before. It was the spring when I was eight—when my mom was dying from pancreatic cancer. It took her quick." Her voice got shaky. "They showed up in that tree one night just after sunset. They stayed about a week and then were gone. Mom died right after. Dad always associated them with losing her, like they were some sort of messengers of doom. And I guess he was right."

"Still, they're just ugly old scavengers, just like turkey buzzards."

Sarah took her eyes off the road to look at me.

"But they're not just scavengers. They're birds of prey. That spring I was just finishing third grade. I was out riding with Dad in the same field where our first-calf heifers are now. He was worried because he'd lost two calves in as many days. The calves were picked clean, and he thought we had a predator problem. Maybe coyotes, maybe even a big cat. We were riding down that willow thicket along the main ditch when we saw a little calf sitting in the sun about fifty feet from its mama. Couldn't have been more than a day old. Then we saw shadows coasting over us and heard creepy wing flaps, and about five of those birds landed all around the calf. He was so little he just froze. They moved right in on him and started pecking his eyes out, then his mouth and tongue, and he went into shock. Then he just disappeared under those birds, black wings flapping and beaks pecking. The heifer bellowed and ran up when it first started, but those nasty things backed her off. We galloped up and Dad tried to scare them away, but they spooked his horse off instead. He was afraid they'd come after me the same way so he got me out of there. It still gives me nightmares."

"Damn, Sarah."

I told her about the vultures moving in on the calf the morning before and how I pushed it and its mother into the willow ditch.

"I know the birds showing up was just some natural occurrence," she said. "Some anomaly in their migratory patterns with a perfectly sound scientific explanation. But you can understand how Dad was freaked out to see them again."

"That's hard."

She looked me right in the eye. "Some people never get over losing their one true love."

We didn't say another word till we got to Dan's truck. An FBI pickup blasted by us as we loaded the horses in the trailer. The driver nodded but didn't stop. They didn't even slow down. A Forest Service truck brought up the rear in no particular hurry. The driver gave us a wave and a sort of here-we-go-again look. They were the poor bastards who'd have to clean up the mess the pot farmers left.

We headed straight across the valley on the dirt lane when we were opposite the ranch and pulled into the yard about five. We'd drive back for Sarah's truck at the other end of the valley later. I wanted to get the horses squared away and be with her before the questions came. I rounded the barn and saw the Impala parked in front of Dave's house and Agent Fuchs sitting on the steps playing with the pup.

"I'll take care of the horses. You go on in."

Fuchs and Sarah went inside the house. The pup followed me as I doctored the mare's wire cut and stowed our saddles. I saw that Kip's saddle rack was empty. I turned the horses out and gathered up the dog. His dish on the porch had some soggy kibble in it that he tried to get to, but it looked nasty so I set it up on an outside shelf where he couldn't reach it.

Inside the house, I got us some beers and listened as Fuchs questioned Sarah about her dad, the pot farm, Jedediah Boone, and Hoyt Berglund. He had a quiet, all-business approach that made it easier for Sarah to talk about the bad things. He said he'd sent some Bureau lab staff up to False Spring to help the county medical examiner. Those would have been the folks we saw hauling ass up the road. He admitted his crew's job was to keep the county folks from trashing the crime scene or touching the body, much less removing it, until his guys gave everything a major going-over. He was especially concerned with ballistic and dental evidence and time of death.

Sarah asked him if his people could look at Hoyt's truck, too, as Hoyt was working on a federal project.

"Between federal drug law, two missing persons and possible kidnappings, probable homicide, another county in on the Ragazino murder two days ago, and the attempted murder of you two," he said, "you've got yourself a jurisdictional cluster . . . a perfect storm."

He told us he'd let us be for now and would take the point with the other agencies as much as he could. Sarah thanked him and handed him the ziplock with the tissue and fluids trace, then we walked him out to his car. When we crossed the porch to the steps, a pair of magpies fluttered up from the dog dish I'd set on the shelf. I watched them fly away over the ironpumpers' shed. Sarah asked me what was wrong.

"The honyockers' Blazer is gone. Haven't seen it move since I got here."

"They almost never use it," Sarah said.

I explained to Fuchs that though they were pals of Sarah's husband, they were well known to Jedediah Boone, too. He scanned his phone like he just thought of something.

"So where is your husband?" he said.

"He was in Carson last night," Sarah said. "At least that's what he told me. Why?"

Fuchs gave a little shrug like it didn't mean anything. He told her he'd be back in touch in the morning. Then he got in his car and drove off.

"Want me to whip up some steak and eggs or something?"

She gave a nod and walked toward the house. She still moved stiff from her mare falling on her.

I rustled up the dinner, but Sarah didn't eat much. When we were cleaning up I looked out the kitchen window.

"If you're up to it we should check out your double-wide to see if anybody's been messing around."

We left Dave's house and crossed the yard. The sun was going down and the air was getting cool. There was a bit of cloud cover like we might get some weather. Sarah stopped dead as soon as she opened the front door.

"Someone's been here," she said.

"Then don't go in yet."

She waited while I trotted down the steps and scanned the dirt in front of the place. It was easy to see a Dually truck had been parked there and that the driver had got out and climbed the steps, then turned around, the new tire tracks semi-wiping out the boot prints.

"Do you want me to get your rifle?"

"Nah. Whoever was here is gone."

I walked around a bit more, then we went inside. The living room and kitchen seemed the same, but Sarah looked around like she was seeing it all for the first time. She went into the kitchen and opened the fridge and stared at the food. When she shut it she just stood there shivering. She asked me to come with her while she checked out the bedroom. I followed her down the hall and watched her slip her 9mm out of its holster. She stepped inside and turned on a bedside lamp. The room was trashed and the bed was stripped, an expensive Pendleton blanket on the floor. There was a handwritten note from a yellow legal pad where the pillows had been. Sarah picked it up and read it. She held it out to me. The paper rattled when her hand shook.

I said NEVER leave me. I warned the old bastard what would happen to him if you did...

She handed the note to me then dropped on the bed.

"I guess I knew all along," she said. I could barely hear her. "I was so afraid to admit it. At some level I knew he'd hurt Dad." She looked me in the eye then. "The random things he said—I knew he blamed Dad for me leaving. Even though it was Dad who threw us together."

She dragged herself up and opened the closets. I just stared down at that big bed of theirs.

"He's taken a lot of his stuff," she said. "Like he's going to be gone a while."

"Try forever." That was cruel and I was sorry I said it as soon as it came out. "What kind of stuff?"

"Work clothes," she said, "not that he ever worked. Outdoor stuff like his Carhartt coat. I don't know. Maybe it's nothing."

"He took his saddle. Or somebody did."

"What—like he's some sort of Old West desperado?" she said. "Like he's going to make his stand horseback?" She closed the closet door. "He must have known about the pot farm," she said. "He and Jedediah and all the rest of them. All the cash Kip threw around—that had to be where it all came from."

"I thought that was from selling his trailer business."

"If he even *had* a trailer business," she said. She looked at me just as calm as could be. "I'll kill them all." Then her eyes flashed red like a damn banshee, and it was a second before I realized it was just the lights off some emergency vehicle.

"That's too close to be out on the highway," she said.

More red light ran along the walls, sliding from one wall to another. We got down the hall to the living room and looked out. The flashing lights were crossing the valley to the north.

"Probably units from the volunteer fire department down by the high school," she said.

We went outside and stood on the deck of the doublewide. We saw the orange flame from Hoyt's truck way out in the dark, and the flashing lights closing the distance across the field. More lights, blue, red, and white this time, flashed in our direction from the Reno Highway.

"That would be Mitch," she said. "And we'll have to go over everything again."

"Except now we have a suspect."

"Yeah," she said. "Now we have a suspect." She stood there on the deck watching the lights come closer, hugging herself like spring would never come.

Mitch and Jack took Sarah into the doublewide for half an hour. I fetched my dad's rifle from Dan's truck, then went into Dave's house. I rooted around the kitchen till I found a bottle of Jim Beam, built myself a drink and sat on the porch. I had this idea that the burned body at False Spring wasn't the end of this—that Kip had just begun a rampage, and that the fire at the end of the valley tonight was probably only a little part of it, and that we wouldn't find Hoyt alive. I thought that even half an hour after Sarah drove into her dad's yard back on Monday morning Dave was already dead. I knew her well enough that she probably was thinking the same thoughts on her own. And to believe her when she said she'd kill them all.

Mitch and Jack finally left. I met her in the yard and she took my hand and we walked back toward the house.

"Mitch has a theory," she said. "He thinks Hoyt is a person of interest in Dad's . . . in his killing. Hoyt and Jedediah."

"Why the hell?"

"Because Dad backed out of the water deal."

"That is eight kinds of stupid."

"It gets better," she said. "He thinks that it was Hoyt's pot farm as well as Boone's, and now that it's discovered,

Hoyt's hiding out." She almost smiled. "He says we have to be open to any possibility."

"Roger that."

She kept hold of my hand as we walked the rest of the way back to Dave's. At the foot of the porch steps I stopped and let her trot up without me. She looked back at me with her hand on the screendoor.

"You're not coming in?" she said.

"I don't know if I should."

Her eyes were puffy from crying but I could see I was pissing her off.

"I'm going to set up the coffee for morning and get the pup situated for the night," she said. "Is there somewhere else you need to be?"

I stood there like a kid.

"Well?" she said.

I started up the steps after her. I paused half a second when I saw one of the magpies lying dead in the dirt by a hops vine that was just leafing out over the porch. I took the last two steps and Sarah slipped her arm around my waist, leaned on me and walked me inside. She started to cry again. Telling her about the poisoned bird could wait until morning, but I'd have to keep my eye on the pup.

Chapter Thirteen

When I wake up in the middle of the night, I usually know within a few minutes what time it is. I don't know how that works, but I just lie there a minute and then I know. Most nights I'm pretty close. That night was no different when I woke up a little before one. Sarah had taken me down the hallway to her room just like I pictured her doing when I was a teenager. And the way she looked and how she felt was just the way I remembered her when I'd wake up in some cave or sewer or barracks in a place like Jalalabad or Kandahar or even Columbus, Georgia. I'd try to conjure her image, then, or remember how she felt or her scent from those couple of months we'd had together. Of course, in Jalalabad, that was after I'd figured exactly what hour of the night it was, Zulu time.

Now I slipped out without waking her and pulled on my jeans and went out to the living room. In her school-girl bed we hadn't talked, but I still felt like I was taking advantage of her on the worst night of her life. After, she'd basically just cried herself to sleep, holding me hard.

I found my jacket, then poked around in the half dark and located the bottle of Jim Beam in the kitchen and built myself another drink. The pup was outside in his run for the night and I didn't want to stir him up, so I left the lights off. He was a pretty nice pup but didn't seem real bonded to Sarah as he probably missed Dave. The yard light by the barn made it bright enough in the living room to see things pretty clear. I sat on the couch and thought that another reason to keep the lights off inside was to not make a target for Kip or his honyocker pals if they were out there in the dark, but I knew they wouldn't be. Kip had made his first strike, then put his cards on the table, showing us what he had and what he had done, and was likely pretty proud of it. Now he'd be putting some distance between us, though not in that new Ram as it'd be too easy to spot. He'd hunker down somewhere to see how we'd react and probably be just as excited as hell, even though he'd need to plan his next play. If he shot us now, the chase would be over too soon and what fun would that be? Jim Beam wasn't my usual, but I liked the glow.

I sat in the half-light for a long time. I pulled my skinning knife, rolling it around in my fingers, feeling the hard sharpness of the blade, the nice roughness of the brass-riveted stag handle, finding comfort in it all and not really thinking about where it had been or who it had killed before it ever found its way to me. I thought about dinner here at the Cathcarts' with Mom and Dad one time when I was twelve and Sarah was in high school. I told myself I'd be in love with her just about forever if only I was a few years older—or if I had a truck. Pretty soon she'd broke my heart dozens of times—every time she'd show up with some new ski instructor or college professor or pilot or mountain climbing guide. At least she never brought any of those bastards into that bedroom. Dave wouldn't have stood for it. That's what I told myself, anyway. When I got out of her bed tonight in the dark and looked down at her asleep, I made a promise that I'd never let myself be away from her again, but that was an idea fit for a twelve-year-old, too. I looked at the table where Dave's breakfast had been set out a few mornings earlier, and where Dad's rifle lay in the scabbard instead. She and I both had other worries now.

I set down my drink, sheathed my knife, and took the rifle and walked outside barefoot, picking my footing in the yard light. At the barn I flipped off the switch and let the dark settle over the yard. I stood out there in the late spring cold, measuring the distances of the black shapes of the buildings, trees and fences, then walking back to the house over the rocky ground. I sat back in the living room and texted my Marine buddy at Pendleton again. Then I texted Captain Cruz that there'd been a family emergency and I might be gone longer than I'd figured, and might have to get my leave extended. She sent a *WTF???* right back to me. It was 04:23 hours in Fort Benning, and Ofelia was still wide awake and ready to spit in your eye. What a wild woman. She sent another text right after the first. *Be true, Lover.* Even sending a text to her now made me feel like I was sneaking around behind Sarah's back. I tossed off the last of my drink and slipped back into her bed.

"My boss wants to know when you're gonna release that body," Roger Parrott said. "That guy was killed in Douglas County."

"He was found in your jurisdiction," Fuchs said. "Where he was killed, when and how he was killed—yet to be determined."

We were sitting around a table at the Frémont County Sheriff's office. It was ten in the morning, and the fluorescent lights in the interview room were giving me a whiskey headache. Sarah and I had had a quick word with Fuchs before we'd gone inside. I'd let him read a text on my phone from the guy at Pendleton.

"The identity of the deceased hasn't been confirmed either," Fuchs said. "We should be getting word later today."

"Jeeso," Mitch said, "it's pretty dang obvious it's Dave."

I reached toward the middle of the table and picked up the note we found on Sarah's bed. It was in an evidence bag, but they'd all read it and had an opinion.

"Let's get back to Isringhausen," Fuchs said. I handed him the note and he held it up. "He obviously is a player in the disappearance of Dave Cathcart—or wants us to think he is. What do we know about him?"

"He's a real well-liked guy around here," Mitch said. "Doing a lot of good for our vets."

"He didn't mean that as a real question, boss," Jack said.

Fuchs opened a file on the table and started to read.

"From fingerprints we know that his real name—or one of them—is Kevin Ingles. He went to school in Santa Barbara, California, not Kingsburg in Fresno County. I'm waiting for more specifics from Santa Barbara PD and Sheriffs on his criminal history, which apparently was substantial. As Kevin Ingles he got an Other Than Honorable discharge from the Marine Corps six years ago. He'd set his Camp Pendleton barracks on fire cooking meth in the head about two o'clock one morning. He was three months out of boot camp at the San Diego Recruit Depot, and both he and half the barracks suffered substantial burns."

I caught Sarah giving me a glance.

"He'd been selling the stuff on base and in Oceanside bars," Fuchs said. "He could have done some real time in the brig, but with psych evaluations all over the map from an abusive childhood and a history of violence going back to Santa Barbara High, the Corps just wanted him gone."

"I think we're totally taking our eye off the pot farm and known actors like Jedediah Boone," Mitch said.

"That drug operation's not even in your jurisdiction, Sheriff," Roger said. "Just sayin'."

"Let's stick with Dave Cathcart's disappearance and Kevin Ingles's possible role in it," Fuchs said. He looked from Roger to Mitch to Jack. "Just think of me as a facilitator here."

"Like we got any choice," Roger said.

"As to his bank records," Fuchs said. "As Isringhausen, he had an account for his five-oh-one-C-three. Jobs-for-vets. That account was cleaned out yesterday afternoon."

"How much we talking?" Mitch said.

"Just under a hundred thousand," Fuchs said.

"Dang," Mitch said. "That boy raised some coin."

"He didn't raise anything," Fuchs said. "We think there's a chance he used that nonprofit to launder drug money."

"What about his trailer business?" Mitch said. "He made major bank selling that puppy. Guy's a respectable businessman."

"Tule Lake Trailers has never been sold," Fuchs said, "and the owners never heard of Kip Isringhausen or Kevin Ingles."

"Well, I'll be goddamned," Mitch said.

"So, Sarah," Fuchs said. "Why do you think he emptied that account and not his joint account with your father?"

"I don't know," she said. "Too small to trifle with?"

"Tommy?" Fuchs said.

"He kept it open on the outside chance he could get that water money flowing."

"Oh, please," Mitch said. "Why is this civilian even here?"

"Because Deputy Cathcart values his input," Fuchs said.

Mitch started to say something crass, then didn't.

"I think this note is pretty clear that your husband felt betrayed by your father and reacted violently," Fuchs said. He looked over at me. "Any thoughts on Kip's next move, Tommy?"

"Torment or rampage. He'll either lay low and mess with Sarah in little ways without exposing himself, then move on so he don't get caught. Or he'll go balls out—show us what a sick badass he really is."

"What do you mean, little ways?" Mitch said.

I got up and went out to the squad room. I'd left a trash bag on an empty desk to give to Fuchs. I took it back to the interview room and pulled the dog dish out of the bag and set it in front of Mitch. It smelled pretty rank.

"Torment—like poisoning Dave's dog. I brought this in so it could get tested."

"God, that stinks," Mitch said.

"What if it's torment *and* rampage?" Fuchs said.

"Then he'll let us know."

When we'd beat every lead to death, I drove Dan's rig out to his ranch with Sarah following in her truck. I'd left the trash bag on the table. Mitch could lick that dog dish for all I cared.

Word about the burned body had spread all over. Becky Tyree was red-eyed but didn't talk much. She and Sarah just hugged and cried like there was nothing left to say and nothing to do but be strong and carry on, so we got on out of there after promising to come back for dinner in a day or two.

Back up at Rickey Junction, I helped Sarah make spaghetti for an early supper. When we'd cleaned up the dishes she dragged me off to bed.

"I had to think Dad was still alive," she said. "I tried to hang on to that."

We were lying there together in the dark and her skin was hot as a stove lid, but right then all she wanted to do was talk.

"What'll he do next, you think?" she said.

"If it's just a game to him, he'll tease us with clues and taunts to keep you scared. If it's a full-on rampage, he'll pull something big."

"It's that second one that I'm afraid of," she said.

"I'm semi-afraid it's probably both."

She rolled up on an elbow and stared down at my face just grim as death.

"I still love you, you bastard," she said. "I wish I didn't, but there you have it."

It was another long while before we fell off to sleep.

I was lying awake under her about five thirty the next morning when we got our answer. The big explosion sounded like it was right in the barnyard and it knocked Sarah clean off me and almost out of bed. We were both up grabbing for our clothes within seconds and out the door in a couple of seconds more with that huge boom ringing in our ears. Off to the west by the Reno Highway we could see a mess of black smoke with orange flame through the trees. Sarah floored her pickup as I yanked the .270 from the scabbard and checked the magazine. She turned off the lane and flew up the highway toward the explosion. It was pretty clear it was at the Marine housing unit. When we got within a couple hundred feet of the drive, we could see folks running and vehicles backing and turning, then hear the shouts and screams. I saw a secondary blast as a truck caught fire and the gas tank went. Sarah turned up the drive into that mess, and we could see the smoke and flame coming from behind Burt and Mom's apartment, and from where the big propane tank for that part of the complex had sat. There was no trace of that tank now. Other apartments south of Burt's were on fire as well. The truck that had just blown was a Tundra, and I could see messed up bodies on the ground as Sarah hit the brakes and we jumped out. One of the bodies was Eddie, the young Marine packer, and he wasn't moving. Sarah buckled on her service belt and jerked her pistol. Other people on the drive staggered around or just lay there shocked. One was a woman in a bathrobe next to a burning BMW. It was Mom. She was on the pavement in front of her place, trying to raise herself up with one arm mangled and blood pouring into her eyes. Then from out of the smoke an old gray-primered Pontiac GTO came blasting down the hill heading for a highway getaway, and I saw Burt pop up out of nowhere. He was standing over Mom with one lens of his glasses shattered. He was shouting like some hellhound and blasting away at the GTO with an AR-15. Burt's rounds just peppered that car as it headed right for us with the driver shooting back at Burt out the window with a pistol. Since Burt had found his target, I wasn't going to second-guess him. The old feeling came back fast and I didn't think about it. I locked eyes with Jedediah through the windshield and steadied the Remington. Instead of putting one in his brain, I took out a front tire on the GTO and watched it swerve. Sarah braced herself against her truck and got off a couple of rounds, then we both jumped back and watched that GTO zip by us sideways and smash into a Subaru parked in front of the Marine Mart. Jedediah half-stumbled out of the Pontiac with automatics in both fists, close enough for me to read the tattoo on his neck. Burt took a knee and cut Jed down like he was still nineteen and back at the Kuwait City airport with one of Saddam's Republican Guards in his sights.

Chapter Fourteen

Sarah and I ran up to Mom. Burt had already dragged her away from the flames and was holding her, crying and calling her his baby girl. Sarah put pressure on Mom's scalp wound to slow down the bleeding, and I squeezed her hand, scared as hell even though I knew she'd be okay. Scalp wounds are just like that. Mom was crying as she watched an MP twenty feet away cover Eddie's body.

"That poor boy," she said. She said it over and over until some EMTs from the volunteer fire station piled out of their ambulance and tended to her. A second ambulance pulled up, then a California Highway Patrol cruiser, then a fire truck.

Sarah and I stood with Burt as they worked on Mom.

"Well," Sarah said, "I guess we got our answer." She was teary and breathing hard. She knew what all this meant.

Burt looked down the drive to the guy he'd shot. An EMT checked the body with the dark blood-blossoms on the bright white tee shirt, then moved on to someone who wasn't past help.

"Who was that bastard?" Burt said. Other than the broken lens on his glasses, he didn't have a mark on him.

"Jedediah Boone," Sarah said. "I think he was in the pot business with my husband."

"Well, Jesus H. Christ," Burt said.

We stayed with Mom until the Care Flight chopper landed and they loaded her up for the trip to Reno. Burt told us he'd meet us at the hospital after he'd gone to the base up by Sonora Pass to check in and give a report. I talked my way past volunteer firefighters and located my travel bag in Burt's half-burned apartment. Sarah and I started back to the ranch as the housing unit was getting locked down by base MPs. The first FBI personnel drove in as we drove out. They had their vests and ballcaps on and were armed to the nuts, but I didn't see Fuchs among them. A mess like this at government personnel housing might have looked like a foreign terror deal if they didn't know about Kip, but for us his plan was terror just the same.

We drove down to the ranch, showered up, fed the dog, and walked out to Sarah's truck. I looked up at the lone cottonwood streaked with buzzard shit. The black vultures had vanished, gone to wherever black vultures go. I got into the Silverado without a word and we headed to Reno.

At the hospital, Mom was already out of the ER and checked into a room on the second floor off intensive care. Her head was wrapped and her arm was in a sling. She'd seen me in a lot of hospitals in the past few years but never the other way around.

"I'm so glad Burt wasn't hurt," she said. "I don't think I could have stood it."

"He's a good man, Ma."

She reached out with her good arm and squeezed my hand.

"Remind me never to sass you in front of him, though. That old boy can shoot."

Mom was drugged up and starting to fret about Dave, then about Eddie, then about her BMW. If my Mustang had been in California, I'd have signed it over to her right then and there.

I was easing Sarah toward the door when we heard spurs out in the hall. It was Becky Tyree and Harvey's wife, May. They'd been gathering some cows and calves with Harvey and Dan down in Piute Meadows for a branding that morning when they heard about the explosion. Sarah and I waited a bit in the hall so they could be with Mom a while. Becky came out in a few minutes.

"My god," she said, "I've seen a lot of terrible things over the years, but this is worse than anything I could have imagined." She put her arm around Sarah. "You can stay with us anytime, you know, darlin'. Both of you. Just say the word."

"I'll just stay at Dad's," Sarah said. "With Tommy."

She got a text from Fuchs, who said he was in the cafeteria. We said good-bye to Becky and walked out to the elevator. Fuchs was waiting for us with a coffee in his hand.

"You two had breakfast?" he said.

We got trays, and the three of us loaded them up and sat at a table in orange plastic chairs.

"We've got some autopsy results," he said. "The body in your dad's truck wasn't his. It was Hoyt Berglund."

Sarah took a breath. "Okay," she said. "Okay."

"He was probably killed night before last. As there wasn't much left of him, our team estimated time of death from the burn rate of the truck and tires, how long it takes things to melt, what shape they were in, that sort of thing. There were indicators in the cab that Berglund was alive when the fire started and that he was shot later—maybe as it burned. His face had been smashed in pretty bad before the fire or the gunshot. Jack Harney told me of a similar facial injury to that drug associate of Boone's named Ragazino."

"Too grim," Sarah said. "So . . . this leaves us at square one about Dad."

"It means he could still be alive," Fuchs said.

"If they killed Hoyt the first night—right after he discovered what they were up to—I've got to face facts," she said. She was still a minute. "Did Hoyt have any next of kin?"

"A son in Oregon," Fuchs said.

We ate quiet for a minute to let Sarah process things.

"We got our next sign from your husband about an hour ago," Fuchs said. "His Ram truck was found burning out near Monte Cristo Summit. On the Marine airstrip."

"Was anyone—"

"There was no one in it," Fuchs said. "A rancher driving by saw a small plane taking off in the sagebrush while the truck was still burning." He described the plane.

"That sounds like the one we saw fly overhead when we were leaving False Spring," Sarah said. "Kip had a body-building friend who was a pilot." She gave him Delroy's name.

"The other sign from her husband would be that little detail of blowing the crap out of the Marine housing where my mother lives."

"I was getting to that, Sergeant," Fuchs said. "Do you think you were the target?"

"Me or Mom. When I saw him three days ago, Jedediah knew Mom was living there, and that I'd been staying there with her."

"You knew him a long time?" Fuchs said.

"My whole life. Anyway, Hoyt finding the pot farm and us finding Hoyt probably cost Jed a million or two. Kip too if he was a part of it."

"I don't disagree with you on his involvement," Fuchs said, "but so far I've got nothing concrete—just indicators in that direction." He took out his iPad and showed it to Sarah. "This is from Santa Barbara County. Your husband was a drug dealer from down there who'd dropped off the grid. He progressed from selling marijuana out of his high school locker to violent nutcase surfer, conman, drug dealer, sadist, you name it."

"Can you guys not call him my husband anymore?" Sarah said.

"Fair enough. The guy you call Kip did local time when

he was only sixteen. A nonfatal hit-and-run on someplace called Indio Muerto Street. Victim was a boy on the swim team—a romantic rival. The cops thought it was intentional—that Kip tried to run the kid over deliberately with his Corvette."

"What kind of Corvette?"

Sarah hit me on the arm.

"A few years later he was a suspect in the disappearance of some high school beach babe who supposedly burned him on a drug deal," Fuchs said. "He was never charged on that one because they never found the body. The girl vanished without a trace, but Santa Barbara PD still has him as *the* person of interest."

"From when?" Sarah said.

"Years ago," Fuchs said. "Like maybe eight or ten."

"Girl's name wasn't Wendy Hammond, was it?"

Fuchs gave me a funny look. "How the hell do you know that?"

I told him about the cross with that name on it at False Spring.

"I guess we'll be digging that one up," he said. "Leaving that name definitely ties Kip to the pot farm site."

We finished our food and Fuchs walked us to the elevator.

"The good thing is, Kip's associate Boone is dead," Fuchs said, "and Kip's on the run. It makes him more dangerous, but maybe more predictable. Can I ask you something Tommy?"

I nodded.

"You could've killed Boone, but from what Burt Kelly

told the agent who debriefed him at the Marine base this morning, you intentionally did not," he said. "Was it because you and Jedediah were old friends?"

"Nope. I'd a shot him when we were eighteen if I thought I coulda got away with it. Jed went out just the way he always imagined he would—guns blazing. But I figured alive he could tell us more about Kip and the pot business, the water deal, and what they were planning next besides setting fire to pickups."

"And you thought he'd tell us the truth with no fear of reprisal from Kip?" Fuchs said.

"I did. One thing you got to know—Jed wasn't afraid of anything or anybody on this earth. Second thing, he always told the truth. Always."

"Strange for a career criminal," Fuchs said.

"He figured out pretty young that the absolutely scariest thing he could do to somebody was tell them what he was thinking."

Fuchs said he'd be in touch in the morning with more lab results, including anything from the burned-out Ram and airplane tire tracks on the airstrip. Sarah and I drove back south. It seemed like forever before we pulled in to Dave's yard and saw a white Marine Corps pickup parked under the trees.

Burt and a tall lieutenant were waiting on the porch steps of the doublewide. It was late afternoon and the sun was already close to the mountain crest. They sat there talking until we got out of Sarah's truck. I let the pup out of his run, and Burt introduced us all around. The lieutenant's name was Gustafson. He was from the base Provost Marshal's Office and said he had been sent to get some clue as to what the hell had just happened, specifically if the housing unit might be a repeat target. We went up the steps into Sarah and Kip's living room and I rustled up some coffee while the guy questioned Sarah about the Kip–Jedediah Boone connection. With a heads-up from Fuchs, they'd ID-ed Kip as a discharged Marine and were hoping he wasn't organizing some rampage against the Corps. Boone had a prison sheet but no military record, so Sarah's story of him working for Kip as some sort of drug partner eased the lieutenant's mind a bit, although it shouldn't have.

"Jedediah knew Tommy was staying with his Mom at Sergeant Kelly's," Sarah said. "The FBI and my department think the propane explosion was to kill Sergeant Smith here."

"We never considered off-base housing as needing much in the way of security," the lieutenant said. "It's safe to say that because of this mess, we'll have to restrict access in the future. A guard shack, check-in protocols, and so forth." Lieutenant Gustafson finished his coffee and stood up. "Pretty big repercussions," he said, "for what seems to be a domestic spat gone viral. I imagine this Kevin Ingles is to hell and gone by now."

I'd been playing with the pup and studying the photographs on the wall behind where they all sat, only half-listening until he said that. Burt stood up then. He was wearing the glasses with one lens missing. That, plus being pissed, made him look semi-deranged. I kind of thought that old Burt was capable of giving a superior officer a right to the jaw—even one who was bigger than he was, and I thought I just might get to see it right there in the living room.

"Actually, Lieutenant, Isringhausen or Ingles or whatever you want to call him was standing right where you're standing now just a couple of hours ago." I pointed at the wall of photos. Two of them were missing. "Old Sam Elliott and Buck Brannaman have left the building."

Sarah got up and looked at the wall.

"Oh god," she said. "He came back. He was just *here*."

Kip poking around the ranch while the country was crawling with law looking for him spooked her all over again. The lieutenant listened to her explain about Kip and his pictures and his goofy celebrity thing, and looked kind of bored. Then he said his good-byes and left fast. Sarah asked Burt not to go.

"You think he took those photos just to mess with us?" she said.

"Yeah, but mostly I think he just wants to be the star-struck punk in those pictures and couldn't bear to leave 'em."

"Maybe he can hang them in his cell at San Quentin," Burt said.

"What it *does* mean is that he's done with all this. The whole life-on-the-ranch business. He's taken his souvenirs and moved on."

Sarah looked at me. She was quiet. She knew she was the last souvenir.

Chapter Fifteen

Sarah turned to Burt. "You look thrashed," she said. "Where are you going to stay?"

"They got a place for me at the base," he said. "It's awful small, though, and probably not the best for Debbie to recuperate in."

"If it's okay with the Corps, you two can stay here in the doublewide as long as you like," Sarah said. "It'll be months before your apartment's livable. And I'm never going to spend another night in this place."

Burt looked over to me to see what I'd say.

"The more of us here, the less chance that bastard will risk coming around. What d'you think, Burt?"

"Well, thanks then," he said.

"Good," Sarah said. She got up and just stood there looking at the empty places on the wall where the pictures had been. Then she went to the kitchen and brought back ice and glasses and built us some drinks with the Maker's Mark. "Let's kill us some of the bastard's whiskey."

We sat there quiet for a while, just too numb to talk and letting the bourbon numb us more.

She and I were back around the table at the sheriff's office the next morning, but without Fuchs.

"I don't buy the Fed's idea that a guy would set his own fifty K truck on fire," Mitch said. "Guys don't work that hard for a nice truck just to walk away from it."

"He didn't work hard for nothing," Jack Harney said. "He just made stuff up about being this great entrepreneur, and we all believed him because he had money and picked up the tab. I'll miss lunches with him at the JT, and that's a fact."

Sarah handed Mitch a sheet she'd printed out.

"There used to be a Kip Isringhausen from Kingsburg outside of Fresno," she said. "He was a saddle bronc rider in the forties and a rodeo pal of Slim Pickens. He was in the Fifth Marine Regiment and died at Inchon. A place called Red Beach."

"When the hell was that?" Mitch said.

"1950." I took the sheet from Mitch and studied it quick. "This guy was everything the fake Kip wanted to be. Good cowboy, Marine war hero, local celeb."

"Fresno Rotary had a little tribute display case of Isringhausen's stuff at a Kingsburg Swedish bakery," Sarah said. "It was broken into a couple of years ago and a lot of things were taken, including posthumous medals and the wallet with his driver's license and Social Security card that was sent to his folks after he died. That's the Social that Kip uses now."

Fuchs came in then, wearing a suit like he'd been

parlaying with his bosses. He stood there a minute and watched Mitch talk.

"Okay, then," Mitch said, "why would a guy work so hard to become somebody else, then throw *that* new life away?" He looked Sarah up and down. "Kip had a sweet deal going."

"Even if he had big income from the pot farm, that water money of Dave's woulda been real tempting."

"I see where Tommy's going with this," Jack said. "Major fraud. Steal a big chunk of cash all at once."

"But he knew it'd have to be one quick strike—ruin Dave's life, then vamoose. So he was already set to leave the ranch life behind way before things went south for him."

"The wild card was Sarah," Fuchs said. "You moving out set him off. Then your dad bailing on the water sale because you moved out made him nuts."

"And then the old boyfriend here showed up," Mitch said.

"You called it the perfect storm," Sarah said to Fuchs.

"The perfect shit-storm, pard," Jack said. He laughed and gave me a whack on the shoulder.

"So don't go looking at this as somebody who risks his nice normal life. Normal life ain't what this guy wants."

"Well, you'd be the big expert on that normal life stuff, huh, Tommy," Mitch said.

Fuchs sat down then and talked about DNA testing on the goop we'd found at False Spring being a match for Hoyt, not Dave, so the only evidence of Dave at the pot farm was his burned truck. I saw Sarah looking at Fuchs the way women sometimes look at a guy in a nice suit.

Fuchs told us how armor-piercing incendiary tracer rounds could penetrate and ignite a propane tank, and Jack said where a guy like Jedediah might have secured some. Fuchs said his FBI cyber team was going over Kip's jobs-for-veterans website and told Mitch that there was now an official link between the Dave and Hoyt cases, but not the attack on the housing unit, though his department was trying to tie it all together for him. He said Reno and Sacramento TV stations had been given information and photos of Kip to warn the public. All this talk took time. After a while, even the most gruesome stuff gets boring.

"Whether you got concrete evidence against Kip or not, which you sure don't yet," Mitch said, "that old boy could be in LA or San Fran by now."

"Maybe," Fuchs said. "But he doesn't seem in any hurry to vanish."

Then Sarah told Fuchs that Kip had been in the doublewide the morning before while the Marine housing was still burning.

"Did you know he was here just a couple of hours ago?" Fuchs said.

"Where?" Sarah said.

"Here—Piute Meadows. He was buying ammo in the sporting goods store just a block from where we're sitting." He checked his notes. "The store owner's niece, Conchetta de la Huerta, sold him two boxes of twelve gauge shells and one box of nine millimeters about eight fifteen this morning."

"Nickel-jacketed rounds, I suppose."

"Yeah, Tommy," he said. "Nickel-jacketed. Exactly."

"This is nuts," Mitch said. "Missing pictures and snarky notes aren't evidence, and it's just crazy that Kip would want to harm Dave. They were pals. I bet if we get word to him he'll come in and clear all this up."

"He's way past that. He's thrown away the scabbard for sure, now."

"What the hell does that mean, Tommy?" Mitch said.

"Means he plans to fight to the death."

"Whose death?" he said.

"Everybody's."

I drove us out to Becky and Dan's when we were done. They were cooking dinner for us.

"Is this how it's going to be?" Sarah said. "We go on, day after day, doing our best to get back to normal life, to heal little bit by little bit, and every time we do this psycho pops up to taunt us? Is this how we're going to live?"

We pulled into Becky's yard. Harvey was walking up from the barn wearing irrigating boots and splattered with mud. He waved at us, and I pulled up and parked by the kitchen door.

"Maybe we're going about this catching Kip business all wrong."

"Well, that's obvious," Sarah said.

We walked up around the house following Harvey. Dan was barbequing tri-tip in a brick pit over chunks of oak. Becky had ice and Jack Daniel's on a table under the aspen and beer and soda iced in a bucket. We sat and talked while Dan cooked. Becky was old-school, so we ate inside on good plates with good wine in the old dining room. She tried to keep it light, asking about Dave's desert permit—when it needed to be gathered and if Sarah and I would need their help. I noticed Sarah smile a bit bashful when Becky lumped her and me together like that.

"Haven't given it a thought for the last week," Sarah said.

"Well, no reason you should, hon," Becky said. "How's the beef? My dad used to bring oak logs up from around Sonora in his horse trailer because my mom loved that old California barbeque taste. Can you tell the difference?"

I'd been gone from these folks so long I purely forgot that once upon a time this was exactly how I wanted to live my life.

I walked outside with Harvey after dinner to shoot the breeze while he had a smoke. We sat on the kitchen steps enjoying the evening. He fired up a Winston and I checked my phone. I saw I had a text from Captain Cruz that said, *Trouble, Lover? Been a bad boy? The whole base is talking, check it out.* Then she pointed me to Kip's jobs-for-vets website. Harvey stared off across the barnyard talking about his early days as a packer. I stared at my phone saying, "Yeah" or "Wow" or "Uh-huh" while he told about leading a string of mules across a glacier. I was skimming a sort of tirade from Kip that was all about me. It was rambley and crazy. I couldn't stand to finish it, but I got pretty close.

Kip posted about how I got my best friend Lester killed two years before because I was too worried about what folks would think of me. How I'd taken advantage of Sarah's sadness to get her in the sack. How I felt I could just shoot anybody who crossed me. And how acting on my damned pride had made Lester a target for some pretty bad characters. There was a lot of stuff Kip could have only heard from Sarah, and in its way it all had some truth. He ended with a crazy story saying he was in Oregon on business and was just as sorry as could be that Dave had vanished. He said he would contact the authorities when he got back south, and, OJ-style, he'd help solve that tragic mystery. He said the only person who had something to gain from tearing his marriage and Dave's family apart was a guy named Tommy Smith. Then he said that in a just world someone would put a bullet in my brain, as combat had made me too violent to live among decent folks. I guess I actually read more than I wanted to. Anybody checking on that site to see about employment for veterans would be surprised as hell.

"You look shook," Harvey said.

"Lotta crazy people in the world."

"Think I oughtta get myself one of them smart phones?"

"Go for it, Harv."

"You're shittin' me, youngster," he said. "I know you."

I saw I had another text—this one from Fuchs. He told me to check out the same website and get back to him. I told Sarah about it as we drove out Becky's lane. Sarah read it, and I thought she was going to cry. I reached over and took her hand.

"Becky's right."

"About what?" she said.

"You should go out to your permit. Gather your cows and calves before the deadline."

"I can get an extension," she said. "I know folks who have." I could tell it was the last thing she wanted to talk about, much less do. We hit the Reno Highway at the edge of town, and I turned right, not left toward the ranch.

"What're you doing?" she said.

"Fuchs said Kip bought ammo from Rick. I wanted to talk to him about it."

"Isn't he closed?"

"It's not quite eight, yet. You want to come in?"

She shook her head no. I parked opposite the Sporting Goods and jogged across the street. It was dusk, and the lights were on. I saw Nick's niece behind the counter. She looked up and saw me and made for the door. I sort of smiled and waved, but she locked it before I got my hand on the knob. She gave me a scowl and tossed her head and turned around. I could see her turning off lights and walking to the back of the store, fading into the shadows. I walked back across the street.

"What was that all about?" Sarah said.

"No love for the trigger-happy home wrecker. I guess Kip got a chance to work his charms on her in person."

"Right," she said. "Obviously no woman can resist him."

It was dark back in her room, but I could make out her eyes staring at me across the pillow.

"You're up to something," she said. Her voice was soft and kind and earthy, but after that "work his charms" crack I figured I'd best watch what I say, so I pretended I was asleep.

"Faker," she said. She sort of goosed me. "Why did you bring up gathering the permit?"

"Just thinking."

"It's always kind of a big operation, so we'd have to get Becky and our usual crew to help us," she said. "At least Kip wouldn't follow us out there."

"What if he did?"

"What do you mean?"

"What if just the two of us went out. And he knew it was just the two of us. Instead of him being the hare and us being the hound, we swap it around. Make him chase us."

"There's a hundred square miles of rock and sagebrush out there," she said. "It would take the two of us weeks to gather."

"But Kip don't know that. And he doesn't know the country."

Chapter Sixteen

We lay awake a bit longer talking about what we needed to do and what we needed to take on a make-believe cattle gather. How many horses, what camp equipment, hay and human food and such, plus things we would borrow for the trip. We both knew the basics, but there were a million details and just the pair of us, and we were giving ourselves just one day to get it all prepped. One thing we agreed on was getting the word out, telling everyone we knew that we were going by ourselves.

We ran Sarah's horses in right after breakfast. She picked the four we'd take so we wouldn't be riding any of them two days in a row. We wanted to be able to travel fast—us being the hare and all—but not be too hard on the animals. She finished our shopping list and headed up north to Gardnerville. I set to shoeing a dun mare, the one horse that was still barefoot, then headed south to Becky's to let them know our plans and to borrow a propane fridge.

Out at Bonner & Tyree's, Harvey was cleaning a ditch in the mare pasture by the road with the backhoe, getting ready for summer. I met him at the gate, and he got in my truck and we drove down the lane to the ranchyard. All his sawbucks, pack bags and slings, tarps, tents, lash ropes and such, plus things like generators and the fridge that I was there to borrow were semi-organized in the back stalls of Becky's barn. We rooted around, and Harv got me squared away with the little fridge and an almost full propane tank. He offered to ride with us on the gather and bring his aught-six. I told him why the two of us were going it alone and asked him to keep the reason to himself, his wife, Becky, and Dan.

"You and old Sarah like working together," he said. "I can tell."

"I know I do. But with her it's *mas o menos*."

"I know what you mean. My first wife, Francie Over-meyer, she was an ornery old hide, but when we were youngsters she used to work with me every day, too," he said. "Her dad ran some sorry-assed cattle out on that Whiskey Flat country by Hawthorne. That girl went every-where with me and rode like a goddamn Comanche."

"'Fess up, Harv. You must have loved her to take her with you every damn day."

"Naw, she was just too ugly to kiss good-bye."

I could never tell if he was serious or not. He helped me load the fridge and some other stuff into my truck, and he saw the Remington in the scabbard.

"You keep both eyes open, you hear?" he said. "There

are folks around here who wouldn't want to see you survive them two wars just to get yourself shot by that little prick. Not me, you understand, but some folks."

"I'll be careful, you old bastard."

Becky was coming up the lane in her truck as I drove out. We zipped by each other with a wave of the hand like folks do in that country, and I realized I might not see any of them again.

I drove into Dave's ranchyard at Rickey Junction. Sarah had topped off the tank on her Silverado and was checking the tire pressure on her gooseneck. We stowed the fridge in the back of her truck just behind the cab. I unloaded more stuff from my truck and was hanging our saddles in the tack room of the gooseneck when Sarah came out of the doublewide lugging my old bedroll. She hefted it into the back of her truck next to a bale of hay, then lifted a pack saddle I'd just set next to it.

"Why are we taking a sawbuck?" she said, "And lashropes, tarps, hobbles—all this packing crap?"

"Might come in handy."

"Dad gathered that permit for twenty years without that stuff. We don't need it."

"If we were actually planning to gather those cattle, that would surely be the case."

We sorted and packed the food last, then hooked up the trailer. When we were finished, we piled into my truck and headed north for dinner at the JT Bar, then caught visiting hours with Mom in Reno. I told her what I'd be doing and that I wouldn't be seeing her for a few days. We were a pretty teary bunch when we said our good-byes. Sarah and I got back to Rickey Junction to hit the sack way later than we'd planned.

We had the horses grained and loaded before sunup. We got our firearms checked and our slickers, coats, and gloves accounted for before six and then hit the road. A few miles north of the State Line Lodge we turned east off the Reno Highway. We passed a scattering of ramshackley houses and mobile homes and a tattoo parlor with a handmade sign, then a health clinic off in the sagebrush next to a medical pot outfit. We climbed a treeless pass that dropped us down into a ravine. Off to the left I saw the southern base of the Pine Nut Mountains that separated Hudson Valley from Carson Valley and ran north almost to the state capitol. We'd be on the northernmost fringes of the Pine Nuts for the next few days if we lived that long. They were steep rolling mountains with bare ridges and some reefs of exposed rock pushing through those ridges, all scattered with sage and the piñon that gave the range its name. We were barely into Hudson Valley when we turned straight north on a farm road, passing five-acre ranchettes with lights on in the kitchens where retired folks were just stirring, then past older hay ranches with flat fields and irrigation wheel lines or pivots, and headquarters off at the base of the mountains. Everything was so peaceful and normal with another day starting that we felt like a couple of fugitives, armed and red-eyed and ready to take doom itself to the ones hunting us.

"So do you believe Kip's story about being in Oregon?" she said.

"Not a bit."

"A person gets so used to hearing lies," she said. "You think that some of them must be true."

"Lies about me?"

"No," she said. "I don't believe those. You know that."

"Those lies are what guys like him count on."

"His rant bothered you, though," she said.

"There's sure no secrets anymore. Even guys at Fort Benning saw that crap."

"You have people there cyber-stalking Tommy Smith just for the hell of it?"

"Seems like. Enough so that right this minute I'd feel funny going back."

"Then don't," she said.

In another ten minutes we were past the last of the houses, and the first sunlight was coming up over Mount Grant. We were in sparse sagebrush with the last pastures of the valley slipping by us on the right. Up ahead was an alkali flat that would have water and ducks in a wet spring. Beyond that was Buckskin Mountain, brown and barren. Between the Pine Nuts and the Buckskins was a low spot in the ridge. That's where we were headed.

We stopped for a mess of sheep crossing the road tended by a boy. The flock spread across the slope and through the dust we could see the herder's tent and a stake-bed trailer hooked to the camp tender's old International. The camp tender was an ancient man who waved at us. Sarah waved back.

"Eufemio?"

"Yeah," Sarah said. "The kid's his grand-nephew."

"Eufemio must be a thousand years old by now."

She was about to say something else when she jerked upright at the sound of a plane. We scanned the sky till we found it—a common-looking reddish, single engine top-winged two-seater. It could have been the plane we saw four days before heading for Monte Cristo Summit, or it could have been nothing more than some prosperous onion farmer flying to breakfast in Carson City. We watched it until it disappeared. By then the sheep were far behind us. We'd be out in the open early the next morning, and the biggest drawback to the Let-Kip-Chase-Us plan was how damn easy catching us was going to be for him.

Chapter Seventeen

The road forked. To the right it circled past the alkali flat at the foot of the Buckskins and climbed across the valley to the white scar on the bare slope that had been a copper town and railroad terminus until the 1940s. It seemed like every year some tourist or dirt biker exploring that place discovered an old mineshaft the hard way.

We took the left fork into the Pine Nuts. At the BLM sign I geared down as the washboardy road began a climb across open flats with clumps of green Mormon tea and yellow sulfur flower scattered among the sage. Another half mile and the road folded into a canyon, climbing high as the canyon grew steep. Big cottonwoods along the trickle of creek below us reached overhead and spread shade on the road. Along the trickle were willow and bitterbrush and the pink of wild peach, and Nevada elms with fire-black trunks, their dead branches poking up through new leaves. When we got some altitude, I could see the hills that had burned the fall before, where incinerated piñon left charcoal sketch lines outlining the edges of every ridge and the contours of every rise and gully. I'd been in the hospital in Bethesda when it happened, the fourth fire in that range in three years, with the cause split pretty equal between lightning and idiots.

I looked over at Sarah. She was staring out the window with no expression. The road turned, spanning the narrow watercourse under a single elm. The water was clear, and willows grew below the crossing with patches of green at the water's edge. Beyond the creek, tan cheatgrass with purplish tips grew up the slope.

"What are you thinking?" she said.

I'd been wondering again if maybe her dad had been dead since that first morning she found him gone, or if Kip had kept him alive for some water-fraud scheme. "Just wondering how many pair you're running up here."

"Only a hundred and ten," she said. "They cut back the allotment after the fires."

"Letting the range heal?"

"Something like that."

The road now was reddish clay, deep ruts dried solid after hard rain, then climbing through juniper growing from sandy ground. Ahead we saw open country. We came to a cattle guard where the road passed through the drift fence that marked the edge of Dave's grazing allotment. Beyond the fence all the piñon and juniper were gone. Not thinned out, but totally vanished. On either side of the road there were piles of brush. Dead piñon limbs and trunks lay white from the sun, and pine boughs dry and rust-red were spread in clumps into the distance. When we cleared the cattle guard, I stopped the truck and we got out.

"The hell?"

"Wildlife mitigation," Sarah said. "Part of the BLM's new conditions on the permit. Dad hired those two weight-lifters of Kip's last fall to come out here with chain saws and cut down the trees for sage grouse habitat." She sounded pissed just thinking about it.

I looked at the mounds of dead trees. Then I scanned the open sage and bare ridges. "Not bad."

"What's the matter with you?" she said. "This is hor-rid."

"I was just thinking that for us, this ain't so terrible. No cover. Not for amateurs, anyway."

She looked like she was sorry she ever asked me home. We got back in the truck. The road climbed for another treeless quarter mile. The fires hadn't burned this far, so the next trees we came to were healthy and thick. Piñon gray as sage against darker junipers, short trees so close together we couldn't see around the next bend. I drove slow, then stopped altogether. Sarah watched me lay the Remington across my lap with the muzzle out the open window. She slipped her 9mm out of its holster on the seat between us. I started up again, just creeping along in second. Finally, the road straightened and the trees fell away at the top of the rise and we could see the pipe corral and loading chute, and the back of the cabin. The morning was warming up. We were at Dave's cowcamp.

Sage had overgrown the corral. The steel was rusty and the chute looked dicey. There was a lodgepole round corral next to the log cabin and wooden sorting pens below it in the center of a sandy flat. Scattered in the brush, I saw bits of scrap and rolls of wire and rusted steel drums. There was a water pump on its side no longer connected to anything and new galvanized stock tanks in the pens. A tarp covered a ton of hay stacked in one of the pens beyond the reach of grazing cattle.

There was an outhouse and shed and wood pile behind the cabin and a ratty Ford flatbed parked next to them. The camp was set on a rise in an open spot where the dirt road forked. The left fork disappeared into the trees. Beyond them I could see small meadows under burned hills. The right fork skirted the pens into open country.

It took us an hour to unload the truck and trailer. The cabin was low ceilinged, with two iron bunks with rolled mattresses and folded blankets stacked on bare springs, a cast-iron cook stove with a full woodbox next to it, an ice-box, a table and wooden chairs, and shelves for tin goods. It was no different than the thousands just like it that used to be scattered across the West, except maybe a bit bigger. Dave left it unlocked, as was the custom in an earlier age. Those who used it—hunters, four-wheelers, and souvenir scavengers today, drifting cowboys, prospectors, and mustangers in his dad's generation—were expected to leave the place as unmolested as they found it and the woodbox full.

Sarah unrolled the larger of the two mattresses and I set my bedroll on it and unrolled that. She peeled back the canvas tarp and aired out the bedding inside. Neither of us commented that the last time the bedroll had been used a couple of years before was the first night she and I had ever been together. We got busy and set the fridge in a likely spot. I hooked up the propane tank and Sarah stocked the fridge with what Harvey always called the basics—eggs, beef, bacon, butter, and beer. The cabin had two small windows cut into the logs, and I kept checking them, trying the latches and studying how much terrain I could see from inside. I caught Sarah watching me.

"We probably don't want to get cornered in here," she said.

"No. We'll keep moving. Get him to show himself."

"Do you think there's a chance the law might catch him before he follows us out here?" she said.

"There's always that chance."

The cabin was squared away, and we went outside and checked the fencing in the pen where we'd turned out the horses. It was in rough shape, with missing boards and exposed nails. The day was starting to get hot. In the morning we would ride out together, then separate, staying close enough to signal but looking as lonesome and vulnerable as could be. Maybe not my best plan, but I was counting on Kip and whatever crew he'd bring to get lost in all that country. After a day or so of searching, he'd try to hit us at the cowcamp, not far out in the open where they didn't know exactly where the hell we'd be. Then he'd be easier to take. Plus, we'd let those cows and their calves run interference for us. In a normal year, they'd be coming down toward the camp anyway when the feed further back got poor. They were used to getting herded out of the canyon to a ranch in the valley that belonged to Becky's brother. But this wasn't like every other year.

We heard a vehicle coming and scampered back to Sarah's Silverado. We picked up our long guns, then spread out and went back to nailing up loose boards—or pretending to. The driver was only some BLM lady that Sarah and Dave knew. Sarah leaned her shotgun against a post and walked over to the government truck, stopping for gulps from her water bottle. They talked for three or four minutes, then the lady gave me a hell of a nasty look and drove off. Sarah walked back to me with sweat on her forehead and blood in her eye.

"What a bitch," she said.

"What happened?"

"She was hard-assing me about the permit," Sarah said. "All whiney that Dad had put out the salt too close to the tanks and the cattle hadn't spread out enough across the winter, and now they're spread out too much, and one of the floats on a tank was broken and the wild critters had no water. Jesus." She stared right into me. "Basically she was wondering what I was doing camped up here with a man who wasn't my husband."

"So what'd you tell her?"

"I told her to go screw herself."

I watched her pick up the shotgun and head for the cabin. She looked about ready to load the horses and head out of there. I went back to nailing up boards.

I finished a while later. She'd set up kindling and wood in the stove, but the day was too hot to light it until we had to. I got a beer from the fridge and sat at the table.

"What's in the shed out back?"

"Some salt blocks, some wire," she said. "A beat-up old pack rig Dad used to haul the salt. Stuff like that."

"Is it locked?"

"Should be," she said. "Why?"

"One less place for somebody to hide. You have the key?"

"Yeap."

"And the key to that old Ford?"

"That too," she said.

I started fiddling with a Coleman, fueling it from a red can, pumping it up and lighting the mantles and adjusting the flame. When I got the lantern set up I shut it down till dusk. I saw a couple of regular kerosene lamps on the shelf and took those down too, filled them and trimmed the wicks. Most guys would have a generator for electric lights, but not Dave. I hoped the familiar routine took Sarah's mind off things.

At sunset I went out to feed the horses while Sarah packed a stuffsack with a couple days worth of food. When I came back she'd lit the lamps and the stove and started dinner, frying up a mess of sirloin and potatoes, the smell of the kerosene mixing with the good smell of onion and garlic in the hot beef fat. I asked her if I could help and she shook her head. She watched me pull Becky's old gun rig out and set it on the table, then fill the belt loops with the .45s from the green and yellow box.

Dinner was spicy and good. We ate and drank red wine like Basco sheepherders and didn't say much. When we did, we talked about the country we would be riding in the morning and all the old stuff that had happened on this range—mostly mining and boomer camps, but railroads and the Pony Express and Piute wars too. After I cleared the plates and put a bucket on the stove for the dishes, we took our guns and went outside. She held my hand like we were an old couple. The air was cooling and the sky was clear. It was a good while since the sun slipped behind the ridge, but a last bit of its light skimmed the peaks to the east. We walked the perimeter and went inside.

Later, with the lanterns blown out, the woodstove put an orange light inside the cabin. I slipped out of the bedroll and jammed more stove wood into the firebox, but for now we both were hot and not sleepy. When Sarah pulled away the sheet to let me back into the bedroll, her hair was tangled and her skin glistened in the orange light and I covered her with the sheet and she wrapped her arms around my neck.

"Will he come for us tonight, you think?" she said.

"No. He's probably just found out we're here, and he won't have a plan yet or the means even if he did."

She squeezed my neck and started to cry, then stopped herself just as quick.

"Tell me again how we'll find him," she said.

"We get out alone in these empty hills tomorrow like we're gathering that stock, he'll find us. Or think he has. He'll chase us till we catch him."

We would ride that country hard from dark to dark.

Each night we would tend our horses and cook our food with not many words, but each one simple and kind and well chosen, like it was our own language. Then we would get into that big bedroll and be as close as the first two humans on earth. She was so sweet I hated every man she had ever been with and shared that sweetness with, and hated myself for any time of ours I might have wasted. I knew that time was always short. Then she would look at me in the dark, or the orange glow of the fire, just tangled gypsy hair and the shape of her face and those eyes reflecting the dying coals, and then she would wrap her arms around my neck and draw me in and that was all there was and all that mattered, except for the man out there in the dark we'd come to kill.

Chapter Eighteen

At quarter to four I stoked the fire and lit the lamp. I singed my fingers getting the coffee started and jumped back into the bedroll to wait for it to boil. I'd left one window open when we went to bed. I'd remembered a lot of things while I was away, but I forgot how sweet the cool air is in the spring and summer at night in the mountains as you lay under the blankets. Not at all like the sticky, stale nights in Georgia when sleep would never come and a knife fight was a diversion.

When the cabin warmed up, I watched Sarah pull on her clothes and loved her so much I didn't think it could ever last. She bundled up and kissed me and went out to feed and saddle while I started breakfast. She wanted to keep as busy as she could and not talk so I left her to it. I tried to catch a look at her out the front window, but the sky was still moonless and black and she'd vanished into the cold starlight. I got ham and eggs and fried toast ready with the coffee, and sandwiches made for lunch, and had rolled up the bedroll by the time she came back into the cabin. We ate fast and hardly spoke, but she looked positive and strong and ready to tear into the morning. That was just how it was with her.

We dropped our dishes into the water bucket on the stove, buckled on our chinks, strapped on our pistols, and pulled on our coats. I unlatched the second window so I could open them both from the outside when we came back. At the door, she came up to me and grabbed the front of my coat and put her forehead against my chin, pressing into me. Her body felt warm but her coat was cold to the touch. Then she gave me a look. We squared our hats and went outside into the black morning.

It was cold like it always is in that country in the predawn, the stars still out and the morning star bright now in the east. The horses she saddled were tied to the side of the gooseneck eating grain from nosebags. I leaned against the front of the truck with my rifle, scanning the shadows while Sarah fetched the food she'd gathered and stowed it next to the pack equipment in the truckbed. I went back to the cabin and hugged the big bedroll and walked outside with that and tossed it in the truck with the rest. We took off the nosebags and loaded the stock. Sarah got behind the wheel. We headed on the right-hand dirt road going north. I was hoping by the time Kip or his boys got to the cowcamp we'd be long gone and have a chance to scout the country before hell got let off the leash.

Sarah knew the road from riding this ground for years with her father. She pointed to the meadows on the left and told me how the road past them led up to Washoe Pass, and

I could see it steepen and climb before it disappeared into rocks and piñon. She said the meadows would be a good place to hold cattle if we ever got the chance. We hit two forks in the road a mile apart, keeping to the right both times. Before long we were following a rocky wash. Sarah said we could leave the gooseneck off the road well above the cabin and ride further north to see if Kip would take the bait and follow. We would push any cow-calf pairs we ran across down toward the meadows. Usually the stock had been moved below the upper drift fence earlier in the year, but Dave's heart attack had left his cows as scattered and untended as his daughter.

It was sunup when Sarah parked the rig off the road under a cut in a hill facing back the way we'd come. It wouldn't be quite hidden, but a person might miss it from a distance. We unloaded the horses, packed our saddle pockets with lunch and ammo, and hit a long trot north. She was riding the dun I'd shod two days before and I was on the sorrel. They were the younger pair of the four horses, and Sarah said they would do well for a long day's circle. What she didn't say was the two more broke horses might do better when the shooting started. The dun hadn't been ridden much recently except by the big ironpumper and had picked up some willful habits. She bogged her head as soon as we broke out of a walk. Sarah grabbed the stock of her shotgun in the scabbard so it wouldn't jostle out, hollered, and brought that horse's head up sharp, in no mood for foolishness. A mile further on we stopped and scanned the ridges. I saw a patch of ground up against the hills that was covered with pale green and asked Sarah why no cattle were out on it. She said if I got close I could see it was only wild mustard and among the springtime stalks there wasn't a blade of grass. She said I'd have known that if I wasn't such a High Sierra, green meadow, and mountain stream sort of cowboy. She said I had a lot to learn about this desert country, but she said it more hopeful than mean. We saw some pairs down in a draw but kept on riding. We could pick them up later if we didn't get any nibbles from Kip.

With the sun up, the day began to warm and we took our coats off by eight. By nine we were seeing more small groups of cows and calves. By ten we came to a drift fence and a galvanized stock tank. Sarah said we'd split up then, and each circle on a different side of a long ridge, meeting down at the tank in a couple of hours with whatever cattle we'd gathered.

"We'll only be a half-mile from each other most of the time," she said.

I studied the hills and saw white mining scars on the slopes from years before, and reddish tailings spreading below the scars. I didn't see a trace of movement.

"If you hear gunfire, hunt a place to hide."

"Like hell," she said.

I bent toward her in the saddle and kissed her.

"You be careful."

She nodded, looking like we were saying good-bye forever. "You be careful, too," she said.

We split up, still riding north. We stayed within sight of each other for ten minutes, then the country changed and we were each alone with nothing to do but keep our eyes open and ride. I hit a climbing gravel road and could see the first clouds rising white above the Sierra crest. I could pretty much estimate where Carson City and Dayton would be behind the near ridges, but this was mostly new country to me. The road swung right in treeless hills with the dry and rocky riverbed off to the left. Ahead were scattered piñon between the road and the watercourse. I climbed along the base of a burned-over slope where the sage was scorched off and the cheatgrass grew. The riverbed on my left was close now with dry boulders and sand ridges out in the sun, then tangles of willow and wild rose under the cottonwoods right to the edge of the road. I saw fresh sign among the brush in the cattle wallows, and there was shallow water now about five feet wide running along the rocks. On the other side of the creek I saw buildings and corrals left from an old stagecoach relay station that a Piute Meadows Basque had used as a winter lambing camp about twenty years back, and I saw cuts in the bare hills from miners' wagons. The stony road turned dirt with muddy patches. I circled wide with my hand just touching the butt of the .45, keeping my eyes on the nearest shack. There was no sign of horses or vehicles, just cowtracks. Ahead I saw four pair brushed up along the creek. I rode on another mile then stopped where a gully spilled into the canyon from the south. Twenty minutes further on, the feed and the cattle sign were both gone and no human sign had replaced them. I turned around.

Wispy clouds had settled into rows of thunderheads above the crest. I rousted the four pair out of the brush at the stage stop and pushed them on ahead. If I'd been the one hunting me that morning, I would've made myself a little den across the creek bed in the rocks and hid in plain sight until a rider was right on me with his eyes focused on the old shack. One shot should do it. But that was me.

In another half hour the terrain widened back out and the road separated from the creek. It was good to be horseback in open country. I took down my rope and swung a loop over a clump of sage, dallied, and pulled it out by the roots. Then I reminded myself why I was there and how I best keep my hands and eyes free and not dawdle. I coiled my rope and brushed my hand across the walnut grips of the revolver again, looking past the cows and calves to the country ahead.

At first it was only hints and traces—the far-off sound of a motor, maybe from a four-wheeler. The clack of rock-on-rock from someone taking a careless step. Maybe a glint of light hitting reflector shades or glancing off a windshield. Even behind a ridge, the signs were easy enough to read. I got off my horse and was quiet, listening for the sounds I knew were coming.

The sound I didn't expect was a shout from Sarah with a gunshot following right behind. I saw movement on the rim, then Sarah burst into plain sight on the dun, fighting that sow all the way. She saw me downslope, and it looked like she was pointing her pistol at me before she spun that horse. The dun danced on the ridge and I heard a shot ping off a rock about twenty feet behind me as I swung back on the sorrel. I was too surprised to holler before the dun flew sideways, spooked from the gunshot. I could see Sarah keeping that knothead moving forward down the slope and not fighting her anymore.

I shouted Sarah's name and busted the sorrel out, lunging over rocks and brush. When I hit the rim, I saw Sarah spin back to face my direction, her pistol still in her fist. I got close and she looked at me half-crazed, then spun the mare again to look in the other direction. She was watching downslope at a rider on a sorrel horse who was dressed just like me—black Nevada hat, red wild rag, white shirt, and gray vest. It was Kip, and he'd shaved his goatee and mustache. He shook a rifle over his head and yipped like a coyote.

"There were two of you," she said. She looked haunted. "I thought I was crazy." The dun fired out at my horse with both hind feet. Sarah spurred that mare hard, bringing her around.

We could hear Kip whoop-whoop again as he sheathed the rifle, goosed his horse and galloped away from us out of that canyon, leaning back in the saddle half out of control and laughing like hell. He yelled something I couldn't quite make out, but it sounded too much like, "I've got you now."

Sarah looked over at me as wild-eyed as the dun, like she still wasn't sure which of us was which.

"From a distance I really did think it was you. When I rode closer, he laughed at me and I just lost it."

"You're okay now."

"I should've known," she said. "Nobody sits a horse like you. I could've killed you."

The few pairs we'd pushed were scattering from the gunfire, moving down along the riverbed. New cattle followed, all drifting in one direction. We left them as we rode toward the parked gooseneck, then headed up onto a high ridge above a talus slope where we could see country all around. We ate our lunch horseback—outlined against the sky—so anyone could see us but not be able to come at us without grief. More thunderheads gathered in the west.

"What's he waiting for?" Sarah said.

"He thinks he's the hound and we're the hare. Just like we wanted."

"Where do you think he is now?"

"Probably waiting for us between here and the cabin."

The sun was almost down as we followed the drifting cattle toward the corrals, but the air was still warm like rain coming. Dust stirred up by scuffing hooves rose and fell over the ground. The white thunderheads had dropped down until they dissolved into a gray-black sky in the west, and we could see the first sliver of a new moon through that sky. We held back, watching the whole camp for any sign of Kip or his crew.

We left our horses saddled and turned them into the round corral with the other two, scattering hay for them. Some of the cattle had gone past the cabin toward the meadows, and some had stayed behind trying to get to the hay I'd just fed or the bales stacked the empty pen. I opened the gate to the second pen and scattered more hay on the ground. The cows and calves moved in fast. If we were being watched, we would look like a couple of pretty sloppy stockmen, not that those gunsels could tell the difference.

I had Sarah wait by the pens to cover me with her 12 gauge while I checked the cabin. Kip or his boys had made their first reconnoiter. I could see four-wheeler tracks circling in the dirt outside the cabin door. The tread was real similar to tracks on the one I'd unloaded for Hoyt. I didn't see any boot tracks, though, so it was a quick visit. Inside, in the semi-dark, things seemed just as we'd left them. I grabbed two beers, then went out to fire up the flatbed Ford. Sarah got in the passenger door and let me drive. It was an automatic, and I remembered what Harvey had said about Kip ripping off the steering wheel in a rage, and noticed the mismatched junkyard wheel in my hands. It was near dark by the time we got back to the gooseneck. A wind had picked up and the temperature started dropping fast. We stood outside the trucks, watching the road as darkness settled and we went over our plan for the next twenty minutes.

"He doesn't seem in any hurry to kill us," Sarah said.

"Once he thinks he's got the last word in and bloodied our nose, he'll try. When he does, that's our best chance."

We drove both trucks back toward the cowcamp, and I parked the Ford behind the cabin. I left it there with the lights hitting the back wall and the diesel running. Sarah turned the gooseneck around between the cabin and the stock pens, leaving it parked and idling on the road. She killed the lights and led the two horses we'd left saddled out to the trailer, loading them just as relaxed as could be. I haltered the other two and tied them outside the pole corral. We were taking our time, knowing that someone was watching. When we finished, we stood on the road cradling our long guns and eyeing the cabin for any sign of life. The crescent moon was settling horizontal just above the ridge.

"So what do we do if he's inside?" she said.

"Make it uncomfortable as hell for him."

She almost laughed. "Then what do we do once we're inside?"

"Either way this goes down, we won't be inside for long."

She stared up at the moon slipping behind the ridge so fast you could almost see it move. "Look," she said, "the points of the moon are sticking up like horn tips above the crest. And the reflection between them looks like a face."

I had been staring at the cabin, but there wasn't a hint of movement. I looked up at the reflection of the earth laying pale on the nightside of the moon between the points of the crescent.

"Don't go giving yourself the fantods, now."

I circled the cabin and pushed open one window with my rifle barrel, then the other. It was mostly black shapes inside with spots of glare from the headlights, but I got no response. I wasn't sure if Kip was cold-blooded enough to sit still in the dark like that. I was circling back when I heard Sarah yelp.

She was standing by the open door back-lit by truck lights. There was something hanging from the lintel at face level. It was a dead magpie. It swung back and forth on a bit of baling twine after Sarah had walked into it with her face. Its blue wing feathers stood out like neon from its black and white body in the headlight glare. It hadn't been there an hour before.

"Well, we know he's close." When we spoke, we spoke at a whisper.

"What a sicko," she said. "You going inside?"

"Yeah."

"What if he's inside?"

"Then we can get this over quick."

"Tommy . . ."

"I'm just going to grab the Coleman. Then draw his attention outside while you load these horses quick as you can."

"I'll be right behind you," she said. "Just don't get yourself shot."

"Nobody shoots me but you."

With the glare in the background, it was black as hell in the cabin. I could tell somebody was in there with us as soon as I stepped inside. Then I bumped into an iron bunk that had been moved into our path, and Sarah bumped into me. I reached behind me and kind of gathered her close. She knew exactly why. The only sound was the rattle of the diesel outside.

A match head scraped on cast iron and lit the cabin up with yellow-green light. He held it under his chin. When he laughed, his face under his hat jumped in the long shadows and the laugh echoed hollow up the stovepipe like death itself.

"Howdy buckaroos and buckarettes," he said. I saw a pistol in the matchlight pointed at Sarah's head. It looked more like a Beretta than his SIG, but it was too dark to tell or matter. "What can I do you for?"

A noise came out of Sarah, but not because of the gun pointing at her. It was him. He'd changed his outfit again since we'd seen him on the ridge. Now he was wearing a palm leaf hat and plaid shirt with the blood-red wild rag. It was exactly the outfit that Lester Wendover had worn in that photo of Sarah with her French boyfriend, Lester, and me at the Deer Hunters' Dance.

"You be careful with that pistol. Hurt a hair on her head, I slit your eyelids." I held my .270 careful in one hand so he could see it.

"Aw, you wouldn't do that," he said. He held the match higher.

We watched that match burn down in spite of ourselves. I figured I only had a few seconds of light. I could see the glass and green metal of the Coleman lamp on the table.

"I wouldn't go betting on me. I got no clue what I would or wouldn't do right about now."

"So my wife belongs to you now?"

"She belongs to nobody but herself."

"How 'bout that knife?" He held out his free hand. "Who's that belong to, huh?"

I held out my knife. He nodded at the table, and I set it there. His eyes went from the knife down to the match for an instant, like he couldn't help looking at it either.

"Just tell me," Sarah said. She took a step closer to him. Her voice was shaky. "Tell me why you killed my dad."

Her voice broke just as he made a little sound like a whimper when the match flame burned down to his fingertips and the room went dark. His 9mm popped twice—once into the ceiling boards and once through a windowpane. The shots rang in the stovepipe, and I grabbed Sarah and we hit the floor. There was a scrape of a table on the planking and I could see the headlights outline his shadow then blaze off the knife blade for an instant when he yanked the cabin door wide. Then he was gone.

I grabbed the Coleman by the bale with one hand, and with the Remington in the other I scampered out the door after him. I stayed low, keeping out of the truck lights, figuring he wouldn't turn back to look until he had some cover. I ran down to the open pen and slid in with the cows and calves. I pulled up the glass on the lantern, pumped it up and set a match to the mantles. The cattle stirred up with that bright gaslight and I stirred right along with them, setting the lantern on a corner post after I got the flame adjusted.

The wind was picking up like the storm was close. The lantern rattled on the post, the mantles flaring and dimming with every gust. I heard a shot and the rip of a round splintering a corral board. He was still just playing with us like that day shooting at me at the dump. I heard the metal creak of the trailer door closing as I crept along the fence. I disappeared into the dark, and a second shot thunked into a cabin log. I kept my head low and ran up the slope for the Ford.

"Long day, assholes?" somebody yelled. It was hard to hear over the wind, but it wasn't Kip and didn't sound like one of the ironpumping gunsels either. Kip had got himself more help.

I hopped into the Ford, put it in drive and hopped right out again. I almost fell as I slammed the door and watched it roll off down the road. The back window shattered and a second shot clanged off the steel of the flatbed before it chugged off into the piñon. I pulled the .45 and fired twice toward where the voice came from, then ran past the cabin out to the road.

Sarah had her truck moving. I ran parallel and grabbed at the door handle as she picked up speed with lights off. She'd unplugged the trailer from the truck, so even the gooseneck brake lights wouldn't show, only the brake lights on the truck. I jumped in and pulled the door closed but didn't slam it. We were hoping to get out into the darkness before Kip and his guys quite figured who the hell was where. The Silverado took two rounds to the right side of the truck-box behind me, and one to the passenger door just in front of my foot before the road dropped into a gully. The next two or three rounds zipped by over our heads, and by then we were gone into the dark.

"You okay?" Sarah said. She was bent forward, trying to see the dirt road with no headlights.

"Not bad. That kind of looked like we were desperate as hell and running for our lives."

"Weren't we?"

"Yeah, but we knew what we were going to do. Old Kip didn't."

"A pretty scary distinction," she said. "I'm not used to getting shot at. You get used to it, right?"

"Nope."

We pulled out of the gully on our way north for the third time that day. It sounded like one last round nicked the gooseneck, but we couldn't stop to check. We both just peered through the dirty windshield as the first trace of rain spattered it. Sarah turned on the wipers. I saw a bit of paper or something dragging back and forth across the spotted glass.

We couldn't see it, but we could hear the sage brushing the underside of the truck as we wandered off the dirt track. Sarah made a correction and got us back on the road. After a few more minutes she said we were about where the road forked and let the truck roll to a stop. We got out. She examined the ruts, trying to find where they turned off. I went back to see if any of the horses had been hit. They were quiet and seemed untouched, but it was hard to know for certain in the dark. I pulled out my phone to give them a quick look with the dim light and didn't find any injury, so I caught up with Sarah. She said the left fork fish-hooked back to the meadows. From where we stood, we could look toward the cabin and see the glow of the Ford's headlights and see even fainter lights moving around—somebody making sure we weren't up to some mischief in the shadows. The lights didn't appear to be following yet. A low piñon-covered ridge hid the cabin itself and would have blocked their view of us even in daylight. I guessed that the cowcamp was three-quarters of a mile behind us, maybe as much as a mile. I walked down the left fork a bit, studying the contours in the dark that I had seen in daylight that morning, seeing where the land dropped away to the left of the road toward the last of the meadows and how it rose up heading for Washoe Pass. There were already puddles forming on the road. We got back in the cab.

"Where does this left fork go once you top the pass?"

"All the way down to Carson Valley," she said. "Right into the suburbs."

"Is it steep?"

"Steep enough," she said, "and rocky."

"And the fork straight ahead from here?"

"It's the wagon road to Dayton," she said, "but I haven't gone up there since I was a kid."

"And the right fork is that rocky road we took today?"

"Correct."

"Okay. Let's ditch this rig."

The rain was getting slushy like snow on the windshield. I got out and grabbed the piece of notepaper from under the wiperblade. Back in the cab I read it by the light of my phone. The paper was soggy but the writing was clear.

Hey my sexy minx . . . you can run but you can't hide.
Oh by the way, I didn't kill your dad.

Happy Trails, doll . . .

I handed the paper to Sarah. She read it, took a long breath, and handed it back to me.

"What the hell does he mean?" she said. "Does this mean Dad's really—?"

"It means Kip's trying to drive you nuts. Don't let him."

She grabbed the paper back from me. "Dot-dot-dot. What a fruit." She squished it in her hand and threw it in the mud.

Sexy minx, my ass.

Chapter Nineteen

Sarah picked up speed to maybe fifteen miles an hour. I could feel the four horses scramble for footing in the trailer as we rattled along in the dark, sometimes on the road, other times not. We hadn't gone far when my phone chirped in my pocket. For the first time in hours I had service. I saw I had a voicemail from Jack Harney and a text from Fuchs. I was trying to call Jack back when a call came in.

"Hey, Jack. Talk to me."

"Tommy Smith?" somebody said. "This isn't Jack. It's Deputy Parrott, Douglas County."

"Oh, hey, Roger."

"I've been trying to reach you," he said. "Sarah Cathcart's boss wanted me to give you guys a head's-up about trouble in my county. You heard anything about it?"

"We been pretty much out of pocket the past day, Rog."

"Well, first, yesterday a.m. there was a break-in near Cathcart's. A ranch house. Firearms were taken. Then couple hours later there was a shooting at State Line Lodge," he said. "Two guys heisted a cashier's cage in the casino in broad daylight just as one of our deputies walked in for a bite. Heisters shot him down right in the doorway—sauntered out just as cool as you please, okay."

"When was this?"

"Yesterday. About two."

"Who was the deputy?"

"Marco Aurillia. Drug Task Force liaison. Had a taste for the anytime day-or-night three-ninety-nine biscuits and gravy."

"You ID-ed the shooters?"

"Not yet." His phone broke up and he said something I couldn't make out, so I had him repeat it. It sounded like the deputy wasn't conscious, and one of the shooters fit Delroy's description. If the other one was Kip, it wasn't clear. "These guys are known associates of Jedediah Boone, so we got a regular outlaw-gang crime spree. Folks are locking their doors, okay."

"Was one of the shooters Kip Isringhausen?"

"I don't think so," he said. "I thought he was in Oregon."

"He's a mile and a half behind us on the Washoe Pass road. He's well-armed, not alone, and coming on fast."

"Whoa," Roger said. "Are you sure it's Isringhausen? Where are you guys exactly?" Then he broke up again.

I told him our position and told him to pass it on to Mitch and Fuchs ASAP. He said affirmative, then he broke up altogether.

Sarah took her foot off the gas and coasted to a stop at

the fork in the road we had taken that morning. The spattering rain had turned to snow.

"Is this the place?"

"Yeah," she said. "He can't miss the rig if we leave it here."

"This is a good spot. It'll look like we stalled out or panicked and we're running scared."

"Isn't that what we're doing?"

"Not a bit. We got him right where we want him."

She almost laughed at that. We unloaded the horses, leaving saddled the two we'd ridden that day. I threw Harvey's pack saddle on Dave's roan and rigged that up while Sarah cut open the haybale and stuffed flakes of it into the pack bags along with big ziplocks of grain. We hoisted the two bags, slipping the loops over the sawbuck, and set the kitchen stuffsack in the middle. We unrolled the bedroll and spread it folded across the top of the load, covered it with the pack tarp then lashed the whole thing down. We got mounted and headed on out of there, riding back down the road in steady snow.

"Do you think he'll follow us tonight?" Sarah said.

"You know him better than I do. But he'll be thinking he's got us bottled up in those canyons with no way back to the cattle guard except past him."

"If he finds the gooseneck fast, he can track us in this snow," she said. "But I can't picture him slogging out here in the dark very long once the snow covers our tracks. He's too much of a pussy."

"Nice talk for a well brought-up girl."

"So I guess he'll stay warm in the cabin and come at us in the morning."

We didn't ride far. We followed the road back toward the cowcamp then took that first westerly fork that led toward the meadows. Even with no moon to guide us, it wasn't quite full dark so we could see the shapes of the land. We weren't far up that fork when we dropped off to the left onto sandy ground that drained the last meadow. We angled away from the road until we had a small sage-covered ridge on our left and a single huge juniper on our right. The juniper shielded us from the meadow beyond.

We set up a picket line with our lash rope between the juniper and a scrub piñon. We tied and unsaddled, and fed the horses hay. I covered our rigs with the pack tarp as Sarah got out some food. We unrolled the bedroll and huddled, munching on cheese and salami and crackers, washing it down with whiskey and water and not saying a word. I studied the ground around us. We were pretty exposed but it didn't feel that way. We were about halfway between the cabin and the truck, but tucked between the little hill and the big tree it made a good camp. The snow had stopped and we could see a few stars, but there was a big snow cloud wrapped over the ridge like fog. There was a glow to the cloud like moonlight behind a ridge, but I figured it was only the city lights of Carson City lighting it up from the other side of the mountain. We stashed our boots and guns in the folds of the tarp, then crawled in the bed with our clothes on and just held each other for what seemed like a long time.

It was one of those nights when you don't really sleep.

You just doze and wake with a start, then go under deep. And when you wake again it's only been minutes and you wonder what you've done with your life. We were still a long way from midnight when Sarah got a text from Mitch. He told her about the shoot-out at State Line Lodge and about the wounded deputy, but that was all. Nothing about where we were or when he might be coming up behind Kip to put the squeeze on.

She was sniffling as she handed me her phone. I called Mitch back, but she wasn't getting any service. I tried my phone and called Jack. I got him for a second but he broke up, too.

"I can't believe I've come to this," she said. "Less than two weeks ago . . ." She didn't finish and was quiet for a while.

"Tell me it'll get better," she said. "That time heals all wounds. Can you tell me that?"

"Wish I could."

She touched my wet eyes with her fingertips.

"Oh god—your dad," she said. "Is that why you left the first time?" She grabbed me and cried a bit then nodded off.

I tried to let my eyes adjust so I could see her. Her eyebrows stood out pale from her face, and it took me a minute to realize that they were pale with snow. It had started falling again, soft and quiet. I kissed the snow away and pulled the top of the tarp over our heads and snapped the canvas closed and let her cry in my arms until she truly slept. With the phone off it was dark as a tomb under that tarp.

"What's with this magpie crap?" she said. She was

mumbly but wide awake all of a sudden, and me who'd been dozing.

"Beats the shit out of me. Just another scavenger bird."

"But pretty," she said, "in its way."

I found the whiskey in the dark and unscrewed the cap and took a drink. I asked her if she wanted some and I could feel her shake her head no.

"Don't be getting any more bad habits," she said.

I almost said something back, but it seemed sort of crass. What I was about to say reminded me of joking with Ofelia Cruz, and I hadn't thought of her for what seemed like forever.

"So what's with Kip trying to look like me or Lester?"

"Because he can't be Tommy Smith." She rolled and pulled my arm over her and held it as she tried to sleep. "That should be pretty obvious, honey, even to you."

When I finally woke up it was dead quiet and dark under the tarp. Sarah was asleep, and I pushed the canvas back slow as not to wake her. When I'd opened it a foot, snow fell into my face. I brushed it off my cheek and neck and raised my head. It was dawn and there was about four inches of snow on the tarp. Our saddles and pads were buried under it and the horses stood still on the picket line with snow on their butts, their manes and tails bright with spikes of ice. The juniper drooped with snow, and the whole country around us was silent and white.

Cold air on her face woke Sarah. She pulled her head up just a bit to see what I'd seen, then slid back down under the blankets.

"At least our tracks are covered," she said.

The sun wasn't up yet but the sky was clear. "Until we make new ones."

I yawned and stretched and felt around for my hat, rifle, and .45. I drank from a water bottle. I found my boots and pulled them on, got up and climbed into my coat and saw Sarah watching me from the bedroll. I took my rifle and made long steps toward the picket line to leave as few footprints as I might.

When I got close to our horses, I froze. They weren't moving but each was watching, ears up, eyes focused at something out in the meadow beyond the shelter of the juniper. I crouched and angled around, keeping the big tree between me and whatever was out there and never taking my eyes off the horses for more than a second. When I was close against the shaggy juniper trunk, I stopped and scanned the field of snow, then took a second to glance backward. I saw Sarah watching me, worried as she got into her boots and coat and pulled her 12 gauge from the tarp. She was as careful as the horses had been not to make any noise or fast movement. I found a spot between the limbs where I could see out unobstructed. The dun mare quivered on the picket line and let out a little nicker I could barely hear as her forefeet moved in place. Then she raised her tail and dropped her hindquarters a bit and pissed deep yellow into the snow. Sarah looked confused as hell when she saw me touch my lips and motion her over. I was watching bits of color and movement out in the meadow. She reached me in the shelter of the juniper and moved in close as I put a hand on her back.

"Mustangs."

We looked through the limbs across the snow. There
was a small band of wild horses only two hundred or so feet
away. All but one were palomino pintos, white with gold
patches and no dark hair on any of them. I'd never seen a
wild bunch colored so similar like that. There were five or
six in the group with a lead mare, some standing alert and
some trying to paw and graze through the fresh snow. If
there were new foals I didn't see them, but that didn't mean
they weren't there. I saw a stallion, a dark liver chestnut
with a flaxy mane and tail standing apart from the others
like they do, watching our four horses on the picket line
and ready to herd his band out of there at the first hint of
trouble or fight a rival for his mares. When a whiff of wind
would stir up the snow, the mustangs would almost vanish
and all I could make out were the shapes of the pale patches
on their hides just floating out there in all that whiteness,
and not any horses at all, as if they'd bred themselves that
color to blend into the winter like snowshoe rabbits. Of
course they hadn't done any such thing, and it wasn't winter at all, just a freak spring snow and freeze. Across the
ground I could see a low spot where water must have run.
I saw two different horses drop their heads, one at a time
at the same place. I knew there must be fresh ice thick on a
shallow ditch or spring, and guessed they'd made a smooth
round hole in the ice with their breath and the warmth of
their noses so they could get to the water underneath. As
we watched, it was like Sarah and I'd forgot to even breathe.
Mustangs are sometimes common as flies in that country
and can be a nuisance. I remember when I was little, my
dad telling me about a big helicopter roundup he saw in

these same canyons. But this was different. Where I had been the past few years, the only wild things were the people. I'd forgot how much I missed all this and was glad these horses were still here to remind me of how it was. Maybe this wasn't different. Maybe the only thing different was me.

Sarah talked to me in a whisper. "That stud has nice color, but he only looks decent from a distance. Up close he's common as mud. This band grazes the meadow down to dirt, then the BLM hard-asses Dad about overgrazing. He wanted to shoot 'em all." She smiled. "They're still cool to look at, though."

We'd just started back when the horses quivered on the picket line and the sound of a motor exploded over our heads. Before I could move, a red single-engine plane blasted over the hill behind us and over our camp only thirty feet above, grazing the top of the juniper and shaking the sky. The dun pranced in place more than ever and looked ready to uncork as prop wash blew the snow off the juniper boughs. The plane was gone before our horses had a chance to really raise hell, but the wild band was gone in a blink.

"Holy shit," Sarah said. "You think he saw us?"

"If he comes back, then he saw us. But the ridge might've hid us till he passed." I brushed the snow off her hair. "We're pretty much covered up."

"Could you see who it was?" she said.

"I think so. The stout little guy with the chin beard."

"Delroy."

We waited by the bedroll and listened for the plane.

I didn't want to feed and water the horses and leave big rows of tracks you could see from hundreds of feet up. The plane made another pass, this time down the center of the meadow about a quarter of a mile away. Again, the snow and juniper tree gave us camouflage. The sound of the plane seemed like it faded off even though I couldn't see it. I hurried to the picket line and led two of the horses out in the open to the frozen ditch. I crushed the ice with my boot heel so they could drink. Now out in the meadow a couple hundred yards off, instead of wild horses, that red plane just sat with its engine off like it was waiting for us. I looked through my riflescope. Muddy furrows cut through the snow behind it from the rough landing. Tan clay and black mud caked the wheels and was splattered on the red paint.

I cussed to myself and walked those horses quiet as could be back to the picket line.

"Old Delroy is parked out in the meadow."

"Did he see you?" Sarah said.

"Probably."

"Should we saddle up and get the hell out?" she said.

"We better take him on right here. That was the plan."

"We should get saddled anyway," she said, "so we're ready to scoot if things go south."

"Okay. I'll water these other two and keep my scope on him. See what he's up to."

Sarah started working fast, shaking the snow and ice off the pack tarp, brushing horses and saddling. She was saving the bedroll for last, as rolling that up would leave

Cheatgrass

a big dark rectangle on the white ground. If we lived we could always come back for it. I took the two unwatered horses back to the ditch, carrying my rifle. While they drank, I looked Delroy over through the scope. He was sitting in the cockpit pouring coffee from a thermos and eating donuts. I could have taken him out right then, but it would have been hard to explain in court. I walked the horses back to the picket line and tied them with the two Sarah was saddling up. She'd laid out hay, so if we had a long chase they'd have something in their bellies. I looked back to the meadow and could see the color of the plane through the juniper. Even that little bit of walking around had trampled the fresh snow. What would happen next depended on what move Delroy made, and there was the outside chance he'd never seen us at all.

"I figure a little fire wouldn't show too much this early, so how 'bout some coffee?"

"Look at you," she said. "You want to make sure he knows we're here."

"No point in being bashful."

I got a nice fire started with pudding-cup cardboard plus dried duff and juniper twigs from under the tarp. Then I threw on anything that would burn. I brushed the snow off the bedroll and laid the Remington down. We sat on the canvas waiting for the water to boil, then drank our coffee and ate yesterday's sandwiches for breakfast. The sun had just crested the hills. It was a real pretty morning, but still cold.

"You make a big enough circle, you might get to the

cattle guard without being seen. Get there about the same time Mitch and the rest of your crew shows up. You'll be safe with them and Kip will be in a squeeze."

She didn't say anything, just watched the smoke rise. "I think we should stick together."

She was dousing the fire with snow and I was squaring my saddle on Dave's roan when we heard the plane fire up. I circled far to one side of our camp and told Sarah to do the same on the other. I watched the plane lug across that snowy meadow heading away from us with the engine rattling. Then I saw it slow down and turn to face us, and stop. It was all the way across the meadow now. I put the scope on Delroy. He was fiddling with his controls, his ballcap on backwards. He didn't seem to be paying us any mind. I knew he was, though. He looked up toward the juniper and seemed like he was looking right through it, like he was looking me in the eye through that scope. He pushed on something in the cockpit and the motor revved. I saw him shove a magazine into what looked like an AK-47.

I heard Sarah yell, "He's getting a running start at us."

The red plane started slow. It looked like any other airplane trying to take off, but there was a slow-motion feel. Maybe it was only because it was heading straight at us and the distance was foreshortened or something. Then I realized the plane really was going slower than it should. It hit an icy patch and skidded to the side, then overcorrected and straightened itself out. Delroy pushed it until the motor screamed and the prop roared as it closed the gap from the top of the meadow in the direction of the juniper.

I could see he was running out of room. I took a quick look at Sarah and held the .270 up to my shoulder, safety off but not quite sighting yet. The nose of the red plane reared back, and it left the ground with mud spinning off the wheels. It still looked like it was going too slow, even when it was airborne. One wing dipped and the plane lurched in the air, half hidden by the top of the juniper. It was flying that low. The wing clipped a branch and the plane wheeled to the right, tearing sideways through the treetop heading in our direction, but now totally out of control. I heard Sarah shout and saw her dive for cover but couldn't hear what she said. As the plane tore over the horses it finished flipping upside down and swapping ends, pinwheeling and just howling over us as it smashed tail first into the hill only fifty feet past our camp.

The horses went nuts. All four pulled back, then plunged forward. The dun pulled hard enough to somehow slip her halter but the picket line held. I turned from the plane to the horses and saw the dun blast off across the snow and disappear. When I turned back to the plane I could see Delroy hanging upside down, his ballcap fallen off, facing me in a rage, wiggling and trying to get out. I looked through the scope and kept the reticle right on his face, but he was just too close. I lowered the rifle without firing. Then I heard a sort of whoosh, a rushing sound like the air sucking out of something. It could have been the vapor in a fuel tank or the life in Delroy's lungs. Then the red plane was covered with yellow flame and Delroy jerked one way and then the other before he was still. I might have heard him scream, but that might have just been the shriek of twisting metal. The fuselage looked like it was curling and melting into the snowy hillside with the shape of Delroy's big torso shriveling into a sort of crouch.

Sarah trotted over from the far side of the juniper, snow on her knees.

"He looks like a little bat," she said, "hanging upside down." She stepped closer, short of breath. I watched her face staring at Delroy as he looked more and more like the burned body in the truck at the pot farm. Then I watched her turn away.

"You okay?"

"Yeah," she said. "You made sure he knew we were here. That was our plan. Get 'em out in unfamiliar territory. I know."

"Yeah, well. Watching him taxi, I could see the ground was too soft and mucky to get up enough speed for takeoff. I figured he'd have trouble."

"I wasn't complaining," she said.

"Okay."

"Tommy . . ."

My phone chirped. It was Jack, and I put it on speaker.

"Can you hear me, Tommy? Sarah?" he said. "Somebody left something really creepy for Becky. She found an envelope stuck on her screendoor early this morning. Dogs didn't bark or nothing. It was an old newspaper clipping from the *Daily Bodie Standard* in 1905. The headline talked about a ranch hand and part-time prospector who'd fallen into an abandoned mineshaft out at the Monte Cristo mine two years before. He'd been exploring by himself and hadn't told nobody where he was going. Every day he waited to die, he'd write a note to his family about the bad fix he was in with a busted leg, no water, no food, and freezing nights down in that shaft with no way out. Minutes went by like hours—that sort of stuff. Wrote them with a piece of pencil on catalogue scraps. The newspaper printed all of the notes he scribbled along with the story. Some cowhands hunting strays found the guy's skeleton a couple of years later with the eight days of notes he'd written before he'd finally died. So both me and Becky think maybe this was meant for you, Sarah. And that maybe it was from Kip."

"Did he do this to Dad?" she said. "Is that what you're saying?"

"It's kind of sick," Jack said. "He could just be messing with you. Or he could've done it—dropped your dad into that old mineshaft to let him die of thirst or exposure or something. It's pretty grim, but I wanted you to know. So maybe there's a chance Dave could still be alive."

"Oh my god," was all she could say.

I took her by the shoulders. She felt stiff as a board.

"If he is," Jack said, "the sooner we get out of here the better. Becky used to run cattle up in that Monte Cristo country maybe ten years ago. Her and Dan are going to pick me up and we're gonna four-wheel up to the mine right now. We'll let you know what we find. And I've given Fuchs the heads-up."

Sarah thanked him and Jack signed off. She was whip-sawed but more hopeful than she'd been in days.

"You should probably make that circle now, Sarah. Get out of here quick. There'll be more of these boys coming, but you can meet Mitch below the cabin."

"I completely forgot to ask Jack when Mitch expected to get here," she said.

"He should be coming up behind Kip directly. Then you can be closer and hear if they find something at the mine."

A blast of heat from a fuel tank exploding made her jerk her head back. She trotted to the picket line, bridled her mare, untied the sorrel, and got on. I swung up on her dad's roan.

"You know these meadows. If you stick to the trees and circle down past the cowcamp you can spot Mitch on the way up."

"What'll you be doing?" she said.

"I'll be coming straight down the road right where they'll be expecting us."

She spun the mare around and rode close. "You be careful. I don't want to find Dad just to lose you."

She kissed me, then goosed the mare and got out of there, leading the sorrel across the meadow and into the trees. I loped off in the other direction toward the road. I could hear little pops as whatever ammo Delroy had in the cockpit exploded right along with him. We both knew that it could have been us, and that the day was just getting started.

When I got to the fork in the road, I headed away from the cowcamp to look for Kip's sign around Sarah's rig. Her truck and trailer were right where we'd left them, but now there were tracks all around, both horse and human, so I could see where Kip had been scouting after us just like I hoped he would. I didn't linger. I headed back down-canyon. I could travel fast on the hard road, rattling on the snowy tracks Kip's guys had made. I rounded a hill and came within sight of the cowcamp and saw a rider heading my direction about a third of a mile away. He was bigger than Kip and on a horse I didn't recognize, so I thought it might be Delroy's ironpumping partner coming to check on the smoke. Whoever it was rode better than those two gunsels and was wearing an orange hoodie. He might as well have worn a sign that said "Shoot Me Now." As far away as he was, he rode hunched over like he was cold. I turned in the saddle. I could still see the black smoke from the plane.

I pulled off my right glove and put it in my coat pocket as I rode into a shallow sandy wash filled with a foot of snow. I reached for the rifle in the scabbard. I'd been keep-ing my eye on the rider, but I glanced down at the .270 for no more than a second. The roan flinched and was halfway down before I heard the rifle shot. It was still ringing when he fell hard on his right side, landing on my leg and trap-ping me in the wash.

The horse didn't fight or thrash so I figured he was dead when he hit. I squirmed and scrambled to get out from under him, but he had me pinned from hip to boot heel. I had to push to even raise my head, and I'd lost my hat. I could see the rider coming, his horse in a jiggy sort of walk. I was too far away to see if he had a rifle out, but he must have. There had only been the one shot. If this was

Delroy's partner, he was a better marksman than I gave him credit for. But then maybe he'd been aiming for me and not the roan at all. Even that would've been good shooting for a city boy off the back of a horse.

My scabbard was way down under my leg, under the full weight of that poor roan. I'd need a hay squeeze to hoist him enough to get the Remington out. I raised up enough to see the rider. He had already closed the gap some. I tried to pull the .45, but my hip was pressing right on it. I started to dig with my right hand. The ground was sandy, but I could only scoop out little grabs at a time. I looked up, and the guy had stopped to watch. It wasn't Delroy's partner. It looked like one of the Miller brothers. When he saw what I was doing, he over-and-undered his horse and came on fast.

The ground tore up my fingers, but the snow numbed them just as quick. I must have looked frantic scraping handfuls of sand, because when he was only a hundred yards away the guy stopped again. It was one of the Millers all right. I could hear him laugh. He came forward slow now and I could see he carried an AR-15 just like Burt's. I clawed faster. I could've used Burt right about now. I squirmed and tried to reach the .45. When I squirmed too hard the sand filled back in like loose dirt in a posthole.

He was less than a hundred yards now. I kept my eyes on the patch of orange, hauling myself up as much as I could with my left hand pulling on the roan's mane as I dug with my right. I could feel the pistol grip now and move it a bit, but it still wouldn't pull. I set to dig some more. He was about twenty yards off when he stopped and studied my situation. I could see it tickled him. He leveled the AR at me, and that's when I saw Sarah top a ridge a couple of hundred yards behind us. I pulled hard on the roan's mane to ease his weight off me one last time and thumbed back the hammer of the Colt as I slid it free.

"Well, asshole," the Miller brother said, "I guess you weren't as—"

I shot him with the revolver resting on the dead roan's shoulder, not aiming, just pointing at the blotch of orange. That .45 hit hard. The guy started to fall, and his horse caught him out of the corner of his eye and shied. It looked like he would fall clear but one foot hung up in a stirrup. He flopped around on his back and that spooked the horse more. The animal flew out of there with the guy grunting and bouncing under the hooves, the horse running to escape him as he made a furrow in the snowy road. If my shot didn't kill him, then the dragging through the rocks probably did. The grunting turned to screaming, then the screaming stopped and all I could hear were hooves clattering and then that faded to nothing as well.

Chapter Twenty

My leg was still pinned but I lay back and rested, watching Sarah come down off the ridge and hit the level ground on that big mare in a long-strided gallop with the sorrel just behind. She swung off when she got to me and took a knee.

"Oh, god, Rusty," she said. With her dad missing, losing his old ropehorse just made everything that much worse.

She was crying when she took her rope off her horse and snugged the loop over my saddle horn. Then she stepped aboard, dallied, and dragged the horse off me a few feet so I could get up. It took me a minute. My whole side was numb, and my right leg buckled before she steadied me. She wrapped her arms around me so I wouldn't fall.

"I thought you were going to ride that circle and get the hell out of here."

"Didn't want to leave you," she said. Her arms were clamped around me tight, her eyes wet. "Idiot." She kissed me quick.

"Well, I'm glad you didn't."

She stepped back and I started to wobble.

"Do you think Kip's waiting down by the cabin?" she said.

"If he was, he would've come running to see that boob finish me off. But maybe he saw the law coming up-canyon and took off. Who knows?"

She walked over to the roan and knelt by his head. "He was such a good horse." She had trouble getting the words out. "But he had a good life. A *good* life." She ran her hand over his neck and got a funny look. "Where was he hit? I don't see an entry."

"I don't know. He dropped like a rock before I even heard the shot. It was fired from a distance, I know that."

"Just one shot?"

"Just one."

She was slipping back into her suspicious cop thinking. She bent close, feeling with both hands. "Here," she said. "The entry wound is tiny. Just behind the eye." She stood up then. "You think it was Kip who shot him?"

"This drunk would've fired more than once. Made hamburger out of us. So yeah, unless Kip got reinforcements." I bent down and found the entry. I'd seen similar.

"This was either a hell of an accident or he's a great shot," she said.

"Or something."

"Let's just load these two in the trailer and get the hell out of here," she said, "before you kill them all and don't leave any for me. Then we can check in with Jack about . . ." She almost didn't finish. "About the mineshaft."

We pulled my saddle and rifle from the dead horse, then I waited with the sorrel. I saddled him while Sarah rode back to fetch the gooseneck. I looked around for my hat but was too wracked to travel far. I sat on a rock watching the road and stood back up when my butt got too numb. It would take a bit to unstiffen from the fall. We had the horses loaded and were just climbing into the cab when my phone buzzed.

"Hey, Sarge." It was Kip. I was surprised as hell I had service, and kind of creeped out to hear him so loud and clear. I put it on speaker. "I thought you'd wiped out back there," he said. "You be the *man* after all."

"Where are you, asshole?"

"Oh, I'm far away," he said. "Far, far away. I just called to say thanks."

Sarah started breathing hard.

"I'm listening."

"Yeah, you did me a huge favor wasting those two clowns." I could hear him laughing over the phone. "See, I was into Delroy for some major coin when goddamn Hoyt found our little pot plantation. Lawdy-lawdy, de ole plantation."

"We knew it was you who killed him," Sarah said. "But what did you mean about Dad?" She tried to sound tough but her voice shook. "Tell me what you *mean*."

"If he's dead, I sure didn't kill him, doll," he said. "Him and me was pards, remember? Yup. Pards to the end."

I scribbled *Keep him talking* on a sandwich bag and gave it to Sarah, but I guess I didn't have to.

"Hey, Sarge, you know I'd be pretty pissed if I'd actually had to pay a dime for that Cessna burning back there," he said. "We stole it from Van Nuys Airport two months ago, but I guess you'd say we got our money's worth. Did you shoot it down? Pretty good wing-shootin', if you did. Pa-chow! We need to go duck hunting together when this is over." He said it like he actually believed we'd do it.

There was a muffled sound on the phone for a second. "Hold on, I got something to show you."

A picture popped up on my phone. It was Sarah kissing me just thirty minutes earlier.

"You like that?" Kip said. "Damn, folks would think she was your wife, not mine."

Sarah looked like she'd be the next one to rip a wheel off a steering column. "I won't be your *anything*," she said. "Except your damn widow. Tell me about the damned mineshaft."

"How about that. Remember, doll, they say the old ways are the best." He laughed, and the phone went silent.

I picked up the dead guy's AR-15 and stowed it in the bed of her truck. Sarah turned the rig around and drove back up the road, stopping where we'd camped the night before. She backed fast and turned again, jamming the brakes hard. She parked heading out in case we had to leave quick. We got out and picked up the rest of our gear and the bedroll, moving fast. We stopped to catch our breath and stare at the plane crumpled against the hillside. It had burned the earth where it crashed, and the snow had melted in a big oval around it. The ground was still warm in places, and the metal of the fuselage and wings had curled. What was left of Delroy's body looked small and twisted and reminded me of old black-and-white photographs of napalmed Jap soldiers from Guadalcanal or the caves on Iwo Jima in my dad's *Life* magazine box-set history of World War II. Sarah gave a wince, but she didn't look away. It was a man she had known and not liked. He was dead and she was glad he was dead, but I knew Delroy's black corpse was hard for her to take.

We got back into the truck and she drove to the cowcamp as fast as she dared with trailered horses. I rode shotgun with my .270 resting out the open window, gulping cold air like a border collie. We both watched for sign of Kip or any new folks he may have brought up to replace Delroy and the big Indian, and watched for any trace of Mitch or the FBI. I was halfway expecting them by now. The day was windy and cold and the snow hadn't melted much, but it had blown off the boughs of the piñon along the road. So much for spring.

"What do you think he meant," she said, "'the old ways are the best?' Did he mean dying in a mineshaft?"

"I guess he'll let us know." I remembered Jedediah saying the same thing.

At the cowcamp we did a quick reconnoiter before we went inside the cabin. Most of the cattle had drifted out to the meadows, and only a few stayed back. The flatbed Ford I'd set off by itself had been driven back to the pens. There was snow on the seat from the shot-out back window.

"Where's everybody gone?" Sarah said. "I figured it would be like the OK Corral when we got here."

"You have service?"

She dug out her phone. "Looks like," she said.

"Call Roger at Douglas County Sheriff's and get an ETA."

She got on her phone and left Roger Parrott a message when he didn't pick up. She mentioned they'd need a coroner up here, too. She tried to get Mitch but got no service calling south.

The cabin was an empty mess. Just overnight, Kip's guys had eaten our food, drunk our beer, and thrown trash everywhere. We took what we needed and got back into Sarah's truck and headed on down the road toward the drift fence. After a few minutes I checked my phone. Sarah watched me, gripping the wheel like death. We were in the treeless mess above the cattle guard.

"I don't know how much of this I can take," Sarah said.

"Pull over. I got a message from Becky."

She stopped the truck.

"She says they found a body but it's not Dave."

"Bodies everywhere—what the hell?"

We were close enough to the mouth of the canyon so cell service was semi-good. I got Becky on speaker. She and Dan were still at the mine with the Forest Service District Ranger.

"The Forest Service guys found a real old corpse—half skeleton, half mummy," Becky said. "It was in a side shaft you wouldn't find if you didn't know where to look. She must've got trapped in the open shaft and couldn't get out."

"She?" Sarah said. "The medical examiner said it was a female?"

"They haven't got here yet. But you can see bits of blond hair on the scalp. And guys?"

"Yeah?"

"The corpse had been wearing a bathing suit. A bikini. Dan called it the creepiest thing he's ever seen—*Tales from the Crypt* creepy."

They talked a bit more, then she thanked Becky and hung up.

"Mitch needs to call Santa Barbara County about the surfer girl who vanished," Sarah said. "The one who burned Kip in a drug deal." She edged closer and took my hand. "He's done this before. If Dad is in some other cave or shaft at some other mine, where do we even start to look?"

"Jesus, who knows? I wonder why we haven't seen Mitch yet."

She drove down toward the drift fence. I asked her to stop at the edge of the piñon, well back from the cattle guard, so I could look for tracks.

"Are you okay to do that?" she said. "You look horrible."

"I'm fine."

I took the Remington and started hobbling up to the fence. Sarah got out of the cab and drifted toward the trees to cover me with the 12 gauge. I walked along, memorizing the tire tracks and footprints in the road still half-covered with snow and in the red clay that showed through the bare spots, some of it frozen hard, some puddled with slush. The mounds of dead piñon from the wildlife mitigation spread off on either side of the road, boughs poking through snowmelt. I could see that the newest tire tracks came up through the piñon forest from the east, then crossed over those tracks heading back over the cattle guard. I figured those were Kip's. I looked back. Sarah was watching me with an are-you-okay sort of look.

I was thirsty and my head ached. The IED wound in my right femur from a few months before ached like it sometimes did when the weather got cold. I stopped to catch my breath and felt along the leg where the horse landed on it, wondering if maybe I'd cracked something. My right hip hadn't hurt this bad since I bruised it playing football on Astroturf against Virginia City in the eleventh grade. I turned back to Sarah again, but by now she was out of sight in the trees. I walked along the fence line. I could see footprints on top of the tire tracks and bent down to look. I walked slow, following them, my eyes on the ground trying to separate what looked like a second set of tracks and feeling that something was wrong. Holding my head that low made it spin like a bad hangover. When I raised up, the ground all around me swirled and I thought I was going to puke, and one of the swirling piñon piles seemed like it was rising up too. I thought I heard somebody yell my name, then the snap and *thpppt* of a rifleshot. I felt a bullet burn in the same spot on my back thigh that had been ripped by scrap-metal from the IED that winter, then the whole sky spun like I was hallucinating. As I fell, the piñon pile rose up in a manshape like some crazy petroglyph. I heard a shotgun blast and the hallucination vanished in a puff of snow and twigs, and then I was down on thin snow over hard ground hanging on to Dad's rifle but not seeing anything to shoot.

I looked up and saw Sarah walking toward me pumping the 12 gauge, her eyes on the pile of brush about a hundred feet away. She kept the shotgun pointed in that direction as she knelt down and put her hand on my leg.

"The hell?"

"Somebody shot you," she said. "Is it bad?"

"I don't think so. If it'd hit bone or artery I'd know it. Help me up." I let the Remington slip out of my hands like it was too heavy to hold.

She didn't argue, but she had to set the shotgun down and grab me under the armpits to get me on my feet.

"Was it Kip?"

She shook her head and pointed out to the mounds of dead piñon. I leaned on her and we limped the hundred feet over to the pile of brush. When I was still fifty feet away I could see that the brush hid a sniper nest, and what I'd seen moving was a shooter in a ghillie suit rising up out of the hole to take a kill shot. We walked closer. Sarah looked down at the red nail polish on the hand cupped around the pistol grip of an Army M110 sniper rifle.

"Did you know her?" she said.

"Not as well as I thought I did."

Chapter Twenty-One

Sarah rolled the body over with her boot to make sure Captain Cruz was dead. She still held the shotgun with both hands, ready to rip into Ofelia a second time. She looked over at me like I'd be next.

"This was the company commander?" she said. "The one who sent the sexy picture to your phone?"

Nodding was about all I dared.

"What the *hell* is she doing here, Tommy? What have you done?"

"I have no damn idea." I poked around the body. "I never made no secret where I was going. She must have found a way to track me." I touched the rifle with my boot toe. "And to get this thing off the base."

Under the camouflage suit Ofelia Cruz wasn't in uniform, just hunting shirt and pants, and good boots. Well turned out, right to the end. She always kept her phone on her belt unless she was wearing a dress. I peeled back the ghillie suit and found it.

Sarah pushed past me, saw where I was looking, and jerked the phone out of its belt holder.

"I guess we're way past doing the right thing here," she said. She started sliding her finger across the screen, turning away from me like she didn't want me to see. After a minute it was like she remembered that I was shot and bleeding and used her own phone to get the Douglas County dispatcher. She gave a report of the shootings and our location for the EMTs, and asked that they confirm the location with Deputy Parrott. Then she walked me to her truck, unbuckled the .45 gun rig, set it on the floorboards, and sat me down in the passenger side of the cab. It hurt to sit but it was better than trying to stay on my feet. I had to ask her to go back and fetch Dad's Remington from where I'd dropped it in the snow. Sarah came back quick, almost throwing the rifle at me. I slipped it behind the seat. She came around to my door looking cranky and in no mood for comfort. She started to untie her wild rag, but thought twice about it and untied mine instead. She yanked it off my neck when it was only half undone, then wrapped it hard around my thigh to apply pressure on the wound. When she was done with that she set my leg inside the cab with my foot resting on the floorboard. She never said a word except things like, "Hurt?" or "That okay?" as she worked. She never looked me in the eye and was rough as hell. When she had me secured, she turned the rig around and drove back up through the piñon to the cowcamp to wait for help.

She cleared the trash off one of the mattresses in the cabin and got me stretched out. When I was situated, she stood by the window and went back to looking at texts on Ofelia's phone. Then she dropped in a chair, looking hard at me.

"I went back to the beginning," she said. "The morning you flew home. Even before your plane landed, this woman cyber-stalked me and found Kip at his veteran's website. He didn't answer right away, but when he did and he realized who she was, they both just went crazy." She finally looked at me, still mad. "There's a huge bunch of texts here. Hundreds. This is just nuts."

She held the phone and read half out loud, getting more and more raggedy and beside herself while I lay there. She was still reading and muttering about thirty minutes later when we heard the county ambulance coming up the road. By then I'd already taken a few pulls from the whiskey bottle and had to listen to Sarah give me little bits of text-swapping between Ofelia Cruz and Kip Isringhausen. I won't deny it was some crazy stuff.

She looked out the cabin window as the ambulance rolled toward us, then read some more, looking disgusted. "Your girlfriend says she'll cut your heart out if you don't come back to her." She looked at me hard. "They were taunting each other, playing this poor-me game so whatever they do to us, they think *we* had it coming." She threw the phone on the bed. "What kind of people are these? My god, he even tried to poison Dad's dog."

"I never should've come back."

"You never should've *left*."

"I know. Look, I reenlisted so I'd be—I don't know—worthy of you. Get a degree. Some kind of career. All the stuff that you have. I wanted you—" I slowed down. I didn't want to screw this up. "I wanted you to be proud."

"I was *always* proud of you," she said. "I never cared about the rest. How can you not have known how I felt? Then you left me, and you never did *any* of those things, did you? No college, no nothing. Except trade me for that woman and almost get yourself killed." She was mad and crying, both at once. "You left me alone. And I am no *good* alone."

She shouted as the ambulance passed by the open window. "Over here, idiot." She put her hand on the wild rag bandage to feel for bleeding, looking down at the blood seeping through my jeans. "You're just lucky she's not a better shot."

The captain had examined me up close where I'd been wounded by the IED, and she'd drilled me right there in the same fleshy part of the leg about four inches below my privates.

"She hit what she aimed at."

The ambulance started backing up.

"You saved my life, Sarah."

"Don't flatter yourself," she said. "I shot that woman because she killed a perfectly harmless horse. Anyway, I assume it was her." She finished poking at the oozy wild rag. "I told you I'd kill them all." She looked up at the ambulance backing to the cabin door.

"They only sent one guy," she said. "That's retarded." She looked at me like she didn't know who to kill next.

I leaned up as best I could and looked out the door.

An EMT in a white uniform shirt and Wranglers was open-ing the rear of the ambulance and pulling out a gurney. I remember thinking most of those departments wear black pants. The guy had his back to us, but he was real recogniz-able.

"Hey, surfer boy."

Sarah pulled her pistol just like I hoped she would as she jerked around to see who I was talking to.

"Your lady sharpshooter's dead."

Sarah saw Kip turn to face us with a 9mm in his hand before she got her pistol raised. He looked more pumped up than ever. The front of the EMT shirt was torn and cov-ered with blood, and way too tight around Kip's chest and shoulders. He looked chipper as hell, though, his eyes just bulging, so I guessed the blood belonged to somebody else. And there was already a body on the gurney. He reached out his free hand for Sarah's 9mm, took it, and tossed it careless-like on the table.

"She was, I believe, *your* lady sharpshooter, Sarge," Kip said. He was grinning. "And she ain't the only one died today."

The body on the gurney looked like one of the EMTs who'd met us at the pot farm. She was face down and had a knife sticking out of her lower back just below her ponytail. It looked like my skinning knife.

"My god, you killed them?" Sarah said. She could barely talk.

"Yeah," he said. "They told me they were friends of yours—saw you two guys on an emergency call up at False

Spring a couple days ago." He took a couple of steps closer and looked at me on the bunk with the wild rag around my thigh.

"This guy," he said to Sarah. "This freakin' guy. He must be something special, huh, doll. Before Ofelia knew he was boinking you, I offered her some major coin to cap him, but she says no." He started talking in a bad Mexican accent. "'He is my man,' she says, 'I only kill heem for love, no for money.' Damn, son, that wildcat was crazy for your ass. *Ay Chihuahua*, dude, I just had to hit that. You understand." He looked at Sarah all smirky. "Sorry about cheating on you, doll."

He took another step towards her and Sarah hissed at him.

"Hey—you can't blame me for wanting to take Tom's new woman for a spin." He giggled like some girl. "Right after I tried out his new Mustang. That GT's a righteously fine ride, son. Exactly like that hottie that drove it across the country just to mess you up." He got a faraway smile. "Too bad I have to kill you, Tom. You and me coulda grabbed a couple of bottles of Patrón, hopped in that Mustang, and tag-teamed that bitch all the way to Cabo and back."

"Shut up, you pig, shut *up*," Sarah said. "Just tell me where my father is." She was on her feet.

"I'll take you to him," he said. "He'll be real glad to see you."

"Then he's alive?" she said.

Kip grabbed her arm and jerked her to the door. She bumped into him, rubbing against the blood on his shirt.

When she saw the red smear on her own shirt she made a disgusted sound.

"Is he alive?"

He just laughed at her. She planted her boots on the floorboards, putting all her weight against him. He buried the muzzle of the automatic in her cheek.

"You're not very smart," she said. She was panting now. "You just think you are. If Dad's alive, nobody could really prove you killed anybody—till now. Jedediah was blamed for the Marine Housing and Hoyt and Randy Ragazino, too. It was Delroy who died trying to kill us. Then the Miller guy tried to kill Tommy. And the woman who just shot him was just a—a rejected coworker. That's what they'll say on the news."

"Actually, I was the one killed Randy," he said. "So give me my props on that one. He was helping us with your Dad, and he wanted more money or said he was gonna rat me out. Randy the Rat. My boys gave me a heads-up. They held him for me out at the Rez till we could go hands-on. One punch, Jedediah style."

"The Miller boys?"

"Very astute, Tom. Your turn to go hands-on with me is coming right up."

"Don't you threaten him," Sarah said. She was eyeing her pistol on the table.

"Isn't she hot," Kip said. "She just loved it when I'd go hands-on, right, doll?"

Sarah leaned her cheek into the pistol so hard it pushed his arm back. "Be as gross as you want. You've hung yourself now." She looked ready to die right there.

Kip dragged the pistol muzzle across her mouth. "Yeah, doll. Maybe you're right. But it'll sure be confusing for a while, since one of the EMTs got shot with Tom's Beretta here . . ." He pulled the automatic away from her face and held it up for me to see. It left a bloodless white circle on her cheek. "Straight from your desk drawer in Georgia, dude. And it's gonna get found in your Mustang in the next hour or two." He jerked Sarah by the arm. "And the one out here got stabbed with Tom's knife." He stuck his face close to Sarah's. "Now did I say old Dave's still alive? Maybe I got that wrong."

Sarah pretty much caved at that, so he let her go and shoved the pistol in his belt. Sarah slumped on the bed, and I saw her scoop up Ofelia's phone and hide it with her hand.

"And there's still Santa Barbara heat on me on account of that little surfer girl up at the Monte Cristo mine." He laughed. "That was my first trip up to your neck of the woods. Damn, she was almost as much of a wildcat in the sack as you, and she was only sixteen."

Sarah got up and spit in his face. He wiped it with the back of his hand, sort of smiling at her.

"Her name was Wendy Hammond, remember shitbird?"

Kip looked a little blank when I said that. And he wasn't a guy who usually let himself go speechless.

"You like to advertise what you do. Like that fake grave at False Spring with Wendy Hammond's name on it."

"You know something," he said, "you guys give me a major pain in the balls. I always hated it when Sarah or Dave would get all serious like you horse guys have your own code or something that makes you special. Like you never told a lie or stole a dollar or got a girl drunk or did your best friend's woman. Like it's your club and nobody else can join."

"Dad let you join," Sarah said. "He took you in."

"And when you left me, he dropped me like a hot rock." He got crazed remembering that. "Said the water sale was 'none of my business' if I wasn't with you. None of my *business*?"

Kip saw Ofelia's phone in Sarah's hand. He jerked it away. Then he tore Sarah's shirt when he grabbed her phone from her front pocket. He threw both phones on the cold stovelid, then jammed my pistol back in her cheek as she tried to hold her shirt together. He turned to me and snapped his fingers.

"Do *not* dick with me, Tom," he said. He'd got real wild-eyed again.

I held out my phone and he grabbed that, too.

He gathered the other two phones from the stove and shoved them all in his pants pockets.

"Come on, doll." He dragged Sarah out the door and turned to me a last time. "History always repeats, fool," he said, "but remember, you never ride the same wave twice." Then he laughed. "You'll figure it out, smart guy. I'm counting on it."

Kip shoved her with my Beretta to her head. She stumbled, one hand holding the front of her shirt. They stopped at the ambulance, and he rooted around in the back and pulled out Captain Cruz's sniper rifle.

"This already drew first blood on you, dude." He

dropped it on the steel flatbed of the old Ford. "Where's your Remington?"

"Out in the snow under a dead horse."

"Even if you're lying," he said, "I got you outgunned." He held Ofelia's rifle with his free hand, grinning like a crazy person.

He reached in Sarah's truckbed and pulled out the Miller brother's AR-15 and Sarah's 12 gauge. He jabbed the shotgun muzzle in Sarah's ribs and pushed her to the passenger side of the Ford. After he shoved her in, he stashed all the long guns in back and scooted around to the driver's side, fired it up, and rattled out of there in a haze of white diesel smoke. And there wasn't a damn thing I could do about it.

Chapter Twenty-Two

I limped to the door. My head was hot like hard whiskey shots. I found a broom for a crutch and the last beer in the fridge then walked outside to the gurney. I looked down at the woman and thought about the way she'd joked with Roger Parrott at False Spring. She was already starting to cool. I wondered where Roger and Mitch and the rest of them had got to.

I went in the side door to the ambulance and rooted around for something to dress my leg. When I had what I needed I sat down on the passenger seat up front, popped open the beer, dropped my jeans, and went to it. I gave the leg a shot of lidocaine and sipped the beer for a minute while I waited for the numbing to kick in. Then I irrigated the whole area inside the bullet furrow with Betadine. I was staining the seat with the runoff, but with that woman out there on the gurney, it would be the least of Douglas County's worries. I dried the wound, bandaged it snug, pulled my pants up and went inside to start the fire and put on some water for coffee. It had been a long time since breakfast.

The two horses we had left were still saddled in the gooseneck. I dragged myself over to where Sarah had parked it, trying to convince myself that the sick bastard wouldn't hurt her any more until he did whatever he was planning on doing to me. The aluminum sides of the stock trailer were solid for the first five feet and open for about fifteen inches above that, so I could see the horses' backs and ears and see that they were standing quiet. I was wondering if Kip had snagged the .45 from the floorboards of the truck when I swung open the latch of the right-hand trailer door.

"Good afternoons, my friend."

There was a guy standing behind the horses in the shadows, resting a shotgun on the bay's butt. It looked like a Mossberg, and it was pointing at me. The guy wore a dirty ballcap and had a bandage across his face. When he stepped around the horses I could see one foot was bandaged, too. He was the Mexican we'd found up at False Spring. He still looked like crap, but I was keeping my eyes on the Mossberg. Kip must have got a bulk rate on those shotguns at Big 5.

"What the hell do you want?"

"For you to stay right there, I think," he said.

"Why?"

"Mister Kip wants you to wait for the police," he said. "They take you to the *juzgado* pretty soon, so you wait here with me." His voice gurgled.

"I saved your life, you prick."

"I thank you for that," he said. "But Mister Kip can take it from me pretty damn quick. So *perdón*, but I hold you for he."

"Shit." I swung the trailer door shut and yanked the foot-long latch handle around, dropped the keeper in place, and stepped back.

"Señor?" I could see his eyes wild through the slats. Then I saw his arm come out over the solid part of the door as he reached down, feeling around half frantic. His hand was an easy six inches short of the latch, so he was as good as in jail.

"*Señor!*"

I heard the clank of the shotgun barrel against the aluminum sides.

"Don't shoot with that mare in there, goddamnit."

I hit the dirt just as he cut loose with the Mossberg. Some of the pellets ventilated the trailer door so the aluminum got a cheese-grater look to it, and some more of them ricocheted around inside. I heard the guy yelp twice as Sarah's mare almost shrieked at a second shotgun going off close to her in less than a week, and I heard that nasty clank, rattle, and stomp that scared horses make when they scramble in a closed space. Then I heard a sort of grunt, and knew he'd either been kicked or slammed against the trailer wall or trampled. Or all three.

I picked myself up from the ground and brushed the snow off, getting steady as I caught my breath. I pulled myself up on the fender and peeked inside. The guy was lying fetal on the floormats, moaning soft. The horses had settled but were still giving him the stink eye. I swung both rear doors open wide, talking quiet to them as I led the mare out first and tied them to the side of the gooseneck. That bay looked ready to turn herself inside out. She had some blood on her croup and above one hock. I checked the wounds. Neither seemed bad, but I could feel a pellet of buckshot under the skin of her croup that would have to be taken out later. I stepped back into the trailer and picked up the shotgun. It was just like the one from the pot farm. I ejected the five shells it carried just to count them, then reloaded. I patted the guy down looking for more shells, and my leg hurt like hell when I bent over. All I found was a half pack of American Spirit cigarettes, a bottle of prescription Motrin from a Tijuana *farmacia*, and a photograph of a dark little woman standing in front of a crappy-looking house with three sorrowful-looking little kids. I picked up the shotgun and found a saddle blanket in the tackroom of Sarah's trailer. I shook the dust out of it and covered the ungrateful bastard. He was pretty much out of his head, so I left a couple of our plastic water bottles next to him before I shut the trailer doors on him again, locking him in. He might live, but he'd probably never make it back to Mexico.

The pickup's hood was up. When I looked in, I saw the battery cables were cut and the terminal clamps were gone. I looked inside the cab. The gun rig was where I'd left it on the passenger-side floor and the Remington was behind the seat. That was something. Guys like Kip get cocky on the thrill and forget the small stuff. I buckled the gun rig on and checked the cylinder. Then I led the horses to the round corral and turned them loose with the saddles on, as I wasn't sure if I had the strength to hoist the rigs up on their backs again. I threw them hay and went inside where the coffee was boiling. My head was killing me and I was about to pass out, but the coffee helped.

I lay on my back on the bunk and ate an apple while the caffeine kicked in, then shuffled back outside. I knew I didn't have much time. I covered the lady on the gurney with a blanket from the ambulance. When I pulled my skinning knife out of her back, it bothered me way more than I thought it would. I cleaned it with rubbing alcohol from the ambulance before I sheathed it. I was destroying evidence in a homicide case but didn't much care, as there was plenty more evidence to go around. I grabbed the Betadine to squirt in the mare's wounds. She was touchy about that but let me do it. With food, water, and whiskey in my saddle pockets, I tied the Mossberg on Sarah's mare, put the hackamore on the sorrel and climbed up on him. Then I grabbed the mare's leadrope and headed away from that place.

The day was cold. With the wind across my scalp, I wished I had my hat. Some snow from the night before had melted or blown away so there were bare patches, but the sky was stormy-looking and most of the snow was still on the ground. I broke the horses into a trot down the road toward the cattle guard. As smooth as that colt was, I still winced at every step. I knew I had to get past the drift fence and lose myself in the piñon before anybody else came up that road. I stepped off at the cattle guard to lead the horses through the wire gate at the side, but I couldn't keep my eyes off Captain Cruz lying dead in the ghillie suit. Instead of mounting up quick, I tied the horses to the braceposts, pulled out my rifle and went over to her. I fell trying to kneel down. There, on my hands and knees, I did my best to straighten out her body, untwist her clothes, and pull the burlap, leaf and twig camouflage mask away from her head. I took off my jacket and spread it over her, covering her face. It was only a soldier's shroud, but she'd served her country and suffered for it, so she deserved at least that much. Besides, she'd meant something to me once. I stuck my rifle stock-down in the piñon duff to brace myself so I could get back on my feet. I gave her one last nod and closed the wire gate on that whole sorry part of my life. Then I caught up the horses and got moving. Down-canyon I could already hear a vehicle coming.

I drifted uphill, angling through piñon and juniper on the high side of the road until I reached where fire had thinned the trees to almost nothing. I stopped and had a good look downslope all the way to where the canyon spilled into the alkali flat. To the left, Buckskin Mountain, usually bare and brown, was dusted with snow, looking about as nice as it ever would.

I could see a Douglas County sheriff's Chevy Tahoe coming toward up from the valley. I sat my horse on the high slope, hiding in plain sight in the shade of a single juniper. I watched the tracks the SUV made in the snow, then watched it stop. A Douglas deputy got out. It was almost too far to see, but it looked like Roger Parrott— better late than never. He walked around the front of the Tahoe, then stopped. He twisted his body a bit like he was reaching back for something, maybe drawing his weapon, but when he walked forward one slow step at a time almost like he was afraid, his hands swung free. If he knew what was waiting just up the road, he'd be afraid plenty. I could see a shape pale in the dirt and see the deputy stop before he took those last steps. He was looking down at something in the road, and I figured it must be the pale skin of the second EMT. This would be the one that Kip said he killed with my 9mm before he stole the guy's bloody shirt, so the body would have fresh chest wounds. They would be from close range because that's how Kip would have liked it. I could see the deputy look all around as he radioed in. If it was Roger, he looked antsy and unsure. He was a town guy a long way from where he'd feel safe. He looked right at where I sat the sorrel, and he kept on looking across the burned-over hills. Somebody used to hunting stock in open country would have spotted me right away, but I knew I was okay with this clown. Now that he'd radioed in, he'd be stuck out there securing the crime scene until help arrived. I figured that if Kip was trying to pin the two dead EMTs on me, he'd have called Douglas County already with some fake name and bullshit story. No matter what, when Roger's help did arrive, I wanted to be long gone.

I eased the horses down the sandy slope heading into Hudson Valley. I figured I'd cross the dirt road about where we'd run into the sheep the morning we drove up. I wouldn't stay on the road, as real soon it would be full of sheriffs, EMTs, coroners, and maybe a reporter or two. I would drop below the road into pastureland, mingling with grazing cattle until I hit the ranch headquarters of someone I knew, or who knew me. Someone who could lend me a phone or a truck. I had a pretty good idea of where I had to get to and hoped I'd get there before it was too late. I was talking out loud to the horse, figuring my options, when I saw a truck and trailer coming down the dirt road in my direction. I was hunting a gate or a hole in the pasture fence when I saw the rig turn uphill into the sagebrush. I dropped to a walk but kept riding toward it until I saw the brush moving and stirring the dust and could finally tell it was sheep. They were only about a mile down from where they'd been a couple of days before. I saw that the truck was the camp tender's International.

I hit a high trot down the road toward it. When I was about a quarter mile away from the sheep, I could see blue and red lights from a cruiser or ambulance heading my way with dust from the road rising behind. I gigged that sorrel and we rattled south toward the lights, the bay running stride for stride at my knee. The lights were from another SUV and it was rolling right along, closing in on the sheep. When I got closer, I could see the herder in his camp and see a black mule picketed uphill near a tent. I left the road with the horses bounding over the sage, circling uphill as best I could without starting a damn sheep stampede. I waved at Eufemio as I passed close by, scattering ewes and lambs. I pointed at the SUV closing in, then at myself, and I saw Eufemio laugh. Then he ignored me and helped his grand-nephew and a dog settle the sheep as I tucked those horses in close to his stake-bed trailer on its uphill side and jumped off, using it for cover. Eufemio waved at the deputies in the SUV as it cruised by a hundred yards away. I hunkered down, watching the deputies through the wood slats. They were from Douglas County too, so there was a good chance somebody'd called in the first of those corpses. Whether it was Kip or Roger or even the Mexican in the gooseneck before he got stomped, it didn't matter.

Eufemio's trailer looked semi-homemade and it stunk, but it hid me well enough. The powers that be don't pay much mind to guys like Eufemio. They're pretty much just invisible.

The SUV was lost in its own dust. Eufemio came over happy as hell to see me and gave me a big *abrazo*, smelling like sheep dip, Dago red, and cigarettes.

"Mister Tomás—*otra vez tú!*?" he said. "What have you done now, my little drunkard?"

"Nothing so bad this time, you mangy sheep stealer. For now, *viejo*, I just need a ride."

I must have looked like death, because the kid gave me a water jug and I took a long drink. I told Eufemio that there'd been a little misunderstanding with the law that I didn't have time to straighten out. I asked him for a ride south, as close as he could get me to Rickey Junction. He had half a dozen wooly pairs to take to headquarters for doctoring and said I was welcome to ride along, and he'd try to drop me off as close as he could. He said he'd tie the mule in the front with my saddle horses so they'd attract less attention.

We loaded the mule first, then my horses. I sat down in the semi-dry sheepshit as Eufemio loaded the ewes and lambs behind me. He said adios to the boy and climbed into the International and off we went. The sides of the trailer only came up to my horses' briskets, so they were looking all around, just curious and windblown as we rattled down the slope to the dirt road.

We passed the abandoned hot springs and I could see newer houses on five-acre lots uphill in the sage, and see a Copper County, Nevada sheriff's cruiser parked where the pavement began. I'd crossed the Douglas-Copper county line about where the first EMT bought it, so now I had two jurisdictions looking for me. A deputy leaned against the cruiser talking to a retired guy in a ballcap. Eufemio pulled over and lit a cigarette as casual as could be. He made a gesture I couldn't make out and I heard him laugh. I was sitting low, holding the Mossberg across my lap and missing my jacket in the cold. I wasn't about to shoot any law enforcement, but I wasn't above a little threat if it came to that. Finally Eufemio put the truck in gear. We chugged past the deputy and I snuck a look through the slats. He glanced at the two saddle horses riding with the mule, but lucky for me two well-bred quarter horses and six grand in saddles didn't quite register with him as being out of place. He must have been another town guy who only saw the ratty trailer full of animals and the ratty old man behind the wheel.

Eight miles south, we came to a T in the road with cruisers from both counties parked on opposite sides of the junction. Both deputies stayed inside their vehicles out of the wind. The right turn led uphill out of the valley where Eufemio would have no cause to go. That road led to Rickey Junction about twenty highway miles away. The left turn led toward the valley farms where Eufemio's Basque boss had his sheep headquarters. Eufemio turned left as I hugged the floorboards. I didn't know what he had in mind, but he didn't have much choice. Peeking through the slats, I could see the deputies hadn't even looked up. Eufemio slowed as the road passed through some cottonwoods by a farm implement store, a bar, a brick slaughterhouse, and a hairdresser's and such. I knew that on the right would be a big old house next to an even older ranch-country general store. Eufemio surprised me when he turned up past those, staying on a gravel road that followed along the West Frémont into a rocky canyon. That clever old bastard was taking me toward Rickey Junction on a route that wouldn't be watched.

We passed the buildings and entered some cottonwoods along the creek. I stood up next to the mule and held on to the top slat, rocking along and watching the country. I looked back and could see that no one was following. Ahead, the canyon widened out and fell away as the road climbed past old stock pens in the rocks along some meadow. We topped out in open sagebrush where I could see the irrigation reservoir and Reno Highway off in the distance. Eufemio drove slow for another bouncy ten minutes until he found a place to turn the rig around. He stopped and opened the trailer gate and we jumped my horses out.

"This is as far as I can go," Eufemio said, "or the old boss will think I ran off with his granddaughter." Eufemio was close to eighty so he laughed like hell. We looked down into Shoshone Valley. Hills blocked my view of Dave's ranch but I knew it was only about five miles away down the dirt road. Eufemio dug a clear glass half-gallon jug of red wine from the truck cab and we shared a few gulps. It tasted terrible but felt good going down. After the second swig Eufemio put his hand on my shoulder.

"Is something hunting you, Tomás? Besides the sheriffs?"

"Yeah."

"Then may God have mercy on them."

He drove off with a nod like a gravedigger. I checked my cinches and weapons and started the long trot to Dave's. I was hoping Burt was there, because I needed an ally bad. If he wasn't, I was hoping I'd find Kip or some of his crew. I was trying not to be too terrified about what he was doing to Sarah. I knew what my worrying about her was doing to me. It was exactly the thing about me that troubled her the most. Eufemio was right. I wanted people to die.

Chapter Twenty-Three

Somewhere in the sagebrush an hour later I crossed the dry wash that had been False Spring Creek. The creek had buried a three-foot culvert and packed it full of rock and sand like concrete in the days when the water flowed. I could look back into the mouth of the canyon where Sarah and I had explored the spring six days back. That felt like forever. Almost as soon as Eufemio left me, I had to slow to a walk as the road was bad and even shod horses would get footsore fast. The day was getting on. With the slow pace and the wind picking up and me with no hat and no jacket, I was working on a vile mood.

I crossed southwest into California about twenty minutes further on. By then I was in sight of Dave's headquarters, and the sun was dropping behind the mountains.

I stopped way out from the buildings to study things. There was no sign of Burt's Ford, so I figured he was with Mom at the hospital. My Dodge was parked under the cottonwood where I left it. I knew there was a chance that Kip was holding Sarah here, but I doubted it. Still, he knew I'd have to stop here to make sure, so I figured he'd have some sort of welcome planned. I took a gate into the horse pasture and kept the barn between me and the house as I rode. Swarms of cliff swallows flapped from mud nests in barn eaves, cruising and diving for mosquitoes in the sunset afterglow. I tied up behind the barn, pulled the .45 and eased in a side door, making sure that I was alone before I unsaddled and turned the horses out. When the rigs were both stowed I stayed back in the shadows, looking out open doors and barn windows. There were no lights on in the house, but Burt must have left the yard light on earlier in the day because I could see its glow above me in the gathering dusk.

I was too sore and cold to dawdle, so I took the Mossberg from Sarah's saddle and gimped across the middle of the yard to the house. If somebody wanted to start it up, they wouldn't get a better chance. I made it to the porch without incident and dragged up the steps. I held the 12 gauge level when I pushed the front door open. The place was empty and tidy, but I checked every room before I pulled a frozen pizza from the freezer, threw it in the microwave and tracked down that bottle of Jim Beam. While the pizza was nuking, I dug around the porch and found an old chore coat of Dave's and put it on. I took a not-too-grimy hat from the rack, tried it on for size, then set it on the table. I let the pup from his run and gave him some kibble. He was glad for the company and followed me down the hall to Sarah's room. I had five shells for the Mossberg but wanted more to be safe. I rooted around her desk drawers but didn't find any. The 12 gauge pump she carried was sheriff's issue, so she probably got her ammo from the department. I opened a couple of dresser drawers, but looking at her old socks and panties and Navajo jewelry only depressed me. I opened a wooden box on her dresser and saw a clipping from the *Copper County Currier* headlined, "Piute Meadows Boy Reenlists," with a bad picture of me in uniform and lame words from some reporter I'd never met. I slammed it shut and hustled back to the hallway.

I closed the pup in Dave's room out of harm's way and sat at the table with the lights off eating the pizza. My chair faced the open front door, the Mossberg resting next to the whiskey glass at my right hand, a shell chambered and ready.

I was about full and it was about dark when the black GMC with the busted tailgate pulled into the yard. I chewed my pizza and finished my drink, just watching the other Miller boy and the big weightlifter get out, joking as if they were alone in the world. The big guy carried what looked like an AK-47 and wore a camo hoodie. The Miller boy wore a buckaroo hat as big as a beach umbrella and the same revolver I'd seen him packing in Aspen Canyon. Might have been a .357. It looked small against his fat waist. He carried what looked like a nice Browning side-by-side, too. I had the bad thought that if I shot him, I just might take that shotgun from him and keep it. I'd always hankered for one of those old Brownings, but he could die with that hat. I watched them pass a bottle of Cuervo back and forth as they headed around the property together to make their rounds. It didn't seem to occur to them that somebody might have come horseback, and it sure didn't occur to them to check the other buildings. Especially the one with the door wide open and the guy with the 12 gauge watching them from the dark.

I waited for them to walk back into the yard light before I stepped outside with the Jim Beam in one hand and the Mossberg in the other. They still didn't notice me until I tapped the shotgun barrel on the porch rail and hollered at them.

"All right, you honyockers, what'll it be?"

I took a last pull on the bottle and set it on the rail before they fired off a couple of rounds and I dodged for cover. They were scrambling backwards, not even hitting the house. Once they got themselves hid, I heard the big weightlifter laugh.

"You gonna hafta get in close with that shotgun, chump," he said.

I walked down the steps, taking my time.

"Close is good."

I shot out the yard light on the peak of the barn wall. Cliff swallows shrieked and scattered, and I could hear those two yelling as I hustled into the shadows and the dark settled around the buildings.

I heard a bottle break and one of them cuss the other. They started taking random shots like they didn't have a clue where to aim. I could hear them muttering and arguing.

"You never gonna see that yellow-haired girl again," the Miller boy said real loud.

Then the weightlifter hollered something way worse about Sarah, but I was long gone from the place they were shouting at. They both sounded stupid and scared, and so sloshed on tequila I could hear them trying to be quiet. My eyes had adjusted to the dusk, and I knew just where everything on that ranch should be, so I could guess where and how they would come at me. I watched their dark shapes moving as they split up, the weightlifter jogging along the open shed, making random shots with his AR. A couple came too close for comfort. I faded around the barn and followed their muzzle flash as easy as taillights.

At the end of the barn I slipped through the grain chute of the feed bin at the end of a row of work-team stalls. I stopped to listen and could hear a steel corral gate screech and the sound of footsteps scuffing the dirt. I opened the feed bin door and the spring made a squeak, but I made it to the cover of the first stall without seeing anyone. Across the center alley of the barn was another row of stalls with an open door at the far end. I waited in the darkness. I could look past the stalls to that open door and the evening sky beyond it and hear whispers too faint to understand. After a minute the weightlifter stepped up into the open doorway and stopped, holding his Kalashnikov in firing position as he looked right at where I was hidden in the dark. The big fool was framed by that doorway just pretty as a picture. I almost felt bad shooting him.

He flew backwards out the door and fell against draft horse stocks made of four-inch steel pipe. His head hit the pipe so hard I could hear it clang.

The Miller boy shouted the big guy's name. When

he didn't get an answer, he shouted louder like that would bring him back to life. I was in the middle of the barn walking down the center alley facing the house across the yard, chambering another shell. I could see the Miller boy running for his truck, if you could call that running. He yanked open the GMC's door, and the dome light in the cab lit him up. I took his legs out with the next shot as I stepped out of the barn, and told him to keep his hands where I could see them.

He was leaning on one elbow whimpering when I got to him. I pulled his .357 from its holster, ejected the rounds, and picked up the shotgun and set them in the bed of his truck. The barrel of the side-by-side felt rusted and the stock had a wobble to it. So much for stealing it. This guy probably ripped it off from somebody even more wasted than he was.

"So, you the one shouted those things about Sarah Cathcart?"

"Screw you, soldier," he said. Then he puked.

I touched his mangled leg with my boot and he yelled. In the dome light I could see a lot of blood and muscle, maybe a little bone.

"You got something you want to say about her?" I poked him with my boot again, harder this time.

"God*damn*. You gonna call nine-one-one, you prick?"

"Maybe I'll call four-one-one and ask for the number of somebody who gives a shit if you live or die. Jesus, you stink." I jostled him hard.

He yelled really loud then.

"Best tell me where she is."

"I dunno, goddamnit," he said. "Kip never tells me nothin'. That whack job ain't paying me enough for this shit."

"You're a little late coming to that conclusion, bud."

I stepped away from the stink of him and he fell back in the dirt, whimpering louder.

"You got anything to drink?"

"Yeap."

I could see headlights turning down the lane from the Reno Highway about a mile away. If they were Kip's, that didn't leave me much time. I faded back into the dark to wait and see who it was. I still had two shells left, but I drifted toward the barn to get the .270 off my saddle if I needed it.

"I said, you got anything to drink?"

I could tell it was a Ford quick enough. It stopped a ways away from the house as soon as its headlights hit the GMC. The Ford's passenger door opened, but the light didn't show anybody in the cab. Burt had rolled out on that side and I could see his big shape hustling behind a cottonwood with a weapon ready—probably his AR. I liked this guy more and more.

I yelled at Burt and told him things were clear. He came over, and we sat on the porch steps drinking Jim Beam out of the bottle as he told me how well Mom was doing and I told him what had happened the last couple of days. The Miller boy hollered at us once or twice more, then got quiet. He was probably getting a little shocky by now. Burt asked me what I wanted him to do. I handed him a piece of paper with some writing on it.

"We probably need to report this mess and get this piece of crap to a hospital. Here's the number of a Douglas County deputy named Roger Parrott. He'd be the guy to call."

"Being as we're in Frémont County, California," Burt said, "why am I calling the Nevada law?"

I handed the bottle back to him. "Sarah's boss is a chucklehead. First off, Mitch may try to arrest me for a couple of murders, and I don't have time for that tonight."

Then I heard a sound from out of the past and it made me jump. Dave's landline was ringing. I hobbled back into the kitchen and grabbed the phone off the wall.

"Talk to me."

"Tommy Smith?"

It was Aaron Fuchs.

"You're a hard guy to get hold of," he said.

I filled him in on our trip out to Dave's permit, right up to the shooting of the second Miller brother here in the yard. I told him Kip had taken Sarah. He told me the details of the shoot-out at the State Line Lodge, the break-in at the Shoshone Valley ranch house about a mile from where I was sitting, and the BOLO all the local agencies had out on the two weightlifters and the Miller brothers, which he figured he could cancel now.

"There's a BOLO out on you, too, you know," he said.

"Figured."

"Douglas County just found a pretty classy looking Mustang with Georgia plates in the State Line Lodge parking lot. Both the car and the Beretta in the glove box were registered to you."

"Affirmative."

"And the tip to the agency was made from your cell phone about an hour ago."

"I'm a self-destructive sonofabitch."

He laughed until I asked him about the wounded deputy Roger had told me about. Fuchs said the guy died in the Gardnerville hospital that morning.

"So where does that leave us with Kip?"

"He's muddied the water now for sure," he said. "If you were Sarah's boss, you wouldn't know who killed who."

"So you have a bead on him?"

"He left fingerprints all over the ranch house he broke into. Like he wanted us to know he was close to Cathcart's—to you and Sarah." He was quiet a second. "And there was another break-in, this one at a fishing cabin at Piute Meadows called in to the sheriffs there earlier today," he said.

"Where, exactly?"

"On Summers Creek," he said. "Two miles below the lake, where a logging road comes out of a canyon. You know it?"

"Oh, yeah."

"Since both the road to the lake and the logging road up the canyon are dead ends, we figure Kip headed back to Piute Meadows and picked up the Reno Highway. North or south, no telling which direction."

"Was anything taken from the fishing cabin?"

Burt walked in real quiet and stood close enough to listen.

"Not that the fishing camp manager could figure," he said. "Except for the door being smashed open and a busted picture on the floor, he said nothing looked out of place."

"Yeah? A picture of what?"

"It was one of those on-the-set Hollywood glossies of that cowboy actor Sam Elliott. It was signed, but half of it was torn and missing so you couldn't see who it was signed to, or who was in the picture with him."

"That's strange."

"No thoughts?" he said.

"Not right off. Probably nothin."

"Well, we've got a BOLO out on Kip and county law enforcement watching the roads in and out of these valleys," he said. "His best chance to get away was that plane, but you say that's non-operational."

"Oh yeah. He'll only be flying that in his dreams."

"If he had a plane, he could be anywhere from San Diego to Mount Shasta, or San Francisco to Salt Lake by now."

"I think he'll stick around. He's still got unfinished business to take care of."

"That would be you?" Fuchs said.

"And Sarah."

We talked a little more, and I gave him Burt's cell number if he wanted to reach me. Burt was watching me when I hung up the kitchen phone.

"Was that the picture you said Kip took from Sarah's mobile home?" he said.

"Sounds like it."

"What's the point?"

"Kip figured that's something only I would figure out. He's telling me where he is—where he's got Sarah."

"Where?"

"I'd guess right up that logging road at Harvey's old pack station."

"How come?" Burt said. "That canyon's a dead end."

"'Cause that's where I'd be."

"How come you didn't tell the Fed that Kip left that picture? How come you don't want help from the law?" he said.

"They go in there in full SWAT mode, whether it's Fuchs with the best intentions or Mitch with none, Sarah dies."

"What about the Douglas deputy? Still want me to call him?"

"Yeah. We can't leave this clown to die in the yard."

"What else you want from me?" Burt said.

"You can drive me to Piute Meadows."

I went to fetch my .270 while Burt called Roger. Then I went back into the house. I phoned Becky Tyree and told her I'd be by her ranch in an hour to borrow a shod horse, sure-footed in the dark, and a trailer to carry him.

Chapter Twenty-Four

"You want to take my truck?" Burt said. "It's newer."

"No, this'll do fine."

He helped me throw my saddle, weapons, and other stuff in my Dodge. I was starting to fade but Burt was pumped.

"Should we take Dave's dog?" he said. "We don't know when we'll be back. We should take him."

"Hell, I don't know. Sure, whatever you want. The more the merrier."

I pulled on Dave's coat and hat and got in my truck, riding shotgun. In a minute Burt was back with the pup.

"You look like a damn old farmer in those clothes," he said.

He didn't bother with the dog crate, just put the little sucker in the cab with us, got behind the wheel and fired it up. I sprawled there trying to sleep. Burt wound up the West Frémont. The pup stood with his front paws on my wounded leg, licking my ear. I'd be lying if I said the leg wasn't worrying me, but I dozed a bit anyway.

In less than an hour I was standing in Becky's lit-up barn saddling a good gelding of Dan's—a horse he'd used for deer hunting. I told them what I was planning to do, and why.

"I wish you'd let me tag along," Burt said. "I'm gonna feel useless as tits on a boar waiting here. If this thing goes south, I don't know what the hell I'd tell your mom. She dotes on you, in case you hadn't noticed."

I asked them to call the law and the emergency services in both Piute Meadows and on the Nevada side of the line, and call Fuchs, and tell him everything, but not till I got myself a good head start. Becky had a tense look to her and I asked her why.

"I saw something this afternoon that made me absolutely heartsick," she said. "We were pushing some pairs up to Aspen Canyon, Harvey, Dan, and me, when . . ."

"What, Becky?"

"Tommy, I saw your grave."

"The hell?"

"I'm not kidding. Off by the drift fence gate above the old pack station was a freshly dug grave. There was a cross made of pipe stuck in the ground—with your name on it. Actually it was a trophy buckle of yours. It was from a roping, and someone had put a bullet hole right through it."

"Kip."

"I don't scare easily," she said. "But that was creepy. I wasn't even sure if I should tell you."

"It's okay."

"How can it be okay? The man's a psycho."

"You just confirmed my hunch. Just think of that buckle as a brass-edged invitation."

"Tommy, it's an invitation to die," she said. "He means to put you in the ground right there."

I walked back to the horse and checked the box of .270s in my saddle pockets.

"What it means is, he's leaving me a trail so I'll know just where to find him."

Becky was watching me the whole time.

"Tommy Smith," she said. "What've you done with that leg now?"

I told her about getting shot that morning but left out the Captain Cruz part, and told her I'd field-dressed it myself. She wasn't impressed. She marched me across the yard to her kitchen and took a first aid kit out of the cupboard. Burt and Dan followed us from the barn, with Burt leading the pup by a strand of baling twine. I tried to convince her I needed to get moving, but after untying my wild rag from my thigh and seeing the crusty blood and crud on it, Becky wasn't having any of it.

"Drop 'em," she said.

I took off Dave's coat, unbuckled the gun rig and dropped my jeans to my knees.

"We got to make this quick."

"You just hush."

Becky sat on a kitchen chair and peeled off my bandage. She made a face but didn't say anything.

"So?"

"It's red and festering," she said. "I don't want you passing out from septic shock in the middle of a gunfight, young man."

Harvey must have seen the lights, because he came into the kitchen from his trailer smoking a Winston just as she was finishing wrapping the new dressing.

"Do I take a number," he said, "or just stand in line with the rest of the boys?"

"All of you clear out," Becky said. She threw a roll of tape at Harvey without looking up. "And take that cigarette with you." He ducked and it bounced off his back. Burt closed the door behind them as the three guys went outside.

"Well, this is embarrassing."

"Hate to break it to you," she said, "but you're not the first cowboy I've seen in his tighty-whities."

She finished up and slapped my butt. "Besides, I changed your diaper a time or two."

I got buckled up and we headed for the door. Becky stopped me before I could open it.

"Are you sure you want to do this alone?"

"I don't see any other way. We go up there with lights and cops, it's just an excuse for Kip to go out in a blaze of glory."

"He'll try to take you with him either way," she said. She gave me an awkward sort of hug.

"Just want to get my girl back safe." I could barely get the words out.

"I know, honey," she said. "I know."

***

At the barn alley I rechecked my weapons as Dan circled his gooseneck. We went over who would do what down at their end, then I loaded the horse and got into the truck with Dan. The others stood in the barnlight trying to act like this was no big deal. I rolled down the passenger window.

"This'd be a whole lot easier if you three stopped looking like a damned morticians' convention." I turned back to Dan. "Let's get to it."

At the end of the ranch lane Dan turned right towards town, not left toward the junction with the Aspen Canyon logging road. In Piute Meadows we turned left onto the Reno Highway, heading north. About a mile past my old house, as the highway was about to leave the valley, he turned left again up a dirt road. It was a longer, less traveled way into the canyon from the north. Dan and I didn't talk much. The rig dipped into a couple of the shallow canyons I'd packed deer hunters into in years past. Each time as we rolled back out of them, we could see the lights of the town clustered across the valley and headlights marking the highway down below. It was coming on to ten o'clock.

Before the road made its big turn into the canyon I had Dan pull over and kill the headlights. We unloaded the horse where the shoulder of the hill kept us hidden. This road turned up the north side of the creek and paralleled the main road on the other side. After the first Forest Service bridge, the roads merged. I told Dan to follow the one we were on until he hit the junction, then turn down-canyon, drive like hell, and not look back. We shook.

"You be careful, now," he said. He looked up at the sliver of moon. "You got a little light to see by, anyhow."

"Shines the same on sinners as it does on saints."

He laughed. "What the hell's that make us?"

"Beats me. I don't go for that stuff. It's just something to say."

He waited till I was mounted, then turned on his low beams and drove off. I came along after him at a good trot. When I hit the junction where he turned off, I kept on going up-canyon. There was no traffic that time of night, but across the creek, high in the Jeffrey pine, I could see a glow of light in a car camper's tent.

At the second Forest Service bridge the road made a sharp dip back across the creek, then turned up through a government campground and stopped a mile later at the locked drift-fence gate. If Kip was waiting for me at the pack station site like I thought he was, he'd be expecting to see me come up that road.

When I got to that bridge, instead of crossing it I picked up a stock trail that Becky used so's not to push her cows straight through the campground tourists. The trail cut gully after gully up and down through rocky sagebrush and the horse stumbled more than once. Pretty soon pines blocked the little bit of moonlight there was when I rode under them, but by then I was on sandy ground so the horse had easy traveling. After twenty minutes, pulling up now and then to listen and watch, I came up a last hill and stopped. I was looking down through the trees at the pack station bridge.

I could see the meadow along the creek and the road coming down to the bridge and the aspen thick where the buildings had been. Below was a weak patch of light and the humming sound of a gas generator that I could hear before I saw it. A construction light was clamped on top of the generator. It threw a yellowish glow on the bridge and the surface of the creek. Its beam mingled with the silver light from the bit of moon and the shadows of tamarack branches on the current. The bridge was narrow and flat and sat about six feet above the creek, just rough plank and steel plate with no railing, not even a board on the edge to keep truck wheels from sliding over. It was empty except for the kneeling woman at the center of the bridge, right at the edge. She was bound with her head tied down and her bare back facing me, her arms tied behind her, her shirt mostly shreds. There was no sign of Kip himself, just Sarah as the bait in the trap, facing the road he thought I would come down. This was him showing me a slice of that twisted brain of his. Sarah wouldn't have got in that place without a fight too awful to imagine, and that made my breath freeze in my lungs.

Still, I'd expected fancier from Kip. Something even more weird and elaborate. The light and the generator made for a pretty hillbilly setup. Maybe he was running out of ideas, or, more likely, losing interest in the game as it came to its end. I took a breath and kept the horse still, watching the bridge and figuring the surest way to get Sarah off of there safe. I still didn't notice any movement below. I waited until I saw headlights coming up-canyon on the other side of the creek before I got off and tied the horse. I slipped the Remington from the scabbard, patted the holstered .45, and started moving downhill through the sage. Across the creek, the headlights turned toward me down the pack station road. They stopped just as quick as they'd appeared, the beams half hidden by trees. I saw a flash of dome light, then nothing but the headlights again. Except for the generator hum, everything was quiet.

From the creekside willows I heard a rifle shot and a ping like a bullet hitting sheet metal. A second shot took out the left headlight of the truck with a pop of glass. Then two quick shots, one on top of the other. The first ripped pine branches above the cab. The second missed the other headlight but sounded like a hit to the windshield. Somebody was blasting my old truck all to hell. The next noise I heard was a whoop that sounded like Kip. I needed to get him out into the light.

I heard a crack like a tree limb breaking and somebody shouting, "C'mere, goddamnit." Then a semi-automatic pop-pop-pop like from Burt's AR-15 from somewhere out in the trees. These got followed by three more shots, crisp and louder like they were either from heavier caliber rounds, or more close-in.

That's when I saw Kip, or thought I did. There was a howl in the dark, and I saw a guy in battle dress and camo cover carrying a military-style sniper rifle with a pistol on his belt. He walked up to the bridge from the pack station side, kind of striding up and down around Sarah like he was on patrol. When he got into the light I could see it was Kip for sure, but now his head was shaved under the cover and his camo looked like Marine issue BDU. He reached down and grabbed Sarah by the hair with his free hand before he shouted.

"My ears are goddamn *ringing*, goddammit," he said.

I saw him drop the rifle on the planks and pull the automatic. He put the muzzle against Sarah's head. He was looking around into the dark. Then I heard him laugh.

"I know you're out there, Tom. You still got that twelve-gauge? I hear you took out two of my boys with a twelve-gauge at Dave's tonight, so I know you got it. It would be pure arrogance to go against me with that, but *so* like you. Am I right?"

I could see him rack the slide on his automatic but couldn't hear anything until he shouted again.

"So what brings you to this neck of the woods?"

"I came for Sarah." I didn't shout too loud, but I figured he heard me. I saw him looking around into the shadows.

"You be careful, now." I could hear him almost giggle. "You'd hate to come this far just to splatter that sweet flesh of hers all over your bridge, hey, Tom?"

He grabbed Sarah's hair tighter and jerked her head up. He put the pistol muzzle to her mouth.

"You hear me, Tom? Sarah's sweet, sweet flesh. I don't hear you. Talk to me you piece of shit before I kill her right here."

I was making enough noise scrambling down that hill, but with the rounds he'd fired off and the rush of the creek, I wasn't surprised he hadn't heard me rustling in the sagebrush. From where he was standing, I'd be needing a straight shot at him down the length of the bridge. I got to where the pack station road curved out of the aspen toward the creek and stopped, waiting for him to position himself for me.

He straightened up, the pistol still on Sarah. He was sort of preening like he knew I was watching him. He looked around, trying to find me in the shadows as he holstered the pistol and picked up the rifle again. When he finally had it he held it up, turning it in his hands like he was trying to sell it to me. It was Captain Cruz's sniper rifle.

"So is this how it's done?" he said. "I got me a state-of-the-art M-one-ten that's already taken a piece of you, I got a better pistol than you ever had, I'm here on your old bridge, and I got your woman." He spread both arms out for a second. "I'm a regular Tom freakin' Smith."

That's when I stepped out of the trees and into the semi-light on the road where he could see me. I was about a hundred feet away.

"You hear me, Tom?" He was jacked—shrieking and laughing at the same time. "She's so *su-weeet*." He set the rifle down hard a second time and pulled the automatic again like he just couldn't decide which one looked better.

Standing in the tree shadows, it took a second for me to catch his eye. He stood frozen for another second, but kept the 9mm close to Sarah's head so I didn't dare shoot. Then he screamed.

"You! You're not *Tom*. How did *you* get out? Why aren't you dead, you old bastard? Dead-dead-DEAD?"

Kip twisted his upper body and swung his right hand with the pistol away from Sarah's head. He was looking back up the hill where my truck sat with one headlight still showing. I figured out that he was mistaking me for Dave, and I almost laughed. I took two steps and dropped prone. Kip swung back and pointed the 9mm my way, but from the lip of the bridge on my side of the creek, the road sloped down just enough to give me cover. He peered into the shadows, all wild and jerky, starting and stopping. I heard rustling and limb-snapping in the trees behind me but tried to ignore it and just wait to take my shot. That's when he stopped, holding the pistol in both hands in the combat stance he'd shown me back at the dump. He whipped way to the right, then way back to the left, and that's when I shot him in the right elbow with Dad's .270.

He yelped and the SIG dropped on the bridge. The second shot blew out his right knee. I was careful not to clip his femoral artery on the inside of his thigh. I didn't want him bleeding out and dying on me. I stood up then and brushed a little dust off my clothes. I walked up to the bridge carrying the Remington in one hand. Kip was trying to crawl toward the SIG lying on the steel. He looked up when I stopped, the stupid shop light clamped on the generator at the far end of the bridge hitting me with a weak glow.

"So it's you," he said. He took deep, shocky breaths. "It's always you."

I started down the bridge toward Sarah and saw Kip squirm close enough to his 9mm to fumble his left hand around it. A headshot would've been safer for her, but I shot him in the forearm instead, breaking at least one of the bones. I still wasn't ready to kill him, though he was screaming at me to finish him off. I stepped over him and set the rifle down, then wrapped an arm around Sarah and cut her free with my skinning knife. She was so cold to the touch I was afraid she was already dead.

"My ears ring like shit," Kip said, more to himself than to me. He was panting hard.

Sarah moaned, and I grabbed her with both arms. A sob hit me so hard I almost lost it. She gasped when she saw me wearing her father's hat and coat, then almost passed out again when she saw it was me. She was bruised bad and so cut and bloodied I could tell she'd fought him till she dropped. I wrapped her in her dad's coat and pulled her to her feet. I could see her knees, bloody through the tears in her jeans.

"You lied to me about earmuffs," Kip said like he couldn't believe that someone besides him would lie. He was trying to steady himself on his good elbow, but a splinter of bone stuck up above it and his whole body shook until he fell back on his side. "That's not fair, goddamn you."

Sarah couldn't stand on her own, so I picked her up and carried her toward my shot-out truck as best I could with my bunged-up leg. I could hear a barking dog and one gunshot, then the creaking of wood and screeching of metal. I was starting to figure things out when I felt steps behind me on the bridge.

"Put her down," somebody said. "Okay?"

"Hey, Roger." I turned around and shifted Sarah's body in my arms.

"It wasn't supposed to work out this way," Roger said.

"What—you gonna shoot us?"

"If you're all gone," he said, "I'm free and none of this happened, okay?"

Kip said something nasty I couldn't quite make out.

"We got some sort of moral compass problem here, Rog."

"I got no choice."

I kissed Sarah on the forehead and pulled her close.

"Hey," he said, "how come you knew it was me?"

"Get real. You've been covering Kip's action since day one when you were first on the scene at False Spring—and up to and including tonight. Want a list? You didn't pull your weapon at the dead EMT 'cause you knew who shot him. You didn't call in the shooting at Dave's after Burt phoned you. If you did, this place would be crawling with cops. Plus this whacko was up here expecting me and he knew all about his boys getting shot at Cathcart's. And you called me Tom. Everybody but Kip calls me Tommy."

"I got this army gun," Roger said. He pointed Captain Cruz's weapon in my general direction. He looked down at it like he wasn't totally sure just how it worked.

"You never fired at a real live person, I bet."

"I got no choice," he said again.

"Yeah, you do. You got kids. A guy can choose to live if he wants."

"I got an ex," he said. "Things add up fast."

"Don't sweat it. You're not the first hick cop who had his head turned by drug money, then died for it."

"Just shut up." He was talking louder to hear himself

over the flowing water. "Shut up and put her down and face me."

I kissed Sarah again and set her as soft as I could against a tamarack growing near the bridgehead. I saw my rifle on the planks about twenty feet away.

"What's the matter, Rog? 'Fraid you'll miss?" I straightened up and stepped away from Sarah, but I only gave him a left-side profile.

He brought the buttstock up to his cheek, but the muzzle wobbled. "Nobody was supposed to get hurt. I was just supposed to look the other way. And the occasional heads-up, okay?"

"And now you got just a few seconds to live."

We both heard another screeching sound like wood and metal tearing.

"What is that?" Roger sounded agitated as hell.

We heard a yapping and Dave's pup ran up on the bridge. He ran past Roger and stopped to give Kip a curious look because he was moaning so loud. The pup growled at him, then ran around me to Sarah. He was just tickled as hell to see her propped under the tamarack.

Roger steadied Ofelia's rifle. "Okay," he said, pointing it toward Sarah. "Goddamn dog. It won't be me who . . ."

In the noise and pale light he hadn't noticed me pull the .45 on the side not facing him. He hadn't heard the hammer over the sound of the creek and the thump of his own heartbeat when I cocked it. He was concentrating the rifle on Sarah and by then it was too late for him to hear anything at all.

Roger fell hard on the edge of the bridge then tumbled into the creek. The .45 had just boomed on that steel before the sound faded in the water's rush. Kip rolled over to look at Roger spinning in the current. He was grinning with blood everywhere as he rolled back, facing me.

"Terrific, dude," he said. "You shot a *cop*." Kip spoke so soft I could barely hear him until he laughed and fell back down on the planks. "Finish it. Sweet Jesus, *finish* it."

I heard him say that nice and clear. One part of me did dearly want to empty that revolver into him. But I slid the Colt back in the gun rig and went over to Sarah. We both looked up at the sound of trucks and saw flashing red and blue and white lights in the Jeffrey pine along the logging road. Then we heard a shout from the other end of the bridge. The pup looked up.

Burt Kelly stumbled toward us, his pants wet to his thighs from wading the creek. His AR was slung over his shoulder and he carried someone in his arms. It was Dave.

"He's almost done for," he said. "But the tough old bastard is still alive."

Chapter Twenty-Five

The Frémont County EMTs and sheriff's staff piled out of their ambulances and SUVs and were all over the wounded and dead. Becky Tyree pulled up behind them. She made sure that Sarah and Dave were tended to before Kip. Dave was unconscious, and one foot and some fingers had bad frostbite, but he wasn't as dehydrated as they thought he might be. Sarah's cuts and bruises from Kip beating her senseless and dragging her along the bridge weren't life-threatening, but they bundled her tight to warm up her body core before they started cleaning her abrasions, as they were worried about hypothermia. I sat with her and held her hand while they worked. She cried from pure exhaustion when she saw her dad wasn't dead. Pretty soon she started giving the county people a hard time, and I knew she was going to be fine.

Burt had to back what was left of my truck up the hill as it was blocking the road. I was surprised the thing still ran. He walked back down toward the bridge with Jack, who was the senior Frémont County officer on the scene. I asked Burt to show the two of us just where he'd found Dave.

We followed Jack's flashlight across the bridge and down the old pack station road.

"I bet you could walk this in the pitch black just from memory," Jack said.

"Pretty much."

I knew where Burt was leading us. Jack shined the beam on the old refrigerated truck box tucked back in the aspen. Burt had tried to shoot the padlock and chain first. When that didn't work he tried to pry the doors apart with a piece of pipe. The chain tore a bit more of the sheet metal, but he couldn't force a wide enough space to push his big self through. Finally, he smashed and jacked the hinges on one side so hard they tore loose from the frame. The whole mess was hanging there off to the side when Jack ran his flashlight beam over it.

"I gotta tell you," Burt said, "going in there with no light except my phone was some spooky deal. I've seen some pretty rank shit in my life, but I didn't want to step into Dave's rotting corpse or anything."

"How did you know to look there?" Jack said.

"The dog," he said. He sort of laughed. "Tommy told me to park his truck on the slope to get Kip's attention and then get the hell out of there. I tripped in a hole, and the damn pup got away from me. Didn't you hear me yell? The little shit has a mind of his own. I was sure he was gonna get one of us shot, but he came right here. Maybe he smelled his pal."

We looked around inside. I could see bits of tack and rope and a couple of old saddles past repair, and the mostly empty saddle racks bolted to the wall. There was a torn-open grain sack half eaten by mice, the husks scattered everywhere, plus lots of trash. A ruined set of canvas pack bags lay in the corner. The whole place stunk.

"How many days was he in here, you figure?" Burt said.

"Could maybe be a week," Jack said. "Depending on when they brought him."

"It's a miracle he survived," Burt said.

"You can go a week without food," Jack said, "but not water."

We poked around the mess. There were wet spots on the sheet-metal floor, and a couple of holes in the ceiling where the rain and snow had puddled over the years and rusted through. We could see where Dave had positioned the pack bags to catch the little bit of condensation and snowmelt from the storm a couple of days before. Burt picked up a rotted canvas nosebag. There was soggy grain pasted to the inside.

"What the heck?" he said.

"Looks like he was softening up some cereal to eat. Yum."

"Are those black flecks what I think they are?" Jack said.

"Those would be mouse turds, yeah."

"What a tough old bird," Burt said.

"You got that right. Dying was not an option."

We went back outside and walked through the trees.

"I remember this was a nice place once," Burt said.

"It's still a nice place." I stopped at the edge of the bridge, looking back across the meadow all lit up now with jagged shadows from the lights of the county vehicles. Jack waited with me as Burt walked on ahead.

"Wouldn't be so nice if your future father-in-law died in that box," Jack said.

I laughed at that. "So where's old Mitch? I'd expect to see him with a bullhorn, kicking ass and taking names."

"He was at a county emergency preparedness dinner down at Mammoth," Jack said, "sucking up to the ski-resort money he'll need come next election. But he'd been on the radio with that Douglas County guy you shot, so he's real happy to think you turned psycho killer. Said he always knew you were a bad one. He told me to keep you here or know the reason why."

I held my arms out, wrists together so he could cuff me. Jack laughed.

More emergency crews appeared at the trailhead and rolled down to the bridge as we finally walked back—so many that it got hard for them to turn around. Flashing lights lit up the pines overhead, and the meat-wagon carrying Roger Parrott's body got stuck in the soft grass by the creek where they'd pulled him out. I saw Fuchs and another agent getting out of his FBI Impala. They talked with Burt for a minute, then the second agent walked with Jack to the ambulance and Fuchs came over to me.

"I hear you got shot by your old army girlfriend this morning," he said.

"She only hurt my pride."

"So it wasn't you who shot her?"

I waited a minute to answer. "No. Sarah took her out to save my life."

"Did you always think Dave Cathcart was alive?" he said.

"I wanted to for Sarah's sake. But until a couple of hours ago when I finally figured Kip was keeping him here, I was pretty damned doubtful."

There was loud talk and cussing as an ambulance spun its wheels in the soggy grass. It was getting close to midnight. I told Fuchs I'd catch up with him and hobbled back to Sarah's ambulance. She sat in the front seat, bundled in blankets. I stood just outside, holding her as best I could as she talked about her father. We watched Jack getting non-essential vehicles turned around and headed back up the hill where there was open space at the trailhead. I could see him talking with Becky and some EMTs. He came over to us when he was done.

"Becky's gonna unlock the gate and lead the ambulances to that meadow about a mile up the canyon," he said. "She thinks the Care Flight chopper can set down there, and we can light up the landing site with headlights. Sarah, I think you oughtta ride with your dad in the chopper to Reno. It's not SOP, but I talked to 'em and they'll let you. It'll make him happy if you're the first one he sees."

Sarah nodded and put her arms around Jack's neck for a second and kissed his cheek, which embarrassed the hell out of him. When he left, she and I were alone for a minute. She made me take her dad's jacket back and put it on, then slid her arms inside the jacket and held me. I could hear her sniffle against my chest. When she did that, it just tore me apart all over again.

"You did it," she said. "You got him back."

"We were just lucky."

She shushed me and pulled back.

"Baby?"

"Yeah?"

She made a face. "You smell like sheep."

We laughed and I held her tight. I said I'd drive to Reno as soon as I could and spend what was left of the night with her in her hospital room. She nodded and squeezed me again hard. The ambulance pulled out, and Burt and I followed it up the hill on foot. Sarah and I said our good-byes then, and Becky led the convoy up the canyon to wait for the chopper. There was nothing left to see but dust and tail lights.

Burt showed me the hole he'd fallen in when he ran away from my truck. It sat just off the pack station turnoff among aspen and pine, below the road where the headlights didn't reach. It was about where I'd flushed the Miller brothers that morning eight days before. I borrowed Burt's phone and used the light. After a second or two I hollered for Jack to bring his big flash. He was closing the drift fence gate and came over and put the beam where Burt had tripped.

We looked down into the fake grave. I saw the cross made of pipe painted white, just like the one at False Spring. I saw my old trophy buckle baling-wired to the cross with a bullet hole in it through my name. We all stared down at the body in the shallow hole, at the straw hat still on the head, and at the rubber irrigating boots turned down below the knee.

"Aw shit," Jack said. "That's Francisco, the irrigator at Dominion's."

"I wondered why the pack station gate was wide open," Burt said. "Dominion always keeps their pastures and barns locked up tight. Was he shot?"

Jack looked closer. "We'll have to wait for the medical examiner to move him, but it looks like he's got blood on his shirt. Shot or stabbed."

"Kip must've caught Francisco coming to change the water on the meadow when he was setting up his psycho-drama on the bridge."

We walked back down toward the creek. A deputy wearing plastic gloves had already put Kip's SIG in an evidence bag and fished Ofelia's sniper rifle out of the creek, but they hadn't got to Dad's Remington yet. I saw it still lying on the planks. I went to fetch it before it disappeared, then walked back to where Jack and Fuchs were standing with the last ambulance crew. At Jack's orders they had Kip restrained, lashed to the gurney with straps, and a deputy keeping watch.

Burt was looking at Kip's BDU. The camo cloth was soaked with blood and torn but still recognizable.

"What a disgrace to the Corps," Burt said. "I oughtta rip that off you."

"We'll all look the other way," Jack said. "Get 'er done, big guy."

Kip made a major deal of ignoring them. He kept his

eyes on me, breathing hard as they worked on the smashed forearm. He'd already jerked out the first IV they'd stuck in his other arm.

"I told you to finish it," he said. He sounded weak and faraway.

"Didn't much feel like it."

"Don't give me that shit," Kip said. "You got medals for killing."

I talked to Jack with my back to Kip. "If I had finished him, nobody'd believe what a crazy mother he was. Now he's *my* character witness."

"Plus you wanted him to suffer," Burt said.

"If I wanted him to suffer I'd have done way worse."

Jack looked at me like he wondered what that could be.

"I've done enough of this for one lifetime."

Messed up as he was, Kip still had that predator's radar.

"You remember you said that," he said. His voice was scratchy and faint. "You remember you said you've had enough when I break out of wherever they put me and I come for you and that blond whore some night when you don't expect it. You'll remember I said this, I *promise*."

Blood bubbled out of his mouth when he tried to talk, like maybe he'd bit his tongue. The EMT working on him was as sick of hearing him talk as the rest of us. He nodded to the driver. Then he rolled the gurney hard into the back of the ambulance and slammed the door.

I asked Burt to hold the .270 while I crossed the bridge and climbed the hill to get my horse. Ten minutes later I was still horseback, and Jack was taking a statement from me while Fuchs stood by just listening, watching Dan turn his gooseneck around. That's when Mitch finally pulled up. He was wearing a tie with his uniform and looked about as good as he ever would. He pulled cuffs from his service belt and walked over to me. He said he was arresting me for the murders of the big weightlifter earlier that night, the first Miller brother I shot on Dave's permit in Nevada, old Roger who I'd just shot here in Mitch's jurisdiction, and Ofelia Cruz, Captain, United States Army, who I hadn't shot at all. To top it off, Mitch kept calling the captain "Olivia." He didn't mention the second Miller boy I'd shot at Dave's, so I figured that one was still alive.

"The voters in the south county won't tolerate another damn bloodbath up here," he said. "Now step off that animal."

I spun Dan's horse around and broke him into an easy lope, heading down the logging road into the dark.

Chapter Twenty-Six

I sat in a chair in Sarah's Reno hospital room the next afternoon checking on flights back to Hartsfield. Jack came in and pulled a chair up next to her bed. She reached out a hand and he took it for a second. He told her how, a couple of hours before, he snuck a six-pack into a guarded hospital room in Gardnerville and interviewed the surviving Miller brother, as he said, Indian to Indian.

"The guy'd been ambulanced north to the nearest emergency ward from Dave's yard where Tommy and Burt left him," Jack said. "His legs were pretty messed up, but it's a long way from his heart. Once I got a couple beers in him, he told me whatever I asked about the stuff he'd done for Kip over the past year—since before you married him, Sarah. Then all the stuff with your dad."

Jack said the Miller boys weren't on the ranch when Dave was taken, but the big weightlifter told the surviving one all about it—how Dave was knocked down in his own kitchen while he was cooking breakfast. Sarah had been close when it happened, so close she almost caught them. Dave was unconscious when they tied him up and threw him into the bed of his own truck. The big weightlifter drove the truck away from the Reno Highway toward the Monte Cristos while Kip followed in his Ram. Delroy had the red Cessna waiting at the Marine airstrip out in the sagebrush at Monte Cristo Summit, along with both the Millers. The guy told Jack how they'd stuffed Dave into the plane and Delroy had flown him two hundred miles south to the airstrip below Lone Pine, then waited for the Millers to meet him. Kip figured that would be far enough away from any law enforcement looking for Dave in the first few hours. The Millers piled him into their GMC and drove him back north that night, circling east through Hawthorne, then north to the Frémont Lake Rez where they stashed him for the next couple of days. Kip had gone back to Dave's to play concerned husband with Sarah but had snuck out to the Rez to check on her dad. That's when he killed Randy Ragazino.

"I couldn't get a good answer about when they took Dave back to the old pack station," Jack said. "But they were all pretty busy guys."

Sarah turned her face to the window, just staring, taking it all in, knowing how close they'd come.

The guy told Jack he and his brother weren't surprised when maybe a week later Kip told them to bring saddle horses and meet him out by Dave's cowcamp. The guy said Kip went nuts when he'd found out we were heading out to gather cattle. He'd wanted to see us all frantic, running around looking for him, which is how I figured he'd react. The Miller boy said Kip went full butcher-shop mode then, and they all figured Sarah and I were dead meat. By then even his boys were afraid of him.

"Usually, folks want something when they skip the traces like that," Jack said. "Money or dope or some damn thing. I never seen anything like this in twenty years with the department. All this for revenge."

"I think it was more than that. I think he kept Dave alive in that refrigerator box on the outside chance he could still get that water money going."

"Could be," Jack said.

"He always thought he was smarter than the rest of us. Still does."

"Do you have Mitch straightened out yet," Sarah said, "so he doesn't jail my—" She turned back to look at us with a funny look on her face. "—boyfriend?"

"Oh yeah," Jack said. "After Tommy galloped off last night, Agent Fuchs set Mitch straight."

"I thought Mitch was gonna start shooting at me."

"No way," Jack said. "He's too afraid of Sarah. Mitch knows he got nothing on you. You just piss him off."

Even with a split lip and a shiner, that made Sarah smile.

"You ride that horse all the way back to Becky's?" Jack said.

"No. I just sat tight in the pines till I heard Dan's truck. I was so fried I almost passed out in the saddle."

"You still look fried," Sarah said.

Since the day I landed in Reno a week and a half before, I'd tied a big knot for us all to untangle. CID at Fort Ben-

ning had already called to say they wanted me back as soon
as I was medically cleared to travel and to expect to make
myself available for questioning when I landed. Otherwise,
they'd be paying me a visit in California. They wanted to
know why the captain was shot, and about the woman who
shot her, and how the M110 made the trip from Georgia
to California. Sarah made sure I had the gunshot wound
to my leg looked at right there in the hospital, and told me
she'd be going to Georgia with me if it wasn't for her dad.
My mom was out of the hospital now, and Dave was in
it. For a cobbled-together family, we were starting out as
pretty much a mess.

We were both dozing, Sarah in the bed and me in the
chair next to it when her dad's doctor came in. The woman
briefed Sarah on the frostbite surgery performed on Dave's
right foot and left hand, and of the tests they had run on his
heart. She told Sarah that Dave did have a second attack. The
doctor called it an "event," and said it was mostly because
Kip had dragged Dave off without his meds before he put
him through his week of hell. She said his strong constitu-
tion had saved him, and as he was back on his meds now,
his prognosis was good.

"Between your father, the beating you took, and
Sergeant Smith's wound going untended," she said, "I'll say
this for you people—you are all a pretty hardy bunch."

"At least you didn't cut off any fingers from his roping
hand," Sarah said.

The doc said Dave was still in the ICU, but we could

go up and see him for a few minutes whenever Sarah was up to it. She warned Sarah that they couldn't be sure how long it would take before he was out of the woods.

We were heading down the hallway on the floor above Sarah's. We walked slow, she from the beating Kip gave her, me from the fresh stitches on the back of my thigh. We noticed two deputies from Washoe County sitting outside one of the rooms with the door closed. One of them was looking at his phone, the other was watching us, sort of amused. Sarah said hey to that one, and he said hey back like he knew who she was.

"What can I say," Sarah said after they were behind us. "It's a brotherhood."

We didn't say anything more until we got to the ICU. The two of them hugged and cried, and Dave wanted to know just what day it was. Sarah told him. She told him about Hoyt, the Marine Housing shoot-out, the deaths of his tormentors except for his son-in-law, and her plans to gather his permit. It would be his first year not running things, and she told him not to worry about anything, but I could tell that she was worrying. She told him that she wasn't going to think of starting until he was in better shape. He started to argue, then just sighed and lay back. He was weak, but he still looked better than you'd expect, even lying in that bed with wires and IVs stuck all over him.

"We've got the Tyrees and Lindermans," she said, "just like always. And Jack's taking a day off to help us, too."

"And Tommy?" Dave said after staring at me a bit.

"Yeap."

"You getting out of the service for good, then?"

Sarah took my hand.

"I expect so."

Dave's eyes watered, and he tried to rub them with his bandaged hand. "Well, damn, girl. *Damn*."

Sarah was eating some sort of mystery chicken when Jack came back to her room about five thirty. He told us that he'd been up to see Dave.

"Him and me'll be team roping before you know it," Jack said. "That mouse shit he ate must have put some lead in his pencil."

Sarah asked him about departmental stuff, and if I was cleared to travel out of the territory. Jack told us that Fuchs had more talks with Mitch and the CID people at Fort Benning, and he'd got them all pretty much on the same page.

"As long as Mitch thinks his ass is covered," Jack said, "he's happy."

"If he's happy," Sarah said, "we're happy."

"Well," Jack said, "I bet you'll be glad to get out of this building and back to the ranch."

"Sure thing," Sarah said.

"I mean," he said, "with Kip and all."

"What do you mean?"

"With him being just upstairs." Jack got a funny look. "Didn't you see those Washoe deputies standing guard three doors down from Dave's room? They got old Kip chained to his bed on a twenty-four hour watch."

Our feet hit the floor at three forty-five, ten mornings later. We loaded horses, gear, and food, ready to start the gather of

Dave's cattle for real. Sarah cooked breakfast while I grained and saddled and packed outside in the dark, as some careless bastard had shot out the yard light. Harvey and May Linderman had picked up some battery cables at the NAPA at Piute Meadows the day before and driven out to Dave's cowcamp to get Sarah's Silverado up and running after Kip had disabled it, so we had her truck and gooseneck back at Dave's ready to load.

We were convoying out to the permit by five thirty with Harvey, May, and Jack, who'd told Mitch he was taking a sick day. Becky and Dan had started the gather the day before. It was the Saturday of Memorial Day weekend. There were three days left in the month of May.

I hadn't booked a flight until I knew when we'd be finished gathering, and that all depended on Sarah feeling she could leave Dave for a few days. Becky said they'd do the whole job for us, but Sarah wouldn't have it. Her cuts and bruises were healed and she was itching to get this done for her dad. Plus she didn't want to give Kip the satisfaction of leaving any job undone, even if he was locked down under guard on his Reno hospital bed and so sedated he'd never know or care.

We got mounted by seven thirty, with Becky and Dan waiting for us, their first day's gather already bawling in the pens. More cattle had followed and were spread close above the cowcamp on the meadows. The day before, while Harvey had worked on Sarah's truck, May had straightened up and cleaned the cabin after the mess Kip's boys had made. When we were ready to head out the next morning, Harvey asked Sarah if he could hold our horses for us while we stepped aboard, as he said we both were as stiff and slow as a couple of overworked yoga instructors. Sarah laughed and told him as nice as could be to go to hell. The day was warming up like summer.

The others drifted out toward the Dayton road. Sarah and I headed toward the Washoe Pass country. She was riding the bay mare, and I was on the sorrel just like before. We followed the road out past where I'd been trapped when her dad's horse got shot and I'd killed the first Miller brother. Then we passed our campsite where Delroy crashed and burned. We didn't look close at either place, but the dead had been carried away. The Cessna still sat upside down where it had burned black. Somebody'd get that hauled out soon enough. The spring snow from a couple of weeks before had melted off and the meadows were already grazed down. We headed up the wagon road toward some spring-fed willow and piñon against a bluff. We'd been riding without talking, each of us just processing the last few wild days.

"Can I ask you something?" she said.

"Sure."

"After Burt found Dad, you could've killed Kip and he would've deserved it. Why didn't you?"

"If we end up together, I didn't think it'd look right for me to be killing your husband just before."

"If?"

"You know what I mean. Folks would talk."

"Yes," she said. "That is so like you, though."

"After what he did to you, letting him live was about the hardest thing I ever had to do. Second hardest, anyway."

Sarah just nodded, eyes on the road ahead.

"Can I ask you something, then?"

"Sure," she said.

I rubbed the sorrel's neck. "How come you quit riding this big old goof?"

"Because he reminded me of everything I loved about you," she said. "With you gone, I couldn't stand to be around him. I would've sold him but Dad wouldn't let me."

"Fair enough."

Branches snapped then, and horses squealed. Our two guys spooked as the spotted mustangs we'd seen all those days ago out in the snow came busting out of the willows past us and rattled down through the rocks toward the meadows. Sarah's mare reared. We laughed at how we'd flushed them without meaning to, and how close the mustangs had come. We watched the stallion circle and bunch his mares at a safe distance, halfway between us and the nearest cattle.

"Well, looky there."

The dun mare who'd been scared away by Delroy's plane was with the bunch now. She looked raggedy and bitten and kicked, like the other mares had tried to run her off—like she'd had a rough time.

"You're not going to say something stupid, are you?" Sarah said, "Like 'now she's free?'"

We both laughed at the whole idea.

"No, I was going to say you should leave her out here 'cause she's too stupid to feed."

"An extra feral horse with Dad's brand," she said. "The

BLM would love that. The meadows already look like crap. You can help me rope her when we're done here."

We watched them a bit longer. The dun drifted close to the stud.

"Make that two extra horses. Bet she's already bred."

I was half laughing, but Sarah got quiet.

"She might not be the only one."

She had a look on her face I'd never seen. I started to say something, but no words came. She moved her mare out and we rode side-by-side toward the pass.

"Obviously, it's way too early to know for sure," she said. "But either way, whatever you say next, whatever question you think you need to ask, it'll probably be the most important words that come out of your mouth for a long time." She gave me a look. "Just sayin.'"

She rode along, serious as hell, but calm at the same time. I must have looked happier than I could remember.

"Then I guess 'holy shit' won't cut it."

She shook her head no.

"I dreamed about you every night of my life since I was twelve years old." I reached my hand out. "And I've loved you since before I even knew what that meant."

She stuck out her hand and hooked one of my fingers with one of hers. We rode that way until we hit the next bunch of cows. Then we got back to work.

That night all of us ate in the cabin. Harvey fired up a bunch of steaks on a grill out by the woodpile and Becky and Dan cooked fried potatoes and corn and sourdough garlic toast on the woodstove inside. May Linderman had brought salad fixings, some California red, and some ice cream. Without anyone saying anything and with one more hard day ahead of us, it was still like we were all celebrating, like it was the end of something. Afterward, May and I did the dishes and talked about Mom and Burt over the racket of the cows and calves out in the pens, and how I planned on surprising Mom with the pink slip to my Mustang, and such things as that. When we were putting the pots away, May dried her hands and said she'd see us in the morning. I looked outside. Harvey was already waiting in their truck, motor running and headlights on. Becky and Dan and Jack were heading for the door before Sarah really noticed.

"Where are you going?" she said. "You're not leaving me alone with this guy, are you?" She was standing next to me with her arm around my waist. She kissed me in front of them, which wasn't like her.

"My brother's putting us up at his place," Becky said. "We'll make sure he's got his pasture gates set for the cattle tomorrow night. Plus, Jack's on duty at eight a.m., so he needs to get back to Piute Meadows." She gave Sarah's free hand a squeeze. "We'll see you kids back up here about what, four thirty?"

"Coffee'll be on."

Becky gave me a wave, and they were gone.

Sarah didn't say anything. The night was twenty degrees warmer than it had been the last time we were here. I blew out the lamps and let the fire burn down and we lay in the bedroll once again, not the only two people on earth anymore. I knew I would remember everything now. The orange glow. The smell of piñon burning and the feel of the night spring breeze blowing between the chinks in the logs. The creak and clank of the cooling iron stove. The canvas tarp stiff against your cheek when you moved. Every last thing. We would have some time after all, more time than I had hoped. And for the first time we talked about not what had been, but what would be. And how we would ride that country one more time from dark to dark, and ride it until we were done.